Y0-BSL-816

DATE DUE

PRINTED IN U.S.A.

SCRIBNER REPRINT EDITIONS

THE
AMBASSADORS

VOLUME II

HENRY JAMES

AUGUSTUS M. KELLEY · PUBLISHERS

NEW YORK 1971

PRINTED IN THE UNITED STATES OF AMERICA
by THE MURRAY PRINTING COMPANY, FORGE VILLAGE, MASS.

THE AMBASSADORS

VOLUME II

BOOK SEVENTH

THE AMBASSADORS

I

IT was n't the first time Strether had sat alone in the great dim church — still less was it the first of his giving himself up, so far as conditions permitted, to its beneficent action on his nerves. He had been to Notre Dame with Waymarsh, he had been there with Miss Gostrey, he had been there with Chad Newsome, and had found the place, even in company, such a refuge from the obsession of his problem that, with renewed pressure from that source, he had not unnaturally recurred to a remedy meeting the case, for the moment, so indirectly, no doubt, but so relievingly. He was conscious enough that it was only for the moment, but good moments — if he could call them good — still had their value for a man who by this time struck himself as living almost disgracefully from hand to mouth. Having so well learnt the way, he had lately made the pilgrimage more than once by himself — had quite stolen off, taking an unnoticed chance and making no point of speaking of the adventure when restored to his friends.

His great friend, for that matter, was still absent, as well as remarkably silent; even at the end of three weeks Miss Gostrey had n't come back. She wrote to him from Mentone, admitting that he must judge her grossly inconsequent — perhaps in fact for the time odiously faithless; but asking for patience, for a deferred sentence, throwing herself in short on his generosity. For her too, she could assure him, life was complicated — more complicated than he could have guessed; she had moreover made certain of him — certain of not wholly missing him on her return — before her disappearance. If furthermore she did n't burden him with letters it was frankly because of her sense of the other great commerce he had to carry on. He himself, at the end of a fortnight, had written twice, to show how his generosity could be trusted; but he reminded himself in each case of Mrs. Newsome's epistolary manner at the times when Mrs. Newsome kept off delicate ground. He sank his problem, he talked of Waymarsh and Miss Barrace, of little Bilham and the set over the river, with whom he had again had tea, and he was easy, for convenience, about Chad and Madame de Vionnet and Jeanne. He admitted that he continued to see them, he was decidedly so confirmed a haunter of Chad's premises and that young man's practical intimacy with them was so undeniably great; but he had his reason for not attempting to render for Miss Gostrey's benefit the impression of these last days. That would be to tell her too much about himself — it being at present just from himself he was trying to escape.

This small struggle sprang not a little, in its way, from the same impulse that had now carried him across to Notre Dame; the impulse to let things be, to give them time to justify themselves or at least to pass. He was aware of having no errand in such a place but the desire not to be, for the hour, in certain other places; a sense of safety, of simplification, which each

time he yielded to it he amused himself by thinking
of as a private concession to cowardice. The great
church had no altar for his worship, no direct voice
for his soul; but it was none the less soothing even to
sanctity; for he could feel while there what he could n't
elsewhere, that he was a plain tired man taking the
holiday he had earned. He was tired, but he was n't
plain — that was the pity and the trouble of it; he was
able, however, to drop his problem at the door very
much as if it had been the copper piece that he de-
posited, on the threshold, in the receptacle of the
inveterate blind beggar. He trod the long dim nave,
sat in the splendid choir, paused before the clustered
chapels of the east end, and the mighty monument laid
upon him its spell. He might have been a student
under the charm of a museum — which was exactly
what, in a foreign town, in the afternoon of life, he
would have liked to be free to be. This form of sacrifice did at any rate for the occasion as well as another;
it made him quite sufficiently understand how, within
the precinct, for the real refugee, the things of the
world could fall into abeyance. That was the cowardice, probably — to dodge them, to beg the question,
not to deal with it in the hard outer light; but his own
oblivions were too brief, too vain, to hurt any one but
himself, and he had a vague and fanciful kindness for
certain persons whom he met, figures of mystery and
anxiety, and whom, with observation for his pastime,
he ranked as those who were fleeing from justice.
Justice was outside, in the hard light, and injustice
too; but one was as absent as the other from the air of
the long aisles and the brightness of the many altars.

5

THE AMBASSADORS

Thus it was at all events that, one morning some dozen days after the dinner in the Boulevard Malesherbes at which Madame de Vionnet had been present with her daughter, he was called upon to play his part in an encounter that deeply stirred his imagination. He had the habit, in these contemplations, of watching a fellow visitant, here and there, from a respectable distance, remarking some note of behaviour, of penitence, of prostration, of the absolved, relieved state; this was the manner in which his vague tenderness took its course, the degree of demonstration to which it naturally had to confine itself. It had n't indeed so felt its responsibility as when on this occasion he suddenly measured the suggestive effect of a lady whose supreme stillness, in the shade of one of the chapels, he had two or three times noticed as he made, and made once more, his slow circuit. She was n't prostrate — not in any degree bowed, but she was strangely fixed, and her prolonged immobility showed her, while he passed and paused, as wholly given up to the need, whatever it was, that had brought her there. She only sat and gazed before her, as he himself often sat; but she had placed herself, as he never did, within the focus of the shrine, and she had lost herself, he could easily see, as he would only have liked to do. She was not a wandering alien, keeping back more than she gave, but one of the familiar, the intimate, the fortunate, for whom these dealings had a method and a meaning. She reminded our friend — since it was the way of nine tenths of his current impressions to act as recalls of things imagined — of some fine firm concentrated heroine of an old story,

6

something he had heard, read, something that, had he had a hand for drama, he might himself have written, renewing her courage, renewing her clearness, in splendidly-protected meditation. Her back, as she sat, was turned to him, but his impression absolutely required that she should be young and interesting, and she carried her head moreover, even in the sacred shade, with a discernible faith in herself, a kind of implied conviction of consistency, security, impunity. But what had such a woman come for if she had n't come to pray ? Strether's reading of such matters was, it must be owned, confused; but he wondered if her attitude were some congruous fruit of absolution, of "indulgence." He knew but dimly what indulgence, in such a place, might mean; yet he had, as with a soft sweep, a vision of how it might indeed add to the zest of active rites. All this was a good deal to have been denoted by a mere lurking figure who was nothing to him; but, the last thing before leaving the church, he had the surprise of a still deeper quickening.

He had dropped upon a seat halfway down the nave and, again in the museum mood, was trying with head thrown back and eyes aloft, to reconstitute a past, to reduce it in fact to the convenient terms of Victor Hugo, whom, a few days before, giving the rein for once in a way to the joy of life, he had purchased in seventy bound volumes, a miracle of cheapness, parted with, he was assured by the shopman, at the price of the red-and-gold alone. He looked, doubtless, while he played his eternal nippers over Gothic glooms, sufficiently rapt in reverence; but what his thought had finally bumped against was the ques-

tion of where, among packed accumulations, so multi-
form a wedge would be able to enter. Were seventy
volumes in red-and-gold to be perhaps what he should
most substantially have to show at Woollett as the
fruit of his mission ? It was a possibility that held him
a minute — held him till he happened to feel that some
one, unnoticed, had approached him and paused.
Turning, he saw that a lady stood there as for a greeting, and he sprang up as he next took her, securely,
for Madame de Vionnet, who appeared to have recognised him as she passed near him on her way to the
door. She checked, quickly and gaily, a certain confusion in him, came to meet it, turned it back, by an
art of her own; the confusion having threatened him
as he knew her for the person he had lately been observing. She was the lurking figure of the dim chapel;
she had occupied him more than she guessed; but it
came to him in time, luckily, that he need n't tell her
and that no harm, after all, had been done. She herself, for that matter, straightway showing she felt their
encounter as the happiest of accidents, had for him
a "You come here too ?" that despoiled surprise of
every awkwardness.

"I come often," she said. "I love this place, but
I'm terrible, in general, for churches. The old women who live in them all know me; in fact I'm already myself one of the old women. It's like that, at
all events, that I foresee I shall end." Looking about
for a chair, so that he instantly pulled one nearer, she
sat down with him again to the sound of an "Oh, I
like so much your also being fond —!"

He confessed the extent of his feeling, though she

8

left the object vague; and he was struck with the tact,
the taste of her vagueness, which simply took for
granted in him a sense of beautiful things. He was
conscious of how much it was affected, this sense, by
something subdued and discreet in the way she had
arranged herself for her special object and her morning walk — he believed her to have come on foot; the
way her slightly thicker veil was drawn — a mere
touch, but everything; the composed gravity of her
dress, in which, here and there, a dull wine-colour
seemed to gleam faintly through black; the charming
discretion of her small compact head; the quiet note,
as she sat, of her folded, grey-gloved hands. It was,
to Strether's mind, as if she sat on her own ground,
the light honours of which, at an open gate, she thus
easily did him, while all the vastness and mystery of
the domain stretched off behind. When people were
so completely in possession they could be extraordinarily civil; and our friend had indeed at this hour a
kind of revelation of her heritage. She was romantic
for him far beyond what she could have guessed, and
again he found his small comfort in the conviction
that, subtle though she was, his impression must
remain a secret from her. The thing that, once more,
made him uneasy for secrets in general was this particular patience she could have with his own want of
colour; albeit that on the other hand his uneasiness
pretty well dropped after he had been for ten minutes
as colourless as possible and at the same time as
responsive.

The moments had already, for that matter, drawn
their deepest tinge from the special interest excited in

him by his vision of his companion's identity with the person whose attitude before the glimmering altar had so impressed him. This attitude fitted admirably into the stand he had privately taken about her connexion with Chad on the last occasion of his seeing them together. It helped him to stick fast at the point he had then reached; it was there he had resolved that he *would* stick, and at no moment since had it seemed as easy to do so. Unassailably innocent was a relation that could make one of the parties to it so carry herself. If it was n't innocent why did she haunt the churches? — into which, given the woman he could believe he made out, she would never have come to flaunt an insolence of guilt. She haunted them for continued help, for strength, for peace — sublime support which, if one were able to look at it so, she found from day to day. They talked, in low easy tones and with lifted lingering looks, about the great monument and its history and its beauty — all of which, Madame de Vionnet professed, came to her most in the other, the outer view. "We'll presently, after we go," she said, "walk round it again if you like. I'm not in a particular hurry, and it will be pleasant to look at it well with you." He had spoken of the great romancer and the great romance, and of what, to his imagination, they had done for the whole, mentioning to her moreover the exorbitance of his purchase, the seventy blazing volumes that were so out of proportion.

"Out of proportion to what?"

"Well, to any other plunge." Yet he felt even as he spoke how at that instant he was plunging. He had made up his mind and was impatient to get into the air; for his purpose was a purpose to be uttered outside, and he had a fear that it might with delay still slip away from him. She however took her time; she drew out their quiet gossip as if she had wished to profit by their meeting, and this confirmed precisely an interpretation of her manner, of her mystery. While she rose, as he would have called it, to the question of Victor Hugo, her voice itself, the light low quaver of her deference to the solemnity about them, seemed to make her words mean something that they did n't mean openly. Help, strength, peace, a sublime support — she had n't found so much of these things as that the amount would n't be sensibly greater for any scrap his appearance of faith in her might enable her to feel in her hand. Every little, in a long strain, helped, and if he happened to affect her as a firm object she could hold on by, he would n't jerk himself out of her reach. People in difficulties held on by what was nearest, and he was perhaps after all not further off than sources of comfort more abstract. It was as to this he had made up his mind; he had made it up, that is, to give her a sign. The sign would be that — though it was her own affair — he understood; the sign would be that — though it was her own affair — she was free to clutch. Since she took him for a firm object — much as he might to his own sense appear at times to rock — he would do his best to *be* one.

The end of it was that half an hour later they were seated together for an early luncheon at a wonderful, a delightful house of entertainment on the left bank — a place of pilgrimage for the knowing, they were both aware, the knowing who came, for its great renown, the homage of restless days, from the other end of the town. Strether had already been there three times — first with Miss Gostrey, then with Chad, then with Chad again and with Waymarsh and little Bilham, all of whom he had himself sagaciously entertained; and his pleasure was deep now on learning that Madame de Vionnet had n't yet been initiated. When he had said, as they strolled round the church, by the river, acting at last on what, within, he had made up his mind to, "Will you, if you have time, come to déjeuner with me somewhere? For instance, if you know it, over there on the other side, which is so easy a walk" — and then had named the place; when he had done this she stopped short as for quick intensity, and yet deep difficulty, of response. She took in the proposal as if it were almost too charming to be true; and there had perhaps never yet been for her companion so unexpected a moment of pride — so fine, so odd a case, at any rate, as his finding himself thus able to offer to a person in such universal possession a new, a rare amusement. She had heard of the happy spot, but she asked him in reply to a further question how in the world he could suppose her to have been there. He supposed himself to have supposed that Chad might have taken her, and she guessed this the next moment, to his no small discomfort.

"Ah, let me explain," she smiled, "that I don't go about with him in public; I never have such chances — not having them otherwise — and it's just the sort of thing that, as a quiet creature living in my hole, I adore." It was more than kind of him to have thought of it — though, frankly, if he asked whether she had time she had n't a single minute. That however made no difference — she 'd throw everything over. Every duty at home, domestic, maternal, social, awaited her; but it was a case for a high line. Her affairs would go to smash, but had n't one a right to one's snatch of scandal when one was prepared to pay? It was on this pleasant basis of costly disorder, consequently, that they eventually seated themselves, on either side of a small table, at a window adjusted to the busy quay and the shining barge-burdened Seine; where, for an hour, in the matter of letting himself go, of diving deep, Strether was to feel he had touched bottom. He was to feel many things on this occasion, and one of the first of them was that he had travelled far since that evening in London, before the theatre, when his dinner with Maria Gostrey, between the pink-shaded candles, had struck him as requiring so many explanations. He had at that time gathered them in, the explanations — he had stored them up; but it was at present as if he had either soared above or sunk below them — he could n't tell which; he could some-how think of none that did n't seem to leave the appearance of collapse and cynicism easier for him than lucidity. How could he wish it to be lucid for others, for any one, that he, for the hour, saw reasons enough in the mere way the bright clean ordered water-side life came in at the open window? — the mere way Madame de Vionnet, opposite him over their intensely white table-linen, their *omelette aux tomates*, their bottle of straw-coloured Chablis, thanked him for everything almost with the smile of a child, while her grey eyes moved in and out of their talk, back to the quarter of the warm spring air, in which early summer had already begun to throb, and then back again to his face and their human questions.

Their human questions became many before they had done — many more, as one after the other came up, than our friend's free fancy had at all foreseen. The sense he had had before, the sense he had had repeatedly, the sense that the situation was running away with him, had never been so sharp as now; and all the more that he could perfectly put his finger on the moment it had taken the bit in its teeth. That accident had definitely occurred, the other evening, after Chad's dinner; it had occurred, as he fully knew, at the moment when he interposed between this lady and her child, when he suffered himself so to discuss with her a matter closely concerning them that her own subtlety, marked by its significant "Thank you!" instantly sealed the occasion in her favour. Again he had held off for ten days, but the situation had continued out of hand in spite of that; the fact that it was running so fast being indeed just *why* he had held off. What had come over him as he recognised her in the nave of the church was that holding off could be but a losing game from the instant she was worked for not only by her subtlety, but by the hand of fate itself. If all the accidents were to fight on her side — and by the actual showing they loomed large — he could only give himself up. This was what he had done in privately deciding then and there to propose she should breakfast with him. What did the success of his proposal in fact resemble but the

smash in which a regular runaway properly ends?
The smash was their walk, their déjeuner, their
omelette, the Chablis, the place, the view, their present talk and his present pleasure in it — to say nothing, wonder of wonders, of her own. To this tune
and nothing less, accordingly, was his surrender made
good. It sufficiently lighted up at least the folly of
holding off. Ancient proverbs sounded, for his memory, in the tone of their words and the clink of their
glasses, in the hum of the town and the plash of the
river. It *was* clearly better to suffer as a sheep than as
a lamb. One might as well perish by the sword as by
famine.

"Maria's still away?" — that was the first thing
she had asked him; and when he had found the frankness to be cheerful about it in spite of the meaning he
knew her to attach to Miss Gostrey's absence, she had
gone on to enquire if he did n't tremendously miss her.
There were reasons that made him by no means sure,
yet he nevertheless answered "Tremendously";
which she took in as if it were all she had wished to
prove. Then, "A man in trouble *must* be possessed
somehow of a woman," she said; "if she does n't come
in one way she comes in another."

"Why do you call me a man in trouble?"

"Ah because that's the way you strike me." She
spoke ever so gently and as if with all fear of wound-
ing him while she sat partaking of his bounty. "*Are n't*
you in trouble?"

He felt himself colour at the question, and then
hated that — hated to pass for anything so idiotic as
woundable. Woundable by Chad's lady, in respect to

15

whom he had come out with such a fund of indifference — was he already at that point? Perversely, none the less, his pause gave a strange air of truth to her supposition; and what was he in fact but disconcerted at having struck her just in the way he had most dreamed of not doing? "I'm not in trouble yet," he at last smiled. "I'm not in trouble now."

"Well, I'm always so. But that you sufficiently know." She was a woman who, between courses, could be graceful with her elbows on the table. It was a posture unknown to Mrs. Newsome, but it was easy for a *femme du monde.* "Yes — I am 'now'!"

"There was a question you put to me," he presently returned, "the night of Chad's dinner. I did n't answer it then, and it has been very handsome of you not to have sought an occasion for pressing me about it since."

She was instantly all there. "Of course I know what you allude to. I asked you what you had meant by saying, the day you came to see me, just before you left me, that you'd save me. And you then said — at our friend's — that you'd have really to wait to see, for yourself, what you did mean."

"Yes, I asked for time," said Strether. "And it sounds now, as you put it, like a very ridiculous speech."

"Oh!" she murmured — she was full of attenuation. But she had another thought. "If it does sound ridiculous why do you deny that you're in trouble?"

"Ah if I were," he replied, "it would n't be the trouble of fearing ridicule. I don't fear it."

"What then do you?"

"Nothing — now." And he leaned back in his chair.

"I like your 'now'!" she laughed across at him.

"Well, it's precisely that it fully comes to me at present that I've kept you long enough. I know by this time, at any rate, what I meant by my speech; and I really knew it the night of Chad's dinner."

"Then why did n't you tell me?"

"Because it was difficult at the moment. I had already at that moment done something for you, in the sense of what I had said the day I went to see you; but I was n't then sure of the importance I might represent this as having."

She was all eagerness. "And you're sure now?"

"Yes; I see that, practically, I've done for you — had done for you when you put me your question — all that it's as yet possible to me to do. I feel now," he went on, "that it may go further than I thought. What I did after my visit to you," he explained, "was to write straight off to Mrs. Newsome about you, and I'm at last, from one day to the other, expecting her answer. It's this answer that will represent, as I believe, the consequences."

Patient and beautiful was her interest. "I see — the consequences of your speaking for me." And she waited as if not to hustle him.

He acknowledged it by immediately going on. "The question, you understand, was *how* I should save you. Well, I'm trying it by thus letting her know that I consider you worth saving."

"I see — I see." Her eagerness broke through. "How can I thank you enough?" He could n't

17

tell her that, however, and she quickly pursued. "You do really, for yourself, consider it?"

His only answer at first was to help her to the dish that had been freshly put before them. "I've written to her again since then — I've left her in no doubt of what I think. I've told her all about you."

"Thanks — not so much. 'All about' me," she went on — "yes."

"All it seems to me you've done for him."

"Ah and you might have added all it seems to *me!*" She laughed again, while she took up her knife and fork, as in the cheer of these assurances. "But you're not sure how she'll take it."

"No, I'll not pretend I'm sure."

"Voilà." And she waited a moment. "I wish you'd tell me about her."

"Oh," said Strether with a slightly strained smile, "all that need concern you about her is that she's really a grand person."

Madame de Vionnet seemed to demur. "Is that all that need concern me about her?"

But Strether neglected the question. "Hasn't Chad talked to you?"

"Of his mother? Yes, a great deal — immensely. But not from your point of view."

"He can't," our friend returned, "have said any ill of her."

"Not the least bit. He has given me, like you, the assurance that she's really grand. But her being really grand is somehow just what hasn't seemed to simplify our case. Nothing," she continued, "is further from me than to wish to say a word against her; but of course I feel how little she can like being told of her owing me anything. No woman ever enjoys such an obligation to another woman."

This was a proposition Strether could n't contradict. "And yet what other way could I have expressed to her what I felt? It's what there was most to say about you."

"Do you mean then that she *will* be good to me?"

"It's what I'm waiting to see. But I've little doubt she would," he added, "if she could comfortably see you."

It seemed to strike her as a happy, a beneficent thought. "Oh then could n't that be managed? Would n't she come out? Would n't she if you so put it to her? *Did* you by any possibility?" she faintly quavered.

"Oh no" — he was prompt. "Not that. It would be, much more, to give an account of you that — since there's no question of *your* paying the visit — I should go home first."

It instantly made her graver. "And are you thinking of that?"

"Oh all the while, naturally."

"Stay with us — stay with us!" she exclaimed on this. "That's your only way to make sure."

"To make sure of what?"

"Why that he does n't break up. You did n't come out to do that to him."

"Does n't it depend," Strether returned after a moment, "on what you mean by breaking up?"

"Oh you know well enough what I mean!"

His silence seemed again for a little to denote an

understanding. "You take for granted remarkable things."

"Yes, I do — to the extent that I don't take for granted vulgar ones. You're perfectly capable of seeing that what you came out for was n't really at all to do what you'd now have to do."

"Ah it's perfectly simple," Strether good-humouredly pleaded. "I've had but one thing to do — to put our case before him. To put it as it could only be put here on the spot — by personal pressure. My dear lady," he lucidly pursued, "my work, you see, is really done, and my reasons for staying on even another day are none of the best. Chad's in possession of our case and professes to do it full justice. What remains is with himself. I've had my rest, my amusement and refreshment; I've had, as we say at Woollett, a lovely time. Nothing in it has been more lovely than this happy meeting with you — in these fantastic conditions to which you've so delightfully consented. I've a sense of success. It's what I wanted. My getting all this good is what Chad has waited for, and I gather that if I'm ready to go he's the same."

She shook her head with a finer deeper wisdom. "You're not ready. If you're ready why did you write to Mrs. Newsome in the sense you've mentioned to me?"

Strether considered. "I shan't go before I hear from her. You're too much afraid of her," he added.

It produced between them a long look from which neither shrank. "I don't think you believe that — believe I've not really reason to fear her."

BOOK SEVENTH

"She's capable of great generosity," Strether presently stated.

"Well then let her trust me a little. That's all I ask. Let her recognise in spite of everything what I've done."

"Ah remember," our friend replied, "that she can't effectually recognise it without seeing it for herself. Let Chad go over and show her what you've done, and let him plead with her there for it and, as it were, for *you.*"

She measured the depth of this suggestion. "Do you give me your word of honour that if she once has him there she won't do her best to marry him?"

It made her companion, this enquiry, look again a while out at the view; after which he spoke without sharpness. "When she sees for herself what he is —"

But she had already broken in. "It's when she sees for herself what he is that she'll want to marry him most."

Strether's attitude, that of due deference to what she said, permitted him to attend for a minute to his luncheon. "I doubt if that will come off. It won't be easy to make it."

"It will be easy if he remains there — and he'll remain for the money. The money appears to be, as a probability, so hideously much."

"Well," Strether presently concluded, "nothing *could* really hurt you but his marrying."

She gave a strange light laugh. "Putting aside what may really hurt *him.*"

But her friend looked at her as if he had thought of

that too. "The question will come up, of course, of the future that you yourself offer him."

She was leaning back now, but she fully faced him. "Well, let it come up!"

"The point is that it's for Chad to make of it what he can. His being proof against marriage will show what he does make."

"If he *is* proof, yes" — she accepted the proposition. "But for myself," she added, "the question is what *you* make."

"Ah I make nothing. It's not my affair."

"I beg your pardon. It's just there that, since you've taken it up and are committed to it, it most intensely becomes yours. You're not saving me, I take it, for your interest in myself, but for your interest in our friend. The one's at any rate wholly dependent on the other. You can't in honour not see me through," she wound up, "because you can't in honour not see *him*."

Strange and beautiful to him was her quiet soft acuteness. The thing that most moved him was really that she was so deeply serious. She had none of the portentous forms of it, but he had never come in contact, it struck him, with a force brought to so fine a head. Mrs. Newsome, goodness knew, was serious; but it was nothing to this. He took it all in, he saw it all together. "No," he mused, "I can't in honour not see him."

Her face affected him as with an exquisite light. "You *will* then?"

"I will."

At this she pushed back her chair and was the next

moment on her feet. "Thank you!" she said with her hand held out to him across the table and with no less a meaning in the words than her lips had so particularly given them after Chad's dinner. The golden nail she had then driven in pierced a good inch deeper. Yet he reflected that he himself had only meanwhile done what he had made up his mind to on the same occasion. So far as the essence of the matter went he had simply stood fast on the spot on which he had then planted his feet.

II

He received three days after this a communication
from America, in the form of a scrap of blue paper
folded and gummed, not reaching him through his
bankers, but delivered at his hotel by a small boy in
uniform, who, under instructions from the concierge,
approached him as he slowly paced the little court.
It was the evening hour, but daylight was long now
and Paris more than ever penetrating. The scent of
flowers was in the streets, he had the whiff of violets
perpetually in his nose; and he had attached himself to
sounds and suggestions, vibrations of the air, human
and dramatic, he imagined, as they were not in other
places, that came out for him more and more as the
mild afternoons deepened — a far-off hum, a sharp
near click on the asphalt, a voice calling, replying,
somewhere and as full of tone as an actor's in a play.
He was to dine at home, as usual, with Waymarsh —
they had settled to that for thrift and simplicity; and
he now hung about before his friend came down.

He read his telegram in the court, standing still a
long time where he had opened it and giving five minutes afterwards to the renewed study of it. At last,
quickly, he crumpled it up as if to get it out of the way;
in spite of which, however, he kept it there — still kept
it when, at the end of another turn, he had dropped
into a chair placed near a small table. Here, with his
scrap of paper compressed in his fist and further con-

cealed by his folding his arms tight, he sat for some time in thought, gazed before him so straight that Waymarsh appeared and approached him without catching his eye. The latter in fact, struck with his appearance, looked at him hard for a single instant and then, as if determined to that course by some special vividness in it, dropped back into the *salon de lecture* without addressing him. But the pilgrim from Milrose permitted himself still to observe the scene from behind the clear glass plate of that retreat. Strether ended, as he sat, by a fresh scrutiny of his compressed missive, which he smoothed out carefully again as he placed it on his table. There it remained for some minutes, until, at last looking up, he saw Waymarsh watching him from within. It was on this that their eyes met — met for a moment during which neither moved. But Strether then got up, folding his telegram more carefully and putting it into his waistcoat pocket.

A few minutes later the friends were seated together at dinner; but Strether had meanwhile said nothing about it, and they eventually parted, after coffee in the court, with nothing said on either side. Our friend had moreover the consciousness that even less than usual was on this occasion said between them, so that it was almost as if each had been waiting for something from the other. Waymarsh had always more or less the air of sitting at the door of his tent, and silence, after so many weeks, had come to play its part in their concert. This note indeed, to Strether's sense, had lately taken a fuller tone, and it was his fancy to-night that they had never quite so drawn it out. Yet it befell, none the less, that he closed the door to confidence when his companion finally asked him if there were anything particular the matter with him. "Nothing," he replied, "more than usual."

On the morrow, however, at an early hour, he found occasion to give an answer more in consonance with the facts. What was the matter had continued to be so all the previous evening, the first hours of which, after dinner, in his room, he had devoted to the copious composition of a letter. He had quitted Waymarsh for this purpose, leaving him to his own resources with less ceremony than their wont, but finally coming down again with his letter unconcluded and going forth into the streets without enquiry for his comrade. He had taken a long vague walk, and one o'clock had struck before his return and his re-ascent to his room by the aid of the glimmering candle-end left for him on the shelf outside the porter's lodge. He had possessed himself, on closing his door, of the numerous loose sheets of his unfinished composition, and then, without reading them over, had torn them into small pieces. He had thereupon slept — as if it had been in some measure thanks to that sacrifice — the sleep of the just, and had prolonged his rest considerably beyond his custom. Thus it was that when, between nine and ten, the tap of the knob of a walking-stick sounded on his door, he had not yet made himself altogether presentable. Chad Newsome's bright deep voice determined quickly enough none the less the admission of the visitor. The little blue paper of the evening before, plainly an object the more precious for its escape from premature destruction, now lay on the sill of the open window, smoothed out afresh and kept from blowing away by the superincumbent weight of his watch. Chad, looking about with careless and competent criticism, as he looked wherever he went, immediately espied it and permitted himself to fix it for a moment rather hard. After which he turned his eyes to his host. "It has come then at last?"

Strether paused in the act of pinning his necktie. "Then you know — ? You've had one too?"

"No, I've had nothing, and I only know what I see. I see that thing and I guess. Well," he added, "it comes as pat as in a play, for I've precisely turned up this morning — as I would have done yesterday, but it was impossible — to take you."

"To take me?" Strether had turned again to his glass.

"Back, at last, as I promised. I'm ready — I've really been ready this month. I've only been waiting for you — as was perfectly right. But you're better now; you're safe — I see that for myself; you've got all your good. You're looking, this morning, as fit as a flea."

Strether, at his glass, finished dressing; consulting that witness moreover on this last opinion. *Was* he looking preternaturally fit? There was something in it perhaps for Chad's wonderful eye, but he had felt himself for hours rather in pieces. Such a judgement, however, was after all but a contribution to his resolve; it testified unwittingly to his wisdom. He was still firmer, apparently — since it shone in him as a light — than he had flattered himself. His firmness indeed was slightly compromised, as he faced about to his friend, by the way this very personage looked —

27

though the case would of course have been worse had n't the secret of personal magnificence been at every hour Chad's unfailing possession. There he was in all the pleasant morning freshness of it — strong and sleek and gay, easy and fragrant and fathomless, with happy health in his colour, and pleasant silver in his thick young hair, and the right word for everything on the lips that his clear brownness caused to show as red. He had never struck Strether as personally such a success; it was as if now, for his definite surrender, he had gathered himself vividly together. This, sharply and rather strangely, was the form in which he was to be presented to Woollett. Our friend took him in again — he was always taking him in and yet finding that parts of him still remained out; though even thus his image showed through a mist of other things. "I've had a cable," Strether said, "from your mother."

"I dare say, my dear man. I hope she's well."

Strether hesitated. "No — she's not well, I'm sorry to have to tell you."

"Ah," said Chad, "I must have had the instinct of it. All the more reason then that we should start straight off."

Strether had now got together hat, gloves and stick, but Chad had dropped on the sofa as if to show where he wished to make his point. He kept observing his companion's things; he might have been judging how quickly they could be packed. He might even have wished to hint that he'd send his own servant to assist. "What do you mean," Strether enquired, "by 'straight off'?"

28

BOOK SEVENTH

"Oh by one of next week's boats. Everything at this season goes out so light that berths will be easy anywhere."

Strether had in his hand his telegram, which he had kept there after attaching his watch, and he now offered it to Chad, who, however, with an odd movement, declined to take it. "Thanks, I'd rather not. Your correspondence with Mother's your own affair. I'm only *with* you both on it, whatever it is." Strether, at this, while their eyes met, slowly folded the missive and put it in his pocket; after which, before he had spoken again, Chad broke fresh ground. "Has Miss Gostrey come back?"

But when Strether presently spoke it wasn't in answer. "It's not, I gather, that your mother's physically ill; her health, on the whole, this spring, seems to have been better than usual. But she's worried, she's anxious, and it appears to have risen within the last few days to a climax. We've tired out, between us, her patience."

"Oh it isn't *you!*" Chad generously protested.

"I beg your pardon — it *is* me." Strether was mild and melancholy, but firm. He saw it far away and over his companion's head. "It's very particularly me."

"Well then all the more reason. *Marchons, marchons!*" said the young man gaily. His host, however, at this, but continued to stand agaze; and he had the next thing repeated his question of a moment before. "Has Miss Gostrey come back?"

"Yes, two days ago."

"Then you've seen her?"

29

"No — I'm to see her to-day." But Strether would n't linger now on Miss Gostrey. "Your mother sends me an ultimatum. If I can't bring you I'm to leave you; I'm to come at any rate myself."

"Ah but you *can* bring me now," Chad, from his sofa, reassuringly replied.

Strether had a pause. "I don't think I understand you. Why was it that, more than a month ago, you put it to me so urgently to let Madame de Vionnet speak for you?"

"'Why'?" Chad considered, but he had it at his fingers' ends. "Why but because I knew how well she'd do it? It was the way to keep you quiet and, to that extent, do you good. Besides," he happily and comfortably explained, "I wanted you really to know her and to get the impression of her — and you see the good that *has* done you."

"Well," said Strether, "the way she has spoken for you, all the same — so far as I've given her a chance — has only made me feel how much she wishes to keep you. If you make nothing of that I don't see why you wanted me to listen to her."

"Why my dear man," Chad exclaimed, "I make everything of it! How can you doubt — ?"

"I doubt only because you come to me this morning with your signal to start."

Chad stared, then gave a laugh. "And is n't my signal to start just what you've been waiting for?"

Strether debated; he took another turn. "This last month I've been awaiting, I think, more than anything else, the message I have here."

"You mean you've been afraid of it?"

"Well, I was doing my business in my own way. And I suppose your present announcement," Strether went on, "is n't merely the result of your sense of what I've expected. Otherwise you would n't have put me in relation —" But he paused, pulling up.

At this Chad rose. "Ah *her* wanting me not to go has nothing to do with it! It's only because she's afraid — afraid of the way that, over there, I may get caught. But her fear's groundless."

He had met again his companion's sufficiently searching look. "Are you tired of her?"

Chad gave him in reply to this, with a movement of the head, the strangest slow smile he had ever had from him. "Never."

It had immediately, on Strether's imagination, so deep and soft an effect that our friend could only for the moment keep it before him. "Never?"

"Never," Chad obligingly and serenely repeated.

It made his companion take several more steps. "Then *you're* not afraid."

"Afraid to go?"

Strether pulled up again. "Afraid to stay."

The young man looked brightly amazed. "You want me now to 'stay'?"

"If I don't immediately sail the Pococks will immediately come out. That's what I mean," said Strether, "by your mother's ultimatum."

Chad showed a still livelier, but not an alarmed interest. "She has turned on Sarah and Jim?"

Strether joined him for an instant in the vision. "Oh and you may be sure Mamie. *That's* whom she's turning on."

This also Chad saw — he laughed out. "Mamie — to corrupt me?"

"Ah," said Strether, "she's very charming."

"So you've already more than once told me. I should like to see her."

Something happy and easy, something above all unconscious, in the way he said this, brought home again to his companion the facility of his attitude and the enviability of his state. "See her then by all means. And consider too," Strether went on, "that you really give your sister a lift in letting her come to you. You give her a couple of months of Paris, which she has n't seen, if I'm not mistaken, since just after she was married, and which I'm sure she wants but the pretext to visit."

Chad listened, but with all his own knowledge of the world. "She has had it, the pretext, these several years, yet she has never taken it."

"Do you mean *you?*" Strether after an instant enquired.

"Certainly — the lone exile. And whom do you mean?" said Chad.

"Oh I mean *me*. I'm her pretext. That is — for it comes to the same thing — I'm your mother's."

"Then why," Chad asked, "does n't Mother come herself?"

His friend gave him a long look. "Should you like her to?" And as he for the moment said nothing: "It's perfectly open to you to cable for her."

Chad continued to think. "Will she come if I do?"

"Quite possibly. But try, and you'll see."

"Why don't *you* try?" Chad after a moment asked.

32

"Because I don't want to."

Chad thought. "Don't desire her presence here?"

Strether faced the question, and his answer was the more emphatic. "Don't put it off, my dear boy, on *me!*"

"Well — I see what you mean. I'm sure you'd behave beautifully, but you *don't* want to see her. So I won't play you that trick."

"Ah," Strether declared, "I should n't call it a trick. You've a perfect right, and it would be perfectly straight of you." Then he added in a different tone: "You'd have moreover, in the person of Madame de Vionnet, a very interesting relation prepared for her."

Their eyes, on this proposition, continued to meet, but Chad's, pleasant and bold, never flinched for a moment. He got up at last, and he said something with which Strether was struck. "She would n't understand her, but that makes no difference. Madame de Vionnet would like to see her. She'd like to be charming to her. She believes she could work it."

Strether thought a moment, affected by this, but finally turning away. "She could n't!"

"You're quite sure?" Chad asked.

"Well, risk it if you like!"

Strether, who uttered this with serenity, had urged a plea for their now getting into the air; but the young man still waited. "Have you sent your answer?"

"No, I've done nothing yet."

"Were you waiting to see me?"

"No, not that."

"Only waiting" — and Chad, with this, had a smile for him — "to see Miss Gostrey?"

"No — not even Miss Gostrey. I was n't waiting to see any one. I had only waited, till now, to make up my mind — in complete solitude; and, since I of course absolutely owe you the information, was on the point of going out with it quite made up. Have therefore a little more patience with me. Remember," Strether went on, "that that's what you originally asked *me* to have. I've had it, you see, and you see what has come of it. Stay on with me."

Chad looked grave. "How much longer?"

"Well, till I make you a sign. I can't myself, you know, at the best, or at the worst, stay for ever. Let the Pococks come," Strether repeated.

"Because it gains you time?"

"Yes — it gains me time."

Chad, as if it still puzzled him, waited a minute. "You don't want to get back to Mother?"

"Not just yet. I'm not ready."

"You feel," Chad asked in a tone of his own, "the charm of life over here?"

"Immensely." Strether faced it. "You've helped me so to feel it that that surely need n't surprise you."

"No, it does n't surprise me, and I'm delighted. But what, my dear man," Chad went on with conscious queerness, "does it all lead to for you?"

The change of position and of relation, for each, was so oddly betrayed in the question that Chad laughed out as soon as he had uttered it — which made Strether also laugh. "Well, to my having a certitude that has been tested — that has passed through the fire. But oh," he could n't help breaking out, "if within my first month here you had been willing to move with me —!"

"Well?" said Chad, while he broke down as for weight of thought.

"Well, we should have been over there by now."

"Ah but you would n't have had your fun!"

"I should have had a month of it; and I'm having now, if you want to know," Strether continued, "enough to last me for the rest of my days."

Chad looked amused and interested, yet still somewhat in the dark; partly perhaps because Strether's estimate of fun had required of him from the first a good deal of elucidation. "It would n't do if I left you —?"

"Left me?" — Strether remained blank.

"Only for a month or two — time to go and come. Madame de Vionnet," Chad smiled, "would look after you in the interval."

"To go back by yourself, I remaining here?" Again for an instant their eyes had the question out; after which Strether said: "Grotesque!"

"But I want to see Mother," Chad presently returned. "Remember how long it is since I've seen Mother."

"Long indeed; and that's exactly why I was originally so keen for moving you. Had n't you shown us enough how beautifully you could do without it?"

"Oh but," said Chad wonderfully, "I'm better now."

There was an easy triumph in it that made his friend laugh out again. "Oh if you were worse I

35

should know what to do with you. In that case I believe I'd have you gagged and strapped down, carried on board resisting, kicking. How *much*," Strether asked, "do you want to see Mother?"

"How much?" — Chad seemed to find it in fact difficult to say.

"How much."

"Why as much as you've made me. I'd give anything to see her. And you've left me," Chad went on, "in little enough doubt as to how much *she* wants it."

Strether thought a minute. "Well then if those things are really your motive catch the French steamer and sail to-morrow. Of course, when it comes to that, you're absolutely free to do as you choose. From the moment you can't hold yourself I can only accept your flight."

"I'll fly in a minute then," said Chad, "if you'll stay here."

"I'll stay here till the next steamer — then I'll follow you."

"And do you call that," Chad asked, "accepting my flight?"

"Certainly — it's the only thing to call it. The only way to keep me here, accordingly," Strether explained, "is by staying yourself."

Chad took it in. "All the more that I've really dished you, eh?"

"Dished me?" Strether echoed as inexpressively as possible.

"Why if she sends out the Pococks it will be that she does n't trust you, and if she does n't trust you, that bears upon — well, you know what."

BOOK SEVENTH

Strether decided after a moment that he did know what, and in consonance with this he spoke. "You see then all the more what you owe me."

"Well, if I do see, how can I pay?"

"By not deserting me. By standing by me."

"Oh I say —!" But Chad, as they went downstairs, clapped a firm hand, in the manner of a pledge, upon his shoulder. They descended slowly together and had, in the court of the hotel, some further talk, of which the upshot was that they presently separated. Chad Newsome departed, and Strether, left alone, looked about, superficially, for Waymarsh. But Waymarsh had n't yet, it appeared, come down, and our friend finally went forth without sight of him.

III

At four o'clock that afternoon he had still not seen
him, but he was then, as to make up for this, engaged
in talk about him with Miss Gostrey. Strether had
kept away from home all day, given himself up to
the town and to his thoughts, wandered and mused,
been at once restless and absorbed — and all with the
present climax of a rich little welcome in the Quartier
Marbœuf. "Waymarsh has been, 'unbeknown' to
me, I'm convinced" — for Miss Gostrey had enquired — "in communication with Woollett: the consequence of which was, last night, the loudest possible call for me."

"Do you mean a letter to bring you home?"

"No — a cable, which I have at this moment in my
pocket: a 'Come back by the first ship.'"

Strether's hostess, it might have been made out,
just escaped changing colour. Reflexion arrived but
in time and established a provisional serenity. It was
perhaps exactly this that enabled her to say with
duplicity: "And you're going — ?"

"You almost deserve it when you abandon me so."

She shook her head as if this were not worth taking
up. "My absence has helped you — as I've only to
look at you to see. It was my calculation, and I'm
justified. You're not where you were. And the
thing," she smiled, "was for me not to be there either.
You can go of yourself."

"Oh but I feel to-day," he comfortably declared, "that I shall want you yet."

She took him all in again. "Well, I promise you not again to leave you, but it will only be to follow you. You've got your momentum and can toddle alone."

He intelligently accepted it. "Yes — I suppose I can toddle. It's the sight of that in fact that has upset Waymarsh. He can bear it — the way I strike him as going — no longer. That's only the climax of his original feeling. He wants me to quit; and he must have written to Woollett that I'm in peril of perdition."

"Ah good!" she murmured. "But is it only your supposition?"

"I make it out — it explains."

"Then he denies? — or you haven't asked him?"

"I've not had time," Strether said; "I made it out but last night, putting various things together, and I've not been since then face to face with him."

She wondered. "Because you're too disgusted? You can't trust yourself?"

He settled his glasses on his nose. "Do I look in a great rage?"

"You look divine!"

"There's nothing," he went on, "to be angry about. He has done me on the contrary a service."

She made it out. "By bringing things to a head?"

"How well you understand!" he almost groaned. "Waymarsh won't in the least, at any rate, when I have it out with him, deny or extenuate. He has acted from the deepest conviction, with the best conscience and after wakeful nights. He'll recognise that he's fully responsible, and will consider that he has been highly successful; so that any discussion we may have will bring us quite together again — bridge the dark stream that has kept us so thoroughly apart. We shall have at last, in the consequences of his act, something we can definitely talk about."

She was silent a little. "How wonderfully you take it! But you're always wonderful."

He had a pause that matched her own; then he had, with an adequate spirit, a complete admission. "It's quite true. I'm extremely wonderful just now. I dare say in fact I'm quite fantastic, and I should n't be at all surprised if I were mad."

"Then tell me!" she earnestly pressed. As he, however, for the time answered nothing, only returning the look with which she watched him, she presented herself where it was easier to meet her. "What will Mr. Waymarsh exactly have done?"

"Simply have written a letter. One will have been quite enough. He has told them I want looking after."

"And *do* you?" — she was all interest.

"Immensely. And I shall get it."

"By which you mean you don't budge?"

"I don't budge."

"You've cabled?"

"No — I've made Chad do it."

"That you decline to come?"

"That *he* declines. We had it out this morning and I brought him round. He had come in, before I was down, to tell me he was ready — ready, I mean,

40

to return. And he went off, after ten minutes with me, to say he would n't."

Miss Gostrey followed with intensity. "Then you 've *stopped* him ?"

Strether settled himself afresh in his chair. "I 've stopped him. That is for the time. That" — he gave it to her more vividly — "is where I am."

"I see, I see. But where 's Mr. Newsome ? He was ready," she asked, "to go ?"

"All ready."

"And sincerely — believing *you 'd* be ?"

"Perfectly, I think; so that he was amazed to find the hand I had laid on him to pull him over suddenly converted into an engine for keeping him still."

It was an account of the matter Miss Gostrey could weigh. "Does he think the conversion sudden ?"

"Well," said Strether, "I 'm not altogether sure what he thinks. I 'm not sure of anything that concerns him, except that the more I 've seen of him the less I 've found him what I originally expected. He 's obscure, and that 's why I 'm waiting."

She wondered. "But for what in particular ?"

"For the answer to his cable."

"And what was his cable ?"

"I don't know," Strether replied; "it was to be, when he left me, according to his own taste. I simply said to him : 'I want to stay, and the only way for me to do so is for *you* to.' That I wanted to stay seemed to interest him, and he acted on that."

Miss Gostrey turned it over. "He wants then himself to stay."

"He half wants it. That is he half wants to go. My

original appeal has to that extent worked in him. Nevertheless," Strether pursued, "he won't go. Not, at least, so long as I'm here."

"But you can't," his companion suggested, "stay here always. I wish you could."

"By no means. Still, I want to see him a little further. He's not in the least the case I supposed; he's quite another case. And it's as such that he interests me." It was almost as if for his own intelligence that, deliberate and lucid, our friend thus expressed the matter. "I don't want to give him up."

Miss Gostrey but desired to help his lucidity. She had however to be light and tactful. "Up, you mean — a — to his mother?"

"Well, I'm not thinking of his mother now. I'm thinking of the plan of which I was the mouthpiece, which, as soon as we met, I put before him as persuasively as I knew how, and which was drawn up, as it were, in complete ignorance of all that, in this last long period, has been happening to him. It took no account whatever of the impression I was here on the spot immediately to begin to receive from him — impressions of which I feel sure I'm far from having had the last."

Miss Gostrey had a smile of the most genial criticism. "So your idea is — more or less — to stay out of curiosity?"

"Call it what you like! I don't care what it's called —"

"So long as you do stay? Certainly not then. I call it, all the same, immense fun," Maria Gostrey declared; "and to see you work it out will be one of the

sensations of my life. It *is* clear you can toddle
alone!"

He received this tribute without elation. "I shan't
be alone when the Pococks have come."

Her eyebrows went up. "The Pococks are coming?"

"That, I mean, is what will happen — and happen
as quickly as possible — in consequence of Chad's
cable. They'll simply embark. Sarah will come to
speak for her mother — with an effect different from
my muddle."

Miss Gostrey more gravely wondered. "*She* then
will take him back?"

"Very possibly — and we shall see. She must at
any rate have the chance, and she may be trusted to
do all she can."

"And do you *want* that?"

"Of course," said Strether, "I want it. I want to
play fair."

But she had lost for a moment the thread. "If it
devolves on the Pococks why do you stay?"

"Just to see that I *do* play fair — and a little also,
no doubt, that they do." Strether was luminous as he
had never been. "I came out to find myself in presence of new facts — facts that have kept striking me
as less and less met by our old reasons. The matter's
perfectly simple. New reasons — reasons as new as
the facts themselves — are wanted; and of this our
friends at Woollett — Chad's and mine — were at
the earliest moment definitely notified. If any are
producible Mrs. Pocock will produce them; she'll
bring over the whole collection. They'll be," he

added with a pensive smile, "a part of the 'fun' you speak of."

She was quite in the current now and floating by his side. "It's Mamie — so far as I've had it from you — who'll be their great card." And then as his contemplative silence was n't a denial she significantly added: "I think I'm sorry for her."

"I think *I* am!" — and Strether sprang up, moving about a little as her eyes followed him. "But it can't be helped."

"You mean her coming out can't be?"

He explained after another turn what he meant. "The only way for her not to come is for me to go home — as I believe that on the spot I could prevent it. But the difficulty as to that is that if I do go home —"

"I see, I see" — she had easily understood. "Mr. Newsome will do the same, and that's not" — she laughed out now — "to be thought of."

Strether had no laugh; he had only a quiet comparatively placid look that might have shown him as proof against ridicule. "Strange, is n't it?"

They had, in the matter that so much interested them, come so far as this without sounding another name — to which however their present momentary silence was full of a conscious reference. Strether's question was a sufficient implication of the weight it had gained with him during the absence of his hostess; and just for that reason a single gesture from her could pass for him as a vivid answer. Yet he was answered still better when she said in a moment: "Will Mr. Newsome introduce his sister —?"

"To Madame de Vionnet?" Strether spoke the name at last. "I shall be greatly surprised if he does n't."

She seemed to gaze at the possibility. "You mean you 've thought of it and you 're prepared."

"I 've thought of it and I 'm prepared."

It was to her visitor now that she applied her consideration. "Bon! You *are* magnificent!"

"Well," he answered after a pause and a little wearily, but still standing there before her — "well, that 's what, just once in all my dull days, I think I shall like to have been!"

Two days later he had news from Chad of a communication from Woollett in response to their determinant telegram, this missive being addressed to Chad himself and announcing the immediate departure for France of Sarah and Jim and Mamie. Strether had meanwhile on his own side cabled; he had but delayed that act till after his visit to Miss Gostrey, an interview by which, as so often before, he felt his sense of things cleared up and settled. His message to Mrs. Newsome, in answer to her own, had consisted of the words: "Judge best to take another month, but with full appreciation of all re-enforcements." He had added that he was writing, but he was of course always writing; it was a practice that continued, oddly enough, to relieve him, to make him come nearer than anything else to the consciousness of doing something: so that he often wondered if he had n't really, under his recent stress, acquired some hollow trick, one of the specious arts of make-believe. Would n't the pages he still so freely dispatched by the American post have been worthy of a showy journalist, some master of the great new science of beating the sense out of words? Was n't he writing against time, and mainly to show he was kind? — since it had become quite his habit not to like to read himself over. On those lines he could still be liberal, yet it was at best a sort of whistling in the dark. It was unmistakeable moreover that the sense of being in the dark now pressed on him more sharply — creating thereby the need for a louder and livelier whistle. He whistled long and hard after sending his message; he whistled again and again in celebration of Chad's news; there was an interval of a fortnight in which this exercise helped him. He had no great notion of what, on the spot, Sarah Pocock would have to say, though he had indeed confused premonitions; but it should n't be in her power to say — it should n't be in any one's anywhere to say — that he was neglecting her mother. He might have written before more freely, but he had never written more copiously; and he frankly gave for a reason at Woollett that he wished to fill the void created there by Sarah's departure.

The increase of his darkness, however, and the quickening, as I have called it, of his tune, resided in the fact that he was hearing almost nothing. He had for some time been aware that he was hearing less than before, and he was now clearly following a process by which Mrs. Newsome's letters could but logically stop. He had n't had a line for many days, and he needed no proof — though he was, in time, to have plenty — that she would n't have put pen to paper after receiving the hint that had determined her telegram. She would n't write till Sarah should have seen him and reported on him. It was strange, though it might well be less so than his own behaviour appeared at Woollett. It was at any rate significant, and what *was* remarkable was the way his friend's nature and manner put on for him, through this very drop of demonstration, a greater intensity. It struck him really that he had never so lived with her as during this period of her silence; the silence was a sacred hush, a finer clearer medium, in which her idiosyncrasies showed. He walked about with her, sat with her, drove with her and dined face-to-face with her — a rare treat "in his life," as he could perhaps have scarce escaped phrasing it; and if he had never seen her so soundless he had never, on the other hand, felt her so highly, so almost austerely, herself: pure and by the vulgar estimate "cold," but deep devoted delicate sensitive noble. Her vividness in these respects became for him, in the special conditions, almost an obsession; and though the obsession sharpened his pulses, adding really to the excitement of life, there were hours at which, to be less on the stretch, he directly sought forgetfulness. He knew it for the queerest of adventures — a circumstance capable of playing such a part only for Lambert Strether — that in Paris itself, of all places, he should find this ghost of the lady of Woollett more importunate than any other presence.

When he went back to Maria Gostrey it was for the change to something else. And yet after all the change scarcely operated, for he talked to her of Mrs. Newsome in these days as he had never talked before. He had hitherto observed in that particular a discretion and a law; considerations that at present broke down quite as if relations had altered. They had n't *really* altered, he said to himself, so much as that came to; for if what had occurred was of course that Mrs. Newsome had ceased to trust him, there was nothing on the other hand to prove that he should n't win back her confidence. It was quite his present theory that he would leave no stone unturned to do so; and in fact if he now told Maria things about her that he had never told before this was largely because it kept before him the idea of the honour of such a woman's esteem. His relation with Maria as well was, strangely enough, no longer quite the same; this truth — though not too disconcertingly — had come up between them on the renewal of their meetings. It was all contained in what she had then almost immediately said to him; it was represented by the remark she had needed but ten minutes to make and that he had n't been disposed to gainsay. He could toddle alone, and the difference that showed was extraordinary. The turn taken by their talk had promptly confirmed this difference; his larger confidence on the score of Mrs. Newsome did the rest; and the time seemed already far off when he had held out his small thirsty cup to the spout of her pail. Her pail was scarce touched now, and other fountains had flowed for him; she fell into her place as but one of his tributaries; and there was a strange sweetness — a melancholy mildness that touched him — in her acceptance of the altered order.

It marked for himself the flight of time, or at any

rate what he was pleased to think of with irony and pity as the rush of experience; it having been but the day before yesterday that he sat at her feet and held on by her garment and was fed by her hand. It was the proportions that were changed, and the proportions were at all times, he philosophised, the very conditions of perception, the terms of thought. It was as if, with her effective little *entresol* and her wide acquaintance, her activities, varieties, promiscuities, the duties and devotions that took up nine tenths of her time and of which he got, guardedly, but the side-wind — it was as if she had shrunk to a secondary element and had consented to the shrinkage with the perfection of tact. This perfection had never failed her; it had originally been greater than his prime measure for it; it had kept him quite apart, kept him out of the shop, as she called her huge general acquaintance, made their commerce as quiet, as much a thing of the home alone — the opposite of the shop — as if she had never another customer. She had been wonderful to him at first, with the memory of her little *entresol*, the image to which, on most mornings at that time, his eyes directly opened; but now she mainly figured for him as but part of the bristling total — though of course always as a person to whom he should never cease to be indebted. It would never be given to him certainly to inspire a greater kindness. She had decked him out for others, and he saw at this point at least nothing she would ever ask for. She only wondered and questioned and listened, rendering him the homage of a wistful speculation. She expressed it repeatedly; he was already far beyond her, and she must prepare herself to lose him. There was but one little chance for her.

Often as she had said it he met it — for it was a touch he liked — each time the same way. "My coming to grief?"

"Yes — then I might patch you up."

"Oh for my real smash, if it takes place, there will be no patching."

"But you surely don't mean it will kill you."

"No — worse. It will make me old."

"Ah nothing can do that! The wonderful and special thing about you is that you *are*, at this time of day, youth." Then she always made, further, one of those remarks that she had completely ceased to adorn with hesitations or apologies, and that had, by the same token, in spite of their extreme straightness, ceased to produce in Strether the least embarrassment. She made him believe them, and they became thereby as impersonal as truth itself. "It's just your particular charm."

His answer too was always the same. "Of course I'm youth — youth for the trip to Europe. I began to be young, or at least to get the benefit of it, the moment I met you at Chester, and that's what has been taking place ever since. I never had the benefit at the proper time — which comes to saying that I never had the thing itself. I'm having the benefit at this moment; I had it the other day when I said to Chad 'Wait'; I shall have it still again when Sarah Pocock arrives. It's a benefit that would make a poor show for many people; and I don't know who else but you and I, frankly, could begin to see in it what I feel. I don't get drunk; I don't pursue the ladies; I don't spend money; I don't even write sonnets. But nevertheless I'm making up late for what I did n't have early. I cultivate my little benefit in my own little way. It amuses me more than anything that has happened to me in all my life. They may say what they like — it's my surrender, it's my tribute, to youth. One puts that in where one can — it has to come in somewhere, if only out of the lives, the conditions, the feelings of other persons. Chad gives me the sense of it, for all his grey hairs, which merely make it solid in him and safe and serene; and *she* does the same, for all her being older than he, for all her marriageable daughter, her separated husband, her agitated history. Though they're young enough, my pair, I don't say they're, in the freshest way, their *own* absolutely prime adolescence; for that has nothing to do with it. The point is that they're mine. Yes, they're my youth; since somehow at the right time nothing else ever was. What I meant just now therefore is that it would all go — go before doing its work — if they were to fail me."

On which, just here, Miss Gostrey inveterately questioned. "What do you, in particular, call its work?"

"Well, to see me through."

"But through what?" — she liked to get it all out of him.

"Why through this experience." That was all that would come.

It regularly gave her none the less the last word. "Don't you remember how in those first days of our meeting it was *I* who was to see you through?"

51

"Remember? Tenderly, deeply" — he always rose to it. "You're just doing your part in letting me maunder to you thus."

"Ah don't speak as if my part were small; since whatever else fails you — "

"*You* won't, ever, ever, ever?" — he thus took her up. "Oh I beg your pardon; you necessarily, you inevitably *will*. Your conditions — that's what I mean — won't allow me anything to do for you."

"Let alone — I see what you mean — that I'm drearily dreadfully old. I *am*, but there's a service — possible for you to render — that I know, all the same, I shall think of."

"And what will it be?"

This, in fine, however, she would never tell him. "You shall hear only if your smash takes place. As that's really out of the question, I won't expose myself" — a point at which, for reasons of his own, Strether ceased to press.

He came round, for publicity — it was the easiest thing — to the idea that his smash *was* out of the question, and this rendered idle the discussion of what might follow it. He attached an added importance, as the days elapsed, to the arrival of the Pococks; he had even a shameful sense of waiting for it insincerely and incorrectly. He accused himself of making believe to his own mind that Sarah's presence, her impression, her judgement would simplify and harmonise; he accused himself of being so afraid of what they *might* do that he sought refuge, to beg the whole question, in a vain fury. He had abundantly seen at home what they were in the habit of doing, and he had not at present the smallest ground. His clearest vision was when he made out that what he most desired was an account more full and free of Mrs. Newsome's state of mind than any he felt he could now expect from herself; that calculation at least went hand in hand with the sharp consciousness of wishing to prove to himself that he was not afraid to look his behaviour in the face. If he was by an inexorable logic to pay for it he was literally impatient to know the cost, and he held himself ready to pay in instalments. The first instalment would be precisely this entertainment of Sarah; as a consequence of which, moreover, he should know vastly better how he stood.

BOOK EIGHTH

I

STRETHER rambled alone during these few days, the effect of the incident of the previous week having been to simplify in a marked fashion his mixed relations with Waymarsh. Nothing had passed between them in reference to Mrs. Newsome's summons but that our friend had mentioned to his own the departure of the deputation actually at sea — giving him thus an opportunity to confess to the occult intervention he imputed to him. Waymarsh however in the event confessed to nothing; and though this falsified in some degree Strether's forecast the latter amusedly saw in it the same depth of good conscience out of which the dear man's impertinence had originally sprung. He was patient with the dear man now and delighted to observe how unmistakeably he had put on flesh; he felt his own holiday so successfully large and free that he was full of allowances and charities in respect to those cabined and confined: his instinct toward a spirit so strapped down as Waymarsh's was to walk round it on tiptoe for fear of waking it up to a sense of losses by this time irretrievable. It was all very funny, he knew, and but the difference, as he often said to himself, of tweedledum and tweedledee — an emancipation so purely comparative that it was like the advance of the door-mat on the scraper; yet the present crisis was happily to profit by it and the pilgrim from Milrose to know himself more than ever in the right.

Strether felt that when he heard of the approach of the Pococks the impulse of pity quite sprang up in him beside the impulse of triumph. That was exactly why Waymarsh had looked at him with eyes in which the heat of justice was measured and shaded. He had looked very hard, as if affectionately sorry for the friend — the friend of fifty-five — whose frivolity had had thus to be recorded; becoming, however, but obscurely sententious and leaving his companion to formulate a charge. It was in this general attitude that he had of late altogether taken refuge; with the drop of discussion they were solemnly sadly superficial; Strether recognised in him the mere portentous rumination to which Miss Barrace had so good-humouredly described herself as assigning a corner of her salon. It was quite as if he knew his surreptitious step had been divined, and it was also as if he missed the chance to explain the purity of his motive; but this privation of relief should be precisely his small penance: it was not amiss for Strether that he should find himself to that degree uneasy. If he had been challenged or accused, rebuked for meddling or otherwise pulled up, he would probably have shown, on his own system, all the height of his consistency, all the depth of his good faith. Explicit resentment of his course would have made him take the floor, and the thump of his fist on the table would have affirmed him as consciously incorruptible. Had what now really prevailed with Strether been but a dread of that thump — a dread of wincing a little painfully at what it might invidiously demonstrate? However this might be, at any rate, one of the marks

of the crisis was a visible, a studied lapse, in Waymarsh, of betrayed concern. As if to make up to his
comrade for the stroke by which he had played pro-
vidence he now conspicuously ignored his movements,
withdrew himself from the pretension to share them,
stiffened up his sensibility to neglect, and, clasping
his large empty hands and swinging his large restless
foot, clearly looked to another quarter for justice.

This made for independence on Strether's part,
and he had in truth at no moment of his stay been so
free to go and come. The early summer brushed the
picture over and blurred everything but the near; it
made a vast warm fragrant medium in which the elements floated together on the best of terms, in which
rewards were immediate and reckonings postponed.
Chad was out of town again, for the first time since
his visitor's first view of him; he had explained this
necessity — without detail, yet also without embarrassment; the circumstance was one of those which,
in the young man's life, testified to the variety of his
ties. Strether was n't otherwise concerned with it
than for its so testifying — a pleasant multitudinous
image in which he took comfort. He took comfort,
by the same stroke, in the swing of Chad's pendulum
back from that other swing, the sharp jerk towards
Woollett, so stayed by his own hand. He had the
entertainment of thinking that if he had for that moment stopped the clock it was to promote the next
minute this still livelier motion. He himself did what
he had n't done before; he took two or three times
whole days off — irrespective of others, of two or
three taken with Miss Gostrey, two or three taken

with little Bilham: he went to Chartres and cultivated, before the front of the cathedral, a general easy beatitude; he went to Fontainebleau and imagined himself on the way to Italy; he went to Rouen with a little handbag and inordinately spent the night.

One afternoon he did something quite different; finding himself in the neighbourhood of a fine old house across the river, he passed under the great arch of its doorway and asked at the porter's lodge for Madame de Vionnet. He had already hovered more than once about that possibility, been aware of it, in the course of ostensible strolls, as lurking but round the corner. Only it had perversely happened, after his morning at Notre Dame, that his consistency, as he considered and intended it, had come back to him; whereby he had reflected that the encounter in question had been none of his making; clinging again intensely to the strength of his position, which was precisely that there was nothing in it for himself. From the moment he actively pursued the charming associate of his adventure, from that moment his position weakened, for he was then acting in an interested way. It was only within a few days that he had fixed himself a limit: he promised himself his consistency should end with Sarah's arrival. It was arguing correctly to feel the title to a free hand conferred on him by this event. If he was n't to be let alone he should be merely a dupe to act with delicacy. If he was n't to be trusted he could at least take his ease. If he was to be placed under control he gained leave to try what his position *might* agreeably give him. An ideal rigour would perhaps postpone the

trial till after the Pococks had shown their spirit; and
it was to an ideal rigour that he had quite promised
himself to conform.

Suddenly, however, on this particular day, he
felt a particular fear under which everything col-
lapsed. He knew abruptly that he was afraid of himself — and yet not in relation to the effect on his
sensibilities of another hour of Madame de Vionnet.
What he dreaded was the effect of a single hour of
Sarah Pocock, as to whom he was visited, in troubled
nights, with fantastic waking dreams. She loomed at
him larger than life; she increased in volume as she
drew nearer; she so met his eyes that, his imagination
taking, after the first step, all, and more than all, the
strides, he already felt her come down on him, already burned, under her reprobation, with the blush
of guilt, already consented, by way of penance, to the
instant forfeiture of everything. He saw himself, under her direction, recommitted to Woollett as juvenile
offenders are committed to reformatories. It was n't
of course that Woollett was really a place of discipline;
but he knew in advance that Sarah's salon at the
hotel would be. His danger, at any rate, in such
moods of alarm, was some concession, on this ground,
that would involve a sharp rupture with the actual;
therefore if he waited to take leave of that actual he
might wholly miss his chance. It was represented
with supreme vividness by Madame de Vionnet, and
that is why, in a word, he waited no longer. He had
seen in a flash that he must anticipate Mrs. Pocock. He
was accordingly much disappointed on now learning
from the portress that the lady of his quest was not in

Paris. She had gone for some days to the country.
There was nothing in this accident but what was natural; yet it produced for poor Strether a drop of all
confidence. It was suddenly as if he should never see
her again, and as if moreover he had brought it on
himself by not having been quite kind to her.

It was the advantage of his having let his fancy lose
itself for a little in the gloom that, as by reaction, the
prospect began really to brighten from the moment
the deputation from Woollett alighted on the platform
of the station. They had come straight from Havre,
having sailed from New York to that port, and having
also, thanks to a happy voyage, made land with a
promptitude that left Chad Newsome, who had meant
to meet them at the dock, belated. He had received
their telegram, with the announcement of their immediate further advance, just as he was taking the
train for Havre, so that nothing had remained for him
but to await them in Paris. He hastily picked up
Strether, at the hotel, for this purpose, and he even,
with easy pleasantry, suggested the attendance of
Waymarsh as well — Waymarsh, at the moment his
cab rattled up, being engaged, under Strether's contemplative range, in a grave perambulation of the
familiar court. Waymarsh had learned from his companion, who had already had a note, delivered by
hand, from Chad, that the Pococks were due, and had
ambiguously, though, as always, impressively, glow-
ered at him over the circumstance; carrying himself
in a manner in which Strether was now expert enough
to recognise his uncertainty, in the premises, as to
the best tone. The only tone he aimed at with confid-

ence was a full tone — which was necessarily difficult in the absence of a full knowledge. The Pococks
were a quantity as yet unmeasured, and, as he had
practically brought them over, so this witness had to
that extent exposed himself. He wanted to feel right
about it, but could only, at the best, for the time, feel
vague. "I shall look to you, you know, immensely,"
our friend had said, "to help me with them," and he
had been quite conscious of the effect of the remark,
and of others of the same sort, on his comrade's sombre sensibility. He had insisted on the fact that Waymarsh would quite like Mrs. Pocock — one could be
certain he would: he would be with her about everything, and she would also be with *him*, and Miss
Barrace's nose, in short, would find itself out of
joint.

Strether had woven this web of cheerfulness while
they waited in the court for Chad; he had sat smoking
cigarettes to keep himself quiet while, caged and leo-
nine, his fellow traveller paced and turned before him.
Chad Newsome was doubtless to be struck, when he
arrived, with the sharpness of their opposition at this
particular hour; he was to remember, as a part of it,
how Waymarsh came with him and with Strether to
the street and stood there with a face half-wistful and
half-rueful. They talked of him, the two others, as
they drove, and Strether put Chad in possession of
much of his own strained sense of things. He had already, a few days before, named to him the wire he
was convinced their friend had pulled — a confidence
that had made on the young man's part quite hugely
for curiosity and diversion. The action of the matter,

moreover, Strether could see, was to penetrate; he saw, that is, how Chad judged a system of influence in which Waymarsh had served as a determinant — an impression just now quickened again; with the whole bearing of such a fact on the youth's view of his relatives. As it came up between them that they might now take their friend for a feature of the control of these latter now sought to be exerted from Woollett, Strether felt indeed how it would be stamped all over him, half an hour later, for Sarah Pocock's eyes, that he was as much on Chad's "side" as Waymarsh had probably described him. He was letting himself, at present, go; there was no denying it; it might be desperation, it might be confidence; he should offer himself to the arriving travellers bristling with all the lucidity he had cultivated.

He repeated to Chad what he had been saying in the court to Waymarsh; how there was no doubt whatever that his sister would find the latter a kindred spirit, no doubt of the alliance, based on an exchange of views, that the pair would successfully strike up. They would become as thick as thieves — which moreover was but a development of what Strether remembered to have said in one of his first discussions with his mate, struck as he had then already been with the elements of affinity between that personage and Mrs. Newsome herself. "I told him, one day, when he had questioned me on your mother, that she was a person who, when he should know her, would rouse in him, I was sure, a special enthusiasm; and that hangs together with the conviction we now feel — this certitude that Mrs. Pocock will take him into her boat. For it's your mother's own boat that she's pulling."

"Ah," said Chad," Mother's worth fifty of Sally!"

"A thousand; but when you presently meet her, all the same, you'll be meeting your mother's representative — just as I shall. I feel like the outgoing ambassador," said Strether, "doing honour to his appointed successor." A moment after speaking as he had just done he felt he had inadvertently rather cheapened Mrs. Newsome to her son; an impression audibly reflected, as at first seen, in Chad's prompt protest. He had recently rather failed of apprehension of the young man's attitude and temper — remaining principally conscious of how little worry, at the worst, he wasted; and he studied him at this critical hour with renewed interest. Chad had done exactly what he had promised him a fortnight previous — had accepted without another question his plea for delay. He was waiting cheerfully and handsomely, but also inscrutably and with a slight increase perhaps of the hardness originally involved in his acquired high polish. He was neither excited nor depressed; was easy and acute and deliberate — unhurried unflurried unworried, only at most a little less amused than usual. Strether felt him more than ever a justification of the extraordinary process of which his own absurd spirit had been the arena; he knew as their cab rolled along, knew as he had n't even yet known, that nothing else than what Chad had done and had been would have led to his present showing. They had made him, these things, what he was, and the business had n't been easy; it had taken time and trouble, it had cost, above all, a price. The result at any rate was now to be offered to Sally; which Strether, so far as that was concerned, was glad to be there to witness. Would she in the least make it out or take it in, the result, or would she in the least care for it if she did? He scratched his chin as he asked himself by what name, when challenged — as he was sure he should be — he could call it for her. Oh those were determinations she must herself arrive at; since she wanted so much to see, let her see then and welcome. She had come out in the pride of her competence, yet it hummed in Strether's inner sense that she practically would n't see.

That this was moreover what Chad shrewdly suspected was clear from a word that next dropped from him. "They're children; they play at life!" — and the exclamation was significant and reassuring. It implied that he had n't then, for his companion's sensibility, appeared to give Mrs. Newsome away; and it facilitated our friend's presently asking him if it were his idea that Mrs. Pocock and Madame de Vionnet should become acquainted. Strether was still more sharply struck, hereupon, with Chad's lucidity. "Why, is n't that exactly — to get a sight of the company I keep — what she has come out for?"

"Yes — I 'm afraid it is," Strether unguardedly replied.

Chad's quick rejoinder lighted his precipitation. "Why do you say you 're afraid?"

"Well, because I feel a certain responsibility. It 's my testimony, I imagine, that will have been at the bottom of Mrs. Pocock's curiosity. My letters, as I 've supposed you to understand from the beginning, have spoken freely. I've certainly said my little say about Madame de Vionnet."

All that, for Chad, was beautifully obvious. "Yes, but you've only spoken handsomely."

"Never more handsomely of any woman. But it's just that tone — !"

"That tone," said Chad, "that has fetched her? I dare say; but I've no quarrel with you about it. And no more has Madame de Vionnet. Don't you know by this time how she likes you?"

"Oh!" — and Strether had, with his groan, a real pang of melancholy. "For all I've done for her!"

"Ah you've done a great deal."

Chad's urbanity fairly shamed him, and he was at this moment absolutely impatient to see the face Sarah Pocock would present to a sort of thing, as he synthetically phrased it to himself, with no adequate forecast of which, despite his admonitions, she would certainly arrive. "I've done *this* !"

"Well, this is all right. She likes," Chad comfortably remarked, "to be liked."

It gave his companion a moment's thought. "And she's sure Mrs. Pocock *will* — ?"

"No, I say that for you. She likes your liking her; it's so much, as it were," Chad laughed, "to the good. However, she does n't despair of Sarah either, and is prepared, on her own side, to go all lengths."

"In the way of appreciation?"

"Yes, and of everything else. In the way of general amiability, hospitality and welcome. She's under arms," Chad laughed again; "she's prepared."

THE AMBASSADORS

Strether took it in; then as if an echo of Miss Barrace were in the air: "She's wonderful."

"You don't begin to know *how* wonderful!"

There was a depth in it, to Strether's ear, of confirmed luxury — almost a kind of unconscious insolence of proprietorship; but the effect of the glimpse was not at this moment to foster speculation: there was something so conclusive in so much graceful and generous assurance. It was in fact a fresh evocation; and the evocation had before many minutes another consequence. "Well, I shall see her oftener now. I shall see her as much as I like — by your leave; which is what I hitherto have n't done."

"It has been," said Chad, but without reproach, "only your own fault. I tried to bring you together, and *she*, my dear fellow — I never saw her more charming to any man. But you've got your extraordinary ideas."

"Well, I *did* have," Strether murmured; while he felt both how they had possessed him and how they had now lost their authority. He could n't have traced the sequence to the end, but it was all because of Mrs. Pocock. Mrs. Pocock might be because of Mrs. Newsome, but that was still to be proved. What came over him was the sense of having stupidly failed to profit where profit would have been precious. It had been open to him to see so much more of her, and he had but let the good days pass. Fierce in him almost was the resolve to lose no more of them, and he whimsically reflected, while at Chad's side he drew nearer to his destination, that it was after all Sarah who would have quickened his chance. What

68

her visit of inquisition might achieve in other directions was as yet all obscure — only not obscure that it would do supremely much to bring two earnest persons together. He had but to listen to Chad at this moment to feel it; for Chad was in the act of remarking to him that they of course both counted on him — he himself and the other earnest person — for cheer and support. It was brave to Strether to hear him talk as if the line of wisdom they had struck out was to make things ravishing to the Pococks. No, if Madame de Vionnet compassed *that*, compassed the ravishment of the Pococks, Madame de Vionnet would be prodigious. It would be a beautiful plan if it succeeded, and it all came to the question of Sarah's being really bribeable. The precedent of his own case helped Strether perhaps but little to consider she might prove so; it being distinct that her character would rather make for every possible difference. This idea of his own bribeability set him apart for himself; with the further mark in fact that his case was absolutely proved. He liked always, where Lambert Strether was concerned, to know the worst, and what he now seemed to know was not only that he was bribeable, but that he had been effectually bribed. The only difficulty was that he could n't quite have said with what. It was as if he had sold himself, but had n't somehow got the cash. That, however, was what, characteristically, *would* happen to him. It would naturally be his kind of traffic. While he thought of these things he reminded Chad of the truth they must n't lose sight of — the truth that, with all deference to her susceptibility to new interests, Sarah would have come out with a high firm definite purpose. "She has n't come out, you know, to be bamboozled. We may all be ravishing — nothing perhaps can be more easy for us; but she has n't come out to be ravished. She has come out just simply to take you home."

"Oh well, with *her* I 'll go," said Chad goodhumouredly. "I suppose you 'll allow *that*." And then as for a minute Strether said nothing: "Or is your idea that when I 've seen her I shan't want to go?" As this question, however, again left his friend silent he presently went on: "My own idea at any rate is that they shall have while they 're here the best sort of time."

It was at this that Strether spoke. "Ah there you are! I think if you really wanted to go —!"

"Well?" said Chad to bring it out.

"Well, you would n't trouble about our good time. You would n't care what sort of a time we have."

Chad could always take in the easiest way in the world any ingenious suggestion. "I see. But can I help it? I 'm too decent."

"Yes, you 're too decent!" Strether heavily sighed. And he felt for the moment as if it were the preposterous erd of his mission.

It ministered for the time to this temporary effect that Chad made no rejoinder. But he spoke again as they came in sight of the station. "Do you mean to introduce her to Miss Gostrey?"

As to this Strether was ready. "No."

"But have n't you told me they know about her?"

"I think I 've told you your mother knows."

70

"And won't she have told Sally?"

"That's one of the things I want to see."

"And if you find she *has* —?"

"Will I then, you mean, bring them together?"

"Yes," said Chad with his pleasant promptness: "to show her there's nothing in it."

Strether hesitated. "I don't know that I care very much what she may think there's in it."

"Not if it represents what Mother thinks?"

"Ah what *does* your mother think?" There was in this some sound of bewilderment.

But they were just driving up, and help, of a sort, might after all be quite at hand. "Is n't that, my dear man, what we're both just going to make out?"

II

STRETHER quitted the station half an hour later in
different company. Chad had taken charge, for the
journey to the hotel, of Sarah, Mamie, the maid and
the luggage, all spaciously installed and conveyed;
and it was only after the four had rolled away that his
companion got into a cab with Jim. A strange new
feeling had come over Strether, in consequence of
which his spirits had risen; it was as if what had
occurred on the alighting of his critics had been something other than his fear, though his fear had yet not
been of an instant scene of violence. His impression
had been nothing but what was inevitable — he said
that to himself; yet relief and reassurance had softly
dropped upon him. Nothing could be so odd as to be
indebted for these things to the look of faces and the
sound of voices that had been with him to satiety, as
he might have said, for years; but he now knew, all
the same, how uneasy he had felt; that was brought
home to him by his present sense of a respite. It had
come moreover in the flash of an eye; it had come in
the smile with which Sarah, whom, at the window
of her compartment, they had effusively greeted from
the platform, rustled down to them a moment later,
fresh and handsome from her cool June progress
through the charming land. It was only a sign, but
enough: she was going to be gracious and unallusive,
she was going to play the larger game — which was

72

still more apparent, after she had emerged from Chad's arms, in her direct greeting to the valued friend of her family.

Strether *was* then as much as ever the valued friend of her family; it was something he could at all events go on with; and the manner of his response to it expressed even for himself how little he had enjoyed the prospect of ceasing to figure in that likeness. He had always seen Sarah gracious — had in fact rarely seen her shy or dry; her marked thin-lipped smile, intense without brightness and as prompt to act as the scrape of a safety-match; the protrusion of her rather remarkably long chin, which in her case represented invitation and urbanity, and not, as in most others, pugnacity and defiance; the penetration of her voice to a distance, the general encouragement and approval of her manner, were all elements with which intercourse had made him familiar, but which he noted to-day almost as if she had been a new acquaintance. This first glimpse of her had given a brief but vivid accent to her resemblance to her mother; he could have taken her for Mrs. Newsome while she met his eyes as the train rolled into the station. It was an impression that quickly dropped; Mrs. Newsome was much handsomer, and while Sarah inclined to the massive her mother had, at an age, still the girdle of a maid; also the latter's chin was rather short, than long, and her smile, by good fortune, much more, oh ever so much more, mercifully vague. Strether had seen Mrs. Newsome reserved; he had literally heard her silent, though he had never known her unpleasant. It was the case with Mrs. Pocock that he had known *her* unpleasant, even though he had never known her not affable. She had forms of affability that were in a high degree assertive; nothing for instance had ever been more striking than that she was affable to Jim.

What had told in any case at the window of the train was her high clear forehead, that forehead which her friends, for some reason, always thought of as a "brow"; the long reach of her eyes — it came out at this juncture in such a manner as to remind him, oddly enough, also of that of Waymarsh's; and the unusual gloss of her dark hair, dressed and hatted, after her mother's refined example, with such an avoidance of extremes that it was always spoken of at Woollett as "their own." Though this analogy dropped as soon as she was on the platform it had lasted long enough to make him feel all the advantage, as it were, of his relief. The woman at home, the woman to whom he was attached, was before him just long enough to give him again the measure of the wretchedness, in fact really of the shame, of their having to recognise the formation, between them, of a "split." He had taken this measure in solitude and meditation; but the catastrophe, as Sarah steamed up, looked for its seconds unprecedentedly dreadful — or proved, more exactly, altogether unthinkable; so that his finding something free and familiar to respond to brought with it an instant renewal of his loyalty. He had suddenly sounded the whole depth, had gasped at what he might have lost.

Well, he could now, for the quarter of an hour of their detention, hover about the travellers as soothingly as if their direct message to him was that he had lost nothing. He was n't going to have Sarah write to her mother that night that he was in any way altered or strange. There had been times enough for a month when it had seemed to him that he was strange, that he was altered, in every way; but that was a matter for himself; he knew at least whose business it was *not;* it was not at all events such a circumstance as Sarah's own unaided lights would help her to. Even if she had come out to flash those lights more than yet appeared she would n't make much headway against mere pleasantness. He counted on being able to be merely pleasant to the end, and if only from incapacity moreover to formulate anything different. He could n't even formulate to himself his being changed and queer; it had taken place, the process, somewhere deep down; Maria Gostrey had caught glimpses of it; but how was he to fish it up, even if he desired, for Mrs. Pocock? This was then the spirit in which he hovered, and with the easier throb in it much indebted furthermore to the impression of high and established adequacy as a pretty girl promptly produced in him by Mamie. He had wondered vaguely — turning over many things in the fidget of his thoughts — if Mamie *were* as pretty as Woollett published her; as to which issue seeing her now again was to be so swept away by Woollett's opinion that this consequence really let loose for the imagination an avalanche of others. There were positively five minutes in which the last word seemed of necessity to abide with a Woollett represented by a Mamie. This was the sort of truth the place itself would feel; it would send her forth in confidence; it would point to her with triumph; it would take its stand on her with assurance; it would be conscious of no requirements she did n't meet, of no question she could n't answer.

Well, it was right, Strether slipped smoothly enough into the cheerfulness of saying: granted that a community *might* be best represented by a young lady of twenty-two, Mamie perfectly played the part, played it as if she were used to it, and looked and spoke and dressed the character. He wondered if she might n't, in the high light of Paris, a cool full studio-light, becoming yet treacherous, show as too conscious of these matters; but the next moment he felt satisfied that her consciousness was after all empty for its size, rather too simple than too mixed, and that the kind way with her would be not to take many things out of it, but to put as many as possible in. She was robust and conveniently tall; just a trifle too bloodlessly fair perhaps, but with a pleasant public familiar radiance that affirmed her vitality. She might have been "receiving" for Woollett, wherever she found herself, and there was something in her manner, her tone, her motion, her pretty blue eyes, her pretty perfect teeth and her very small, too small, nose, that immediately placed her, to the fancy, between the windows of a hot bright room in which voices were high — up at that end to which people were brought to be "presented." They were there to congratulate, these images, and Strether's renewed vision, on this hint, completed the idea. What Mamie was like was the happy bride, the bride after the church and just before going away. She was n't the mere maiden, and yet was only as much married as that quantity came to. She was in the brilliant acclaimed festal stage. Well, might it last her long!

Strether rejoiced in these things for Chad, who was all genial attention to the needs of his friends, besides having arranged that his servant should re-enforce him; the ladies were certainly pleasant to see, and Mamie would be at any time and anywhere pleasant to exhibit. She would look extraordinarily like his young wife — the wife of a honeymoon, should he go about with her; but that was his own affair — or perhaps it was hers; it was at any rate something she could n't help. Strether remembered how he had seen him come up with Jeanne de Vionnet in Gloriani's garden, and the fancy he had had about that — the fancy obscured now, thickly overlaid with others; the recollection was during these minutes his only note of trouble. He had often, in spite of himself, wondered if Chad but too probably were not with Jeanne the object of a still and shaded flame. It was on the cards that the child *might* be tremulously in love, and this conviction now flickered up not a bit the less for his disliking to think of it, for its being, in a complicated situation, a complication the more, and for something indescribable in Mamie, something at all events straightway lent her by his own mind, something that gave her value, gave her intensity and purpose, as the symbol of an opposition. Little Jeanne was n't really at all in question — how *could* she be ? — yet from the moment Miss Pocock had shaken her

77

skirts on the platform, touched up the immense bows of her hat and settled properly over her shoulder the strap of her morocco-and-gilt travelling-satchel, from that moment little Jeanne was opposed.

It was in the cab with Jim that impressions really crowded on Strether, giving him the strangest sense of length of absence from people among whom he had lived for years. Having them thus come out to him was as if he had returned to find them; and the droll promptitude of Jim's mental reaction threw his own initiation far back into the past. Whoever might or might n't be suited by what was going on among them, Jim, for one, would certainly be: his instant recognition — frank and whimsical — of what the affair was for *him* gave Strether a glow of pleasure. "I say, you know, this *is* about my shape, and if it had n't been for *you* —!" so he broke out as the charming streets met his healthy appetite; and he wound up, after an expressive nudge, with a clap of his companion's knee and an "Oh you, you — you *are* doing it!" that was charged with rich meaning. Strether felt in it the intention of homage, but, with a curiosity otherwise occupied, postponed taking it up. What he was asking himself for the time was how Sarah Pocock, in the opportunity already given her, had judged her brother — from whom he himself, as they finally, at the station, separated for their different conveyances, had had a look into which he could read more than one message. However Sarah was judging her brother, Chad's conclusion about his sister, and about her husband and her husband's sister, was at the least on the way not to fail of confidence. Strether

felt the confidence, and that, as the look between
them was an exchange, what he himself gave back
was relatively vague. This comparison of notes
however could wait; everything struck him as de-
pending on the effect produced by Chad. Neither
Sarah nor Mamie had in any way, at the station —
where they had had after all ample time — broken
out about it; which, to make up for this, was what
our friend had expected of Jim as soon as they should
find themselves together.

It was queer to him that he had that noiseless brush
with Chad; an ironic intelligence with this youth on
the subject of his relatives, an intelligence carried on
under their nose and, as might be said, at their expense — such a matter marked again for him strongly
the number of stages he had come; albeit that if the
number seemed great the time taken for the final one
was but the turn of a hand. He had before this had
many moments of wondering if he himself were n't
perhaps changed even as Chad was changed. Only
what in Chad was conspicuous improvement — well,
he had no name ready for the working, in his own
organism, of his own more timid dose. He should
have to see first what this action would amount to.
And for his occult passage with the young man, after
all, the directness of it had no greater oddity than the
fact that the young man's way with the three travellers should have been so happy a manifestation.
Strether liked him for it, on the spot, as he had n't
yet liked him; it affected him while it lasted as he
might have been affected by some light pleasant perfect work of art: to that degree that he wondered if

79

they were really worthy of it, took it in and did it justice; to that degree that it would have been scarce a miracle if, there in the luggage-room, while they waited for their things, Sarah had pulled his sleeve and drawn him aside. "You're right; we have n't quite known what you mean, Mother and I, but now we see. Chad's magnificent; what can one want more? If *this* is the kind of thing —!" On which they might, as it were, have embraced and begun to work together.

Ah how much, as it was, for all her bridling brightness — which was merely general and noticed nothing — *would* they work together? Strether knew he was unreasonable; he set it down to his being nervous : people could n't notice everything and speak of everything in a quarter of an hour. Possibly, no doubt, also, he made too much of Chad's display. Yet, none the less, when, at the end of five minutes, in the cab, Jim Pocock had said nothing either — had n't said, that is, what Strether wanted, though he had said much else — it all suddenly bounced back to their being either stupid or wilful. It was more probably on the whole the former; so that that would be the drawback of the bridling brightness. Yes, they would bridle and be bright; they would make the best of what was before them, but their observation would fail; it would be beyond them; they simply would n't understand. Of what use would it be then that they had come? — if they were n't to be intelligent up to *that* point : unless indeed he himself were utterly deluded and extravagant? Was he, on this question of Chad's improvement, fantastic and away

from the truth? Did he live in a false world, a world
that had grown simply to suit him, and was his present slight irritation — in the face now of Jim's silence
in particular — but the alarm of the vain thing men-
aced by the touch of the real? Was this contribution
of the real possibly the mission of the Pococks? — had
they come to make the work of observation, as *he*
had practised observation, crack and crumble, and to
reduce Chad to the plain terms in which honest minds
could deal with him? Had they come in short to be
sane where Strether was destined to feel that he himself had only been silly?

He glanced at such a contingency, but it failed to
hold him long when once he had reflected that he
would have been silly, in this case, with Maria Gostrey and little Bilham, with Madame de Vionnet and
little Jeanne, with Lambert Strether, in fine, and
above all with Chad Newsome himself. Would n't
it be found to have made more for reality to be
silly with these persons than sane with Sarah and
Jim? Jim in fact, he presently made up his mind,
was individually out of it; Jim did n't care; Jim
had n't come out either for Chad or for him; Jim in
short left the moral side to Sally and indeed simply
availed himself now, for the sense of recreation, of
the fact that he left almost everything to Sally. He
was nothing compared to Sally, and not so much by
reason of Sally's temper and will as by that of her
more developed type and greater acquaintance with
the world. He quite frankly and serenely confessed,
as he sat there with Strether, that he felt his type hang
far in the rear of his wife's and still further, if possible,

in the rear of his sister's. Their types, he well knew,
were recognised and acclaimed; whereas the most
a leading Woollett business-man could hope to achieve
socially, and for that matter industrially, was a certain freedom to play into this general glamour.

The impression he made on our friend was another
of the things that marked our friend's road. It was
a strange impression, especially as so soon produced;
Strether had received it, he judged, all in the twenty
minutes; it struck him at least as but in a minor degree the work of the long Woollett years. Pocock was
normally and consentingly though not quite wittingly
out of the question. It was despite his being normal;
it was despite his being cheerful; it was despite his
being a leading Woollett business-man; and the de-
termination of his fate left him thus perfectly usual
— as everything else about it was clearly, to his sense,
not less so. He seemed to say that there was a whole
side of life on which the perfectly usual *was* for leading Woollett business-men to be out of the question.
He made no more of it than that, and Strether, so far
as Jim was concerned, desired to make no more.
Only Strether's imagination, as always, worked, and
he asked himself if this side of life were not somehow
connected, for those who figured on it, with the fact
of marriage. Would *his* relation to it, had he married
ten years before, have become now the same as Pocock's? Might it even become the same should he
marry in a few months? Should he ever know himself as much out of the question for Mrs. Newsome
as Jim knew himself — in a dim way — for Mrs. Jim?

To turn his eyes in that direction was to be personally reassured; he was different from Pocock; he had affirmed himself differently and was held after all in higher esteem. What none the less came home to him, however, at this hour, was that the society over there, that of which Sarah and Mamie — and, in a more eminent way, Mrs. Newsome herself — were specimens, was essentially a society of women, and that poor Jim was n't in it. He himself, Lambert Strether, *was* as yet in some degree — which was an odd situation for a man; but it kept coming back to him in a whimsical way that he should perhaps find his marriage had cost him his place. This occasion indeed, whatever that fancy represented, was not a time of sensible exclusion for Jim, who was in a state of manifest response to the charm of his adventure. Small and fat and constantly facetious, straw-coloured and destitute of marks, he would have been practically indistinguishable had n't his constant preference for light-grey clothes, for white hats, for very big cigars and very little stories, done what it could for his identity. There were signs in him, though none of them plaintive, of always paying for others; and the principal one perhaps was just this failure of type. It was with this that he paid, rather than with fatigue or waste; and also doubtless a little with the effort of humour — never irrelevant to the conditions, to the relations, with which he was acquainted.

He gurgled his joy as they rolled through the happy streets; he declared that his trip was a regular windfall, and that he was n't there, he was eager to remark, to hang back from anything: he did n't know quite what Sally had come for, but *he* had come for a

good time. Strether indulged him even while wondering if what Sally wanted her brother to go back for
was to become like her husband. He trusted that a
good time was to be, out and out, the programme for
all of them; and he assented liberally to Jim's proposal that, disencumbered and irresponsible — his
things were in the omnibus with those of the others
— they should take a further turn round before going
to the hotel. It was n't for *him* to tackle Chad — it
was Sally's job; and as it would be like her, he felt,
to open fire on the spot, it would n't be amiss of
them to hold off and give her time. Strether, on his
side, only asked to give her time; so he jogged with
his companion along boulevards and avenues, trying
to extract from meagre material some forecast of his
catastrophe. He was quick enough to see that Jim
Pocock declined judgement, had hovered quite round
the outer edge of discussion and anxiety, leaving all
analysis of their question to the ladies alone and now
only feeling his way toward some small droll cynicism.
It broke out afresh, the cynicism — it had already
shown a flicker — in a but slightly deferred: "Well,
hanged if I would if *I* were he!"

"You mean you would n't in Chad's place — ?"

"Give up this to go back and boss the advertising!" Poor Jim, with his arms folded and his little
legs out in the open fiacre, drank in the sparkling
Paris noon and carried his eyes from one side of
their vista to the other. "Why I want to come right
out and live here myself. And I want to live while I
am here too. I feel with *you* — oh you 've been grand,
old man, and I 've twigged — that it ain't right to

84

worry Chad. *I* don't mean to persecute him; I could
n't in conscience. It's thanks to you at any rate that
I'm here, and I'm sure I'm much obliged. You're
a lovely pair."

There were things in this speech that Strether let
pass for the time. "Don't you then think it important
the advertising should be thoroughly taken in hand?
Chad *will* be, so far as capacity is concerned," he
went on, "the man to do it."

"Where did he get his capacity," Jim asked, "over
here?"

"He did n't get it over here, and the wonderful
thing is that over here he has n't inevitably lost it.
He has a natural turn for business, an extraordinary
head. He comes by that," Strether explained, "honestly enough. He's in that respect his father's son,
and also — for she's wonderful in her way too — his
mother's. He has other tastes and other tendencies;
but Mrs. Newsome and your wife are quite right
about his having that. He's very remarkable."

"Well, I guess he is!" Jim Pocock comfortably
sighed. "But if you've believed so in his making us
hum, why have you so prolonged the discussion?
Don't you know we've been quite anxious about
you?"

These questions were not informed with earnestness, but Strether saw he must none the less make
a choice and take a line. "Because, you see, I've
greatly liked it. I've liked my Paris. I dare say
I've liked it too much."

"Oh you old wretch!" Jim gaily exclaimed.

"But nothing's concluded," Strether went on.

"The case is more complex than it looks from Woollett."

"Oh well, it looks bad enough from Woollett!" Jim declared.

"Even after all I've written?"

Jim bethought himself. "Isn't it what you've written that has made Mrs. Newsome pack us off? That at least and Chad's not turning up?"

Strether made a reflexion of his own. "I see. That she should do something was, no doubt, inevitable, and your wife has therefore of course come out to act."

"Oh yes," Jim concurred — "to act. But Sally comes out to act, you know," he lucidly added, "every time she leaves the house. She never comes out but she *does* act. She's acting moreover now for her mother, and that fixes the scale." Then he wound up, opening all his senses to it, with a renewed embrace of pleasant Paris. "We haven't all the same at Woollett got anything like this."

Strether continued to consider. "I'm bound to say for you all that you strike me as having arrived in a very mild and reasonable frame of mind. You don't show your claws. I felt just now in Mrs. Pocock no symptom of that. She isn't fierce," he went on. "I'm such a nervous idiot that I thought she might be."

"Oh don't you know her well enough," Pocock asked, "to have noticed that she never gives herself away, any more than her mother ever does? They ain't fierce, either of 'em; they let you come quite close. They wear their fur the smooth side out — the warm side in. Do you know what they are?" Jim pursued as he looked about him, giving the question, as Strether felt, but half his care — "do you know what they are? They're about as intense as they can live."

"Yes" — and Strether's concurrence had a positive precipitation; "they're about as intense as they can live."

"They don't lash about and shake the cage," said Jim, who seemed pleased with his analogy; "and it's at feeding-time that they're quietest. But they always get there."

"They do indeed — they always get there!" Strether replied with a laugh that justified his confession of nervousness. He disliked to be talking sincerely of Mrs. Newsome with Pocock; he could have talked insincerely. But there was something he wanted to know, a need created in him by her recent intermission, by his having given from the first so much, as now more than ever appeared to him, and got so little. It was as if a queer truth in his companion's metaphor had rolled over him with a rush. She *had* been quiet at feeding-time; she had fed, and Sarah had fed with her, out of the big bowl of all his recent free communication, his vividness and pleasantness, his ingenuity and even his eloquence, while the current of her response had steadily run thin. Jim meanwhile however, it was true, slipped characteristically into shallowness from the moment he ceased to speak out of the experience of a husband.

"But of course Chad has now the advantage of being there before her. If he does n't work that for all it's worth —!" He sighed with contingent pity at his brother-in-law's possible want of resource. "He has worked it on *you*, pretty well, eh?" and he asked the next moment if there were anything new at the Varieties, which he pronounced in the American manner. They talked about the Varieties — Strether confessing to a knowledge which produced again on Pocock's part a play of innuendo as vague as a nursery-rhyme, yet as aggressive as an elbow in his side; and they finished their drive under the protection of easy themes. Strether waited to the end, but still in vain, for any show that Jim had seen Chad as different; and he could scarce have explained the discouragement he drew from the absence of this testimony. It was what he had taken his own stand on, so far as he had taken a stand; and if they were all only going to see nothing he had only wasted his time. He gave his friend till the very last moment, till they had come into sight of the hotel; and when poor Pocock only continued cheerful and envious and funny he fairly grew to dislike him, to feel him extravagantly common. If they were *all* going to see nothing! — Strether knew, as this came back to him, that he was also letting Pocock represent for him what Mrs. Newsome would n't see. He went on disliking, in the light of Jim's commonness, to talk to him about that lady; yet just before the cab pulled up he knew the extent of his desire for the real word from Woollett.

"Has Mrs. Newsome at all given way — ?"

"'Given way'?" — Jim echoed it with the practical derision of his sense of a long past.

"Under the strain, I mean, of hope deferred, of disappointment repeated and thereby intensified."

"Oh is she prostrate, you mean?" — he had his categories in hand. "Why yes, she's prostrate — just as Sally is. But they're never so lively, you know, as when they're prostrate."

"Ah Sarah's prostrate?" Strether vaguely murmured.

"It's when they're prostrate that they most sit up."

"And Mrs. Newsome's sitting up?"

"All night, my boy — for *you!*" And Jim fetched him, with a vulgar little guffaw, a thrust that gave relief to the picture. But he had got what he wanted. He felt on the spot that this *was* the real word from Woollett. "So don't you go home!" Jim added while he alighted and while his friend, letting him profusely pay the cabman, sat on in a momentary muse. Strether wondered if that were the real word too.

III

As the door of Mrs. Pocock's salon was pushed open
for him, the next day, well before noon, he was
reached by a voice with a charming sound that made
him just falter before crossing the threshold. Madame
de Vionnet was already on the field, and this gave the
drama a quicker pace than he felt it as yet — though
his suspense had increased — in the power of any act
of his own to do. He had spent the previous evening
with all his old friends together; yet he would still
have described himself as quite in the dark in respect
to a forecast of their influence on his situation. It was
strange now, none the less, that in the light of this
unexpected note of her presence he felt Madame de
Vionnet a part of that situation as she had n't even
yet been. She was alone, he found himself assuming,
with Sarah, and there was a bearing in that — somehow beyond his control — on his personal fate. Yet
she was only saying something quite easy and independent — the thing she had come, as a good friend
of Chad's, on purpose to say. "There is n't anything
at all — ? I should be so delighted."

It was clear enough, when they were there before
him, how she had been received. He saw this, as
Sarah got up to greet him, from something fairly
hectic in Sarah's face. He saw furthermore that they
were n't, as had first come to him, alone together; he
was at no loss as to the identity of the broad high back

presented to him in the embrasure of the window furthest from the door. Waymarsh, whom he had to-day
not yet seen, whom he only knew to have left the hotel
before him, and who had taken part, the night previous, on Mrs. Pocock's kind invitation, conveyed by
Chad, in the entertainment, informal but cordial,
promptly offered by that lady — Waymarsh had anticipated him even as Madame de Vionnet had done,
and, with his hands in his pockets and his attitude
unaffected by Strether's entrance, was looking out, in
marked detachment, at the Rue de Rivoli. The latter
felt it in the air — it was immense how Waymarsh
could mark things — that he had remained deeply
dissociated from the overture to their hostess that we
have recorded on Madame de Vionnet's side. He had,
conspicuously, tact, besides a stiff general view; and
this was why he had left Mrs. Pocock to struggle
alone. He would outstay the visitor; he would unmistakeably wait; to what had he been doomed for months
past but waiting? Therefore she was to feel that she
had him in reserve. What support she drew from this
was still to be seen, for, although Sarah was vividly
bright, she had given herself up for the moment to an
ambiguous flushed formalism. She had had to reckon
more quickly than she expected; but it concerned
her first of all to signify that she was not to be taken
unawares. Strether arrived precisely in time for her
showing it. "Oh you're too good; but I don't think
I feel quite helpless. I have my brother — and these
American friends. And then you know I've been to
Paris. I *know* Paris," said Sally Pocock in a tone that
breathed a certain chill on Strether's heart.

THE AMBASSADORS

"Ah but a woman, in this tiresome place where everything's always changing, a woman of good will," Madame de Vionnet threw off, "can always help a woman. I'm sure you 'know' — but we know perhaps different things." She too, visibly, wished to make no mistake; but it was a fear of a different order and more kept out of sight. She smiled in welcome at Strether; she greeted him more familiarly than Mrs. Pocock; she put out her hand to him without moving from her place; and it came to him in the course of a minute and in the oddest way that — yes, positively — she was giving him over to ruin. She was all kindness and ease, but she could n't help so giving him; she was exquisite, and her being just as she was poured for Sarah a sudden rush of meaning into his own equivocations. How could she know how she was hurting him? She wanted to show as simple and humble — in the degree compatible with operative charm; but it was just this that seemed to put him on her side. She struck him as dressed, as arranged, as prepared infinitely to conciliate — with the very poetry of good taste in her view of the conditions of her early call. She was ready to advise about dressmakers and shops; she held herself wholly at the disposition of Chad's family. Strether noticed her card on the table — her coronet and her "Comtesse" — and the imagination was sharp in him of certain private adjustments in Sarah's mind. She had never, he was sure, sat with a "Comtesse" before, and such was the specimen of that class he had been keeping to play on her. She had crossed the sea very particularly for a look at her; but he read in Madame de Vionnet's own eyes that this curiosity had n't been so successfully met as that she herself would n't now have more than ever need of him. She looked much as she had looked to him that morning at Notre Dame; he noted in fact the suggestive sameness of her discreet and delicate dress. It seemed to speak — perhaps a little prematurely or too finely — of the sense in which she would help Mrs. Pocock with the shops. The way that lady took her in, moreover, added depth to his impression of what Miss Gostrey, by their common wisdom, had escaped. He winced as he saw himself but for that timely prudence ushering in Maria as a guide and an example. There was however a touch of relief for him in his glimpse, so far as he had got it, of Sarah's line. She "knew Paris." Madame de Vionnet had, for that matter, lightly taken this up. "Ah then you 've a turn for that, an affinity that belongs to your family. Your brother, though his long experience makes a difference, I admit, has become one of us in a marvellous way." And she appealed to Strether in the manner of a woman who could always glide off with smoothness into another subject. Was n't *he* struck with the way Mr. Newsome had made the place his own, and had n't he been in a position to profit by his friend's wondrous expertness?

Strether felt the bravery, at the least, of her presenting herself so promptly to sound that note, and yet asked himself what other note, after all, she *could* strike from the moment she presented herself at all. She could meet Mrs. Pocock only on the ground of the obvious, and what feature of Chad's situation was more eminent than the fact that he had created for

himself a new set of circumstances? Unless she hid
herself altogether she could show but as one of these,
an illustration of his domiciled and indeed of his confirmed condition. And the consciousness of all this in
her charming eyes was so clear and fine that as she
thus publicly drew him into her boat she produced
in him such a silent agitation as he was not to fail
afterwards to denounce as pusillanimous. "Ah don't
be so charming to me! — for it makes us intimate,
and after all what *is* between us when I've been so
tremendously on my guard and have seen you but
half a dozen times?" He recognised once more the
perverse law that so inveterately governed his poor
personal aspects: it would be exactly *like* the way
things always turned out for him that he should affect
Mrs. Pocock and Waymarsh as launched in a relation
in which he had really never been launched at all.
They were at this very moment — they could only be
— attributing to him the full licence of it, and all by
the operation of her own tone with him; whereas his
sole licence had been to cling with intensity to the
brink, not to dip so much as a toe into the flood. But
the flicker of his fear on this occasion was not, as may
be added, to repeat itself; it sprang up, for its moment,
only to die down and then go out for ever. To meet
his fellow visitor's invocation and, with Sarah's brilliant eyes on him, answer, *was* quite sufficiently to
step into her boat. During the rest of the time her
visit lasted he felt himself proceed to each of the
proper offices, successively, for helping to keep the
adventurous skiff afloat. It rocked beneath him,
but he settled himself in his place. He took up an

oar and, since he was to have the credit of pulling, pulled.

"That will make it all the pleasanter if it so happens that we *do* meet," Madame de Vionnet had further observed in reference to Mrs. Pocock's mention of her initiated state; and she had immediately added that, after all, her hostess could n't be in need with the good offices of Mr. Strether so close at hand. "It's he, I gather, who has learnt to know his Paris, and to love it, better than any one ever before in so short a time; so that between him and your brother, when it comes to the point, how can you possibly want for good guidance? The great thing, Mr. Strether will show you," she smiled, "is just to let one's self go."

"Oh I've not let myself go very far," Strether answered, feeling quite as if he had been called upon to hint to Mrs. Pocock how Parisians could talk. "I'm only afraid of showing I have n't let myself go far enough. I've taken a good deal of time, but I must quite have had the air of not budging from one spot." He looked at Sarah in a manner that he thought she might take as engaging, and he made, under Madame de Vionnet's protection, as it were, his first personal point. "What has really happened has been that, all the while, I've done what I came out for."

Yet it only at first gave Madame de Vionnet a chance immediately to take him up. "You've renewed acquaintance with your friend — you've learnt to know him again." She spoke with such cheerful helpfulness that they might, in a common cause, have been calling together and pledged to mutual aid.

Waymarsh, at this, as if he had been in question, straightway turned from the window. "Oh yes, Countess — he has renewed acquaintance with *me*, and he *has*, I guess, learnt something about me, though I don't know how much he has liked it. It's for Strether himself to say whether he has felt it justifies his course."

"Oh but *you*," said the Countess gaily, "are not in the least what he came out for — is he really, Strether? and I had n't you at all in my mind. I was thinking of Mr. Newsome, of whom we think so much and with whom, precisely, Mrs. Pocock has given herself the opportunity to take up threads. What a pleasure for you both!" Madame de Vionnet, with her eyes on Sarah, bravely continued.

Mrs. Pocock met her handsomely, but Strether quickly saw she meant to accept no version of her movements or plans from any other lips. She required no patronage and no support, which were but other names for a false position; she would show in her own way what she chose to show, and this she expressed with a dry glitter that recalled to him a fine Woollett winter morning. "I've never wanted for opportunities to see my brother. We've many things to think of at home, and great responsibilities and occupations, and our home's not an impossible place. We've plenty of reasons," Sarah continued a little piercingly, "for everything we do" — and in short she would n't give herself the least little scrap away. But she added as one who was always bland and who could afford a concession: "I've come because — well, because we do come."

BOOK EIGHTH

"Ah then fortunately!" — Madame de Vionnet
breathed it to the air. Five minutes later they were
on their feet for her to take leave, standing together in
an affability that had succeeded in surviving a further
exchange of remarks; only with the emphasised appearance on Waymarsh's part of a tendency to revert,
in a ruminating manner and as with an instinctive
or a precautionary lightening of his tread, to an open
window and his point of vantage. The glazed and
gilded room, all red damask, ormolu, mirrors, clocks,
looked south, and the shutters were bowed upon the
summer morning; but the Tuileries garden and what
was beyond it, over which the whole place hung, were
things visible through gaps; so that the far-spreading
presence of Paris came up in coolness, dimness and
invitation, in the twinkle of gilt-tipped palings, the
crunch of gravel, the click of hoofs, the crack of
whips, things that suggested some parade of the circus. "I think it probable," said Mrs. Pocock, "that
I shall have the opportunity of going to my brother's.
I've no doubt it's very pleasant indeed." She spoke
as to Strether, but her face was turned with an intensity of brightness to Madame de Vionnet, and there
was a moment during which, while she thus fronted
her, our friend expected to hear her add: "I'm much
obliged to you, I'm sure, for inviting me there." He
guessed that for five seconds these words were on the
point of coming; he heard them as clearly as if they
had been spoken; but he presently knew they had
just failed — knew it by a glance, quick and fine,
from Madame de Vionnet, which told him that she
too had felt them in the air, but that the point had

97

luckily not been made in any manner requiring notice. This left her free to reply only to what had been said.

"That the Boulevard Malesherbes may be common ground for us offers me the best prospect I see for the pleasure of meeting you again."

"Oh I shall come to see you, since you've been so good": and Mrs. Pocock looked her invader well in the eyes. The flush in Sarah's cheeks had by this time settled to a small definite crimson spot that was not without its own bravery; she held her head a good deal up, and it came to Strether that of the two, at this moment, she was the one who most carried out the idea of a Countess. He quite took in, however, that she would really return her visitor's civility: she would n't report again at Woollett without at least so much producible history as that in her pocket.

"I want extremely to be able to show you my little daughter." Madame de Vionnet went on; "and I should have brought her with me if I had n't wished first to ask your leave. I was in hopes I should perhaps find Miss Pocock, of whose being with you I've heard from Mr. Newsome and whose acquaintance I should so much like my child to make. If I have the pleasure of seeing her and you do permit it I shall venture to ask her to be kind to Jeanne. Mr. Strether will tell you" — she beautifully kept it up — "that my poor girl is gentle and good and rather lonely. They've made friends, he and she, ever so happily, and he does n't, I believe, think ill of her. As for Jeanne herself he has had the same success with her that I know he has had here wherever he has turned." She seemed to ask him for permission to say these things, or seemed rather to take it, softly and happily, with the ease of intimacy, for granted, and he had quite the consciousness now that not to meet her at any point more than halfway would be odiously, basely to abandon her. Yes, he was *with* her, and, opposed even in this covert, this semi-safe fashion to those who were not, he felt, strangely and confusedly, but excitedly, inspiringly, how much and how far. It was as if he had positively waited in suspense for something from her that would let him in deeper, so that he might show her how he could take it. And what did in fact come as she drew out a little her farewell served sufficiently the purpose. "As his success is a matter that I'm sure he'll never mention for himself, I feel, you see, the less scruple; which it's very good of me to say, you know, by the way," she added as she addressed herself to him; "considering how little direct advantage I've gained from your triumphs with *me*. When does one ever see you? I wait at home and I languish. You'll have rendered me the service, Mrs. Pocock, at least," she wound up, "of giving me one of my much-too-rare glimpses of this gentleman."

"I certainly should be sorry to deprive you of anything that seems so much, as you describe it, your natural due. Mr. Strether and I are very old friends," Sarah allowed, "but the privilege of his society isn't a thing I shall quarrel about with any one."

"And yet, dear Sarah," he freely broke in, "I feel, when I hear you say that, that you don't quite do justice to the important truth of the extent to which — as you're also mine — I'm *your* natural due. I should like much better," he laughed, "to see you fight for me."

She met him, Mrs. Pocock, on this, with an arrest of speech — with a certain breathlessness, as he immediately fancied, on the score of a freedom for which she was n't quite prepared. It had flared up — for all the harm he had intended by it — because, confoundedly, he did n't want any more to be afraid about her than he wanted to be afraid about Madame de Vionnet. He had never, naturally, called her anything but Sarah at home, and though he had perhaps never quite so markedly invoked her as his "dear," that was somehow partly because no occasion had hitherto laid so effective a trap for it. But something admonished him now that it was too late — unless indeed it were possibly too early; and that he at any rate should n't have pleased Mrs. Pocock the more by it. "Well, Mr. Strether —!" she murmured with vagueness, yet with sharpness, while her crimson spots burned a trifle brighter and he was aware that this must be for the present the limit of her response. Madame de Vionnet had already, however, come to his aid, and Waymarsh, as if for further participation, moved again back to them. It was true that the aid rendered by Madame de Vionnet was questionable; it was a sign that, for all one might confess to with her, and for all she might complain of not enjoying, she could still insidiously show how much of the material of conversation had accumulated between them.

"The real truth is, you know, that you sacrifice one without mercy to dear old Maria. She leaves no room in your life for anybody else. Do you know," she enquired of Mrs. Pocock, "about dear old Maria? The worst is that Miss Gostrey is really a wonderful woman."

"Oh yes indeed," Strether answered for her, "Mrs. Pocock knows about Miss Gostrey. Your mother, Sarah, must have told you about her; your mother knows everything," he sturdily pursued. "And I cordially admit," he added with his conscious gaiety of courage, "that she's as wonderful a woman as you like."

"Ah it is n't *I* who 'like,' dear Mr. Strether, anything to do with the matter!" Sarah Pocock promptly protested; "and I'm by no means sure I have — from my mother or from any one else — a notion of whom you're talking about."

"Well, he won't let you see her, you know," Madame de Vionnet sympathetically threw in. "He never lets *me* — old friends as we are: I mean as I am with Maria. He reserves her for his best hours; keeps her consummately to himself; only gives us others the crumbs of the feast."

"Well, Countess, *I've* had some of the crumbs," Waymarsh observed with weight and covering her with his large look; which led her to break in before he could go on.

"*Comment donc*, he shares her with *you?*" she exclaimed in droll stupefaction. "Take care you don't have, before you go much further, rather more of all *ces dames* than you may know what to do with!"

But he only continued in his massive way. "I can post you about the lady, Mrs. Pocock, so far as you may care to hear. I've seen her quite a number of times, and I was practically present when they made acquaintance. I've kept my eye on her right along, but I don't know as there's any real harm in her."

"'Harm'?" Madame de Vionnet quickly echoed. "Why she's the dearest and cleverest of all the clever and dear."

"Well, you run her pretty close, Countess," Waymarsh returned with spirit; "though there's no doubt she's pretty well up in things. She knows her way round Europe. Above all there's no doubt she does love Strether."

"Ah but we all do that — we all love Strether: it isn't a merit!" their fellow visitor laughed, keeping to her idea with a good conscience at which our friend was aware that he marvelled, though he trusted also for it, as he met her exquisitely expressive eyes, to some later light.

The prime effect of her tone, however — and it was a truth which his own eyes gave back to her in sad ironic play — could only be to make him feel that, to say such things to a man in public, a woman must practically think of him as ninety years old. He had turned awkwardly, responsively red, he knew, at her mention of Maria Gostrey; Sarah Pocock's presence — the particular quality of it — had made this inevitable; and then he had grown still redder in proportion as he hated to have shown anything at all. He felt indeed that he was showing much, as, uncomfortably and almost in pain, he offered up his redness to Waymarsh, who, strangely enough, seemed now to be looking at him with a certain explanatory yearning. Something deep — something built on their old old relation — passed, in this complexity, between them; he got the side-wind of a loyalty that stood behind all actual queer questions. Waymarsh's dry bare humour — as it gave itself to be taken — gloomed out to demand justice. "Well, if you talk of Miss Barrace I've *my* chance too," it appeared stiffly to nod, and it granted that it was giving him away, but struggled to add that it did so only to save him. The sombre glow stared it at him till it fairly sounded out — "to save you, poor old man, to save you; to save you in spite of yourself." Yet it was somehow just this communication that showed him to himself as more than ever lost. Still another result of it was to put before him as never yet that between his comrade and the interest represented by Sarah there was already a basis. Beyond all question now, yes: Waymarsh had been in occult relation with Mrs. Newsome — out, out it all came in the very effort of his face. "Yes, you're feeling my hand" — he as good as proclaimed it; "but only because this at least I *shall* have got out of the damned Old World: that I shall have picked up the pieces into which it has caused you to crumble." It was as if in short, after an instant, Strether had not only had it from him, but had recognised that so far as this went the instant had cleared the air. Our friend understood and approved; he had the sense that they would n't otherwise speak of it. This would be all, and it would mark in himself a kind of intelligent generosity. It was with grim Sarah then — Sarah grim for all her grace — that Waymarsh had begun at ten o'clock in the morning to save him. Well — if he *could*, poor dear man, with his big bleak kindness! The upshot of which crowded perception was that Strether, on his own side, still showed no more than he absolutely had to. He showed the least possible by saying to Mrs. Pocock after an interval much briefer than our glance at the picture reflected in him: "Oh it's as true as they please!—There's no Miss Gostrey for any one but me—not the least little peep. I keep her to myself."

"Well, it's very good of you to notify me," Sarah replied without looking at him and thrown for a moment by this discrimination, as the direction of her eyes showed, upon a dimly desperate little community with Madame de Vionnet. "But I hope I shan't miss her too much."

Madame de Vionnet instantly rallied. "And you know — though it might occur to one — it is n't in the least that he's ashamed of her. She's really — in a way — extremely good-looking."

"Ah but extremely!" Strether laughed while he wondered at the odd part he found thus imposed on him.

It continued to be so by every touch from Madame de Vionnet. "Well, as I say, you know, I wish you would keep *me* a little more to yourself. Could n't you name some day for me, some hour — and better soon than late? I'll be at home whenever it best suits you. There — I can't say fairer."

Strether thought a moment while Waymarsh and Mrs. Pocock affected him as standing attentive. "I did lately call on you. Last week — while Chad was out of town."

"Yes — and I was away, as it happened, too. You

choose your moments well. But don't wait for my next absence, for I shan't make another," Madame de Vionnet declared, "while Mrs. Pocock's here."

"That vow need n't keep you long, fortunately," Sarah observed with reasserted suavity. "I shall be at present but a short time in Paris. I have my plans for other countries. I meet a number of charming friends"— and her voice seemed to caress that description of these persons.

"Ah then," her visitor cheerfully replied, "all the more reason! To-morrow, for instance, or next day?" she continued to Strether. "Tuesday would do for me beautifully."

"Tuesday then with pleasure."

"And at half-past five?— or at six?"

It was ridiculous, but Mrs. Pocock and Waymarsh struck him as fairly waiting for his answer. It was indeed as if they were arranged, gathered for a performance, the performance of "Europe" by his confederate and himself. Well, the performance could only go on. "Say five forty-five."

"Five forty-five— good." And now at last Madame de Vionnet must leave them, though it carried, for herself, the performance a little further. "I *did* hope so much also to see Miss Pocock. May n't I still?"

Sarah hesitated, but she rose equal. "She'll return your visit with me. She's at present out with Mr. Pocock and my brother."

"I see— of course Mr. Newsome has everything to show them. He has told me so much about her. My great desire's to give my daughter the opportunity of making her acquaintance. I'm always on the lookout for such chances for her. If I did n't bring her to-day it was only to make sure first that you'd let me." After which the charming woman risked a more intense appeal. "It would n't suit *you* also to mention some near time, so that we shall be sure not to lose you?" Strether on his side waited, for Sarah likewise had, after all, to perform; and it occupied him to have been thus reminded that she had stayed at home — and on her first morning of Paris — while Chad led the others forth. Oh she was up to her eyes; if she had stayed at home she had stayed by an understanding, arrived at the evening before, that Waymarsh would come and find her alone. This was beginning well — for a first day in Paris; and the thing might be amusing yet. But Madame de Vionnet's earnestness was meanwhile beautiful. "You may think me indiscreet, but I've *such* a desire my Jeanne shall know an American girl of the really delightful kind. You see I throw myself for it on your charity.'

The manner of this speech gave Strether such a sense of depths below it and behind it as he had n't yet had — ministered in a way that almost frightened him to his dim divinations of reasons; but if Sarah still, in spite of it, faltered, this was why he had time for a sign of sympathy with her petitioner. "Let me say then, dear lady, to back your plea, that Miss Mamie is of the most delightful kind of all — is charming among the charming."

Even Waymarsh, though with more to produce on the subject, could get into motion in time. "Yes, Countess, the American girl's a thing that your country must at least allow ours the privilege to say we *can* show you. But her full beauty is only for those who know how to make use of her."

"Ah then," smiled Madame de Vionnet, "that's exactly what I want to do. I'm sure she has much to teach us."

It was wonderful, but what was scarce less so was that Strether found himself, by the quick effect of it, moved another way. "Oh that may be! But don't speak of your own exquisite daughter, you know, as if she were n't pure perfection. *I* at least won't take that from you. Mademoiselle de Vionnet," he explained, in considerable form, to Mrs. Pocock, "*is* pure perfection. Mademoiselle de Vionnet *is* exquisite."

It had been perhaps a little portentous, but "Ah?" Sarah simply glittered.

Waymarsh himself, for that matter, apparently recognised, in respect to the facts, the need of a larger justice, and he had with it an inclination to Sarah. "Miss Jane's strikingly handsome — in the regular French style."

It somehow made both Strether and Madame de Vionnet laugh out, though at the very moment he caught in Sarah's eyes, as glancing at the speaker, a vague but unmistakeable "You too?" It made Waymarsh in fact look consciously over her head. Madame de Vionnet meanwhile, however, made her point in her own way. "I wish indeed I could offer you my poor child as a dazzling attraction: it would make one's position simple enough! She's as good as she can be, but of course she's different, and the question is now — in the light of the way things seem to go — if she is n't after all *too* different: too different I mean from the splendid type every one is so agreed that your wonderful country produces. On the other hand of course Mr. Newsome, who knows it so well, has, as a good friend, dear kind man that he is, done everything he can — to keep us from fatal benightedness — for my small shy creature. Well," she wound up after Mrs. Pocock had signified, in a murmur still a little stiff, that she would speak to her own young charge on the question — "well, we shall sit, my child and I, and wait and wait and wait for you." But her last fine turn was for Strether. "Do speak of us in such a way —!"

"As that something can't but come of it? Oh something *shall* come of it! I take a great interest!" he further declared; and in proof of it, the next moment, he had gone with her down to her carriage.

BOOK NINTH

I

"THE difficulty is," Strether said to Madame de Vionnet a couple of days later, "that I can't surprise them into the smallest sign of his not being the same old Chad they've been for the last three years glowering at across the sea. They simply won't give any, and as a policy, you know — what you call a *parti pris*, a deep game — that's positively remarkable."

It was so remarkable that our friend had pulled up before his hostess with the vision of it; he had risen from his chair at the end of ten minutes and begun, as a help not to worry, to move about before her quite as he moved before Maria. He had kept his appointment with her to the minute and had been intensely impatient, though divided in truth between the sense of having everything to tell her and the sense of having nothing at all. The short interval had, in the face of their complication, multiplied his impressions — it being meanwhile to be noted, moreover, that he already frankly, already almost publicly, viewed the complication as common to them. If Madame de Vionnet, under Sarah's eyes, had pulled him into her boat, there was by this time no doubt whatever that he had remained in it and that what he had really most been conscious of for many hours together was the movement of the vessel itself. They were in it together this moment as they had n't yet been, and he had n't at present uttered the least of the words of alarm or remonstrance that had died on his lips at the hotel. He had other things to say to her than that she had put him in a position; so quickly had his position grown to affect him as quite excitingly, altogether richly, inevitable. That the outlook, however — given the point of exposure — had n't cleared up half so much as he had reckoned was the first warning she received from him on his arrival. She had replied with indulgence that he was in too great a hurry, and had remarked soothingly that if she knew how to be patient surely *he* might be. He felt her presence, on the spot, he felt her tone and everything about her, as an aid to that effort; and it was perhaps one of the proofs of her success with him that he seemed so much to take his ease while they talked. By the time he had explained to her why his impressions, though multiplied, still baffled him, it was as if he had been familiarly talking for hours. They baffled him because Sarah — well, Sarah was deep; deeper than she had ever yet had a chance to show herself. He did n't say that this was partly the effect of her opening so straight down, as it were, into her mother, and that, given Mrs. Newsome's profundity, the shaft thus sunk might well have a reach; but he was n't without a resigned apprehension that, at such a rate of confidence between the two women, he was likely soon to be moved to show how already, at moments, it had been for him as if he were dealing directly with Mrs. Newsome. Sarah, to a certainty, would have begun herself to feel it in him — and this naturally put it in her power to torment him the more. From the moment she knew he *could* be tormented —!

"But *why* can you be?" — his companion was surprised at his use of the word.

"Because I'm made so — I think of everything."

"Ah one must never do that," she smiled. "One must think of as few things as possible."

"Then," he answered, "one must pick them out right. But all I mean is — for I express myself with violence — that she's in a position to watch me. There's an element of suspense for me, and she can see me wriggle. But my wriggling does n't matter," he pursued. "I can bear it. Besides, I shall wriggle out."

The picture at any rate stirred in her an appreciation that he felt to be sincere. "I don't see how a man can be kinder to a woman than you are to me."

Well, kind was what he wanted to be; yet even while her charming eyes rested on him with the truth of this he none the less had his humour of honesty. "When I say suspense I mean, you know," he laughed, "suspense about my own case too!"

"Oh yes — about your own case too!" It diminished his magnanimity, but she only looked at him the more tenderly.

"Not, however," he went on, "that I want to talk to you about that. It's my own little affair, and I mentioned it simply as part of Mrs. Pocock's advantage." No, no; though there was a queer present temptation in it, and his suspense was so real that to fidget was a relief, he would n't talk to her about Mrs. Newsome, would n't work off on her the anxiety produced in him by Sarah's calculated omissions of reference. The effect she produced of representing her

mother had been produced — and that was just the
immense, the uncanny part of it — without her having
so much as mentioned that lady. She had brought no
message, had alluded to no question, had only answered his enquiries with hopeless limited propriety.
She had invented a way of meeting them — as if he
had been a polite perfunctory poor relation, of distant
degree — that made them almost ridiculous in him.
He could n't moreover on his own side ask much
without appearing to publish how he had lately lacked
news; a circumstance of which it was Sarah's profound
policy not to betray a suspicion. These things, all the
same, he would n't breathe to Madame de Vionnet —
much as they might make him walk up and down.
And what he did n't say — as well as what *she* did n't,
for she had also her high decencies — enhanced the
effect of his being there with her at the end of ten
minutes more intimately on the basis of saving her
than he had yet had occasion to be. It ended in fact
by being quite beautiful between them, the number
of things they had a manifest consciousness of not
saying. He would have liked to turn her, critically,
to the subject of Mrs. Pocock, but he so stuck to the
line he felt to be the point of honour and of delicacy
that he scarce even asked her what her personal impression had been. He knew it, for that matter, without putting her to trouble: that she wondered how,
with such elements, Sarah could still have no charm,
was one of the principal things she held her tongue
about. Strether would have been interested in her
estimate of the elements — indubitably there, some
of them, and to be appraised according to taste — but

he denied himself even the luxury of this diversion. The way Madame de Vionnet affected him to-day was in itself a kind of demonstration of the happy employment of gifts. How could a woman think Sarah had charm who struck one as having arrived at it herself by such different roads? On the other hand of course Sarah was n't obliged to have it. He felt as if somehow Madame de Vionnet *was*. The great question meanwhile was what Chad thought of his sister; which was naturally ushered in by that of Sarah's apprehension of Chad. *That* they could talk of, and with a freedom purchased by their discretion in other senses. The difficulty however was that they were reduced as yet to conjecture. He had given them in the day or two as little of a lead as Sarah, and Madame de Vionnet mentioned that she had n't seen him since his sister's arrival.

"And does that strike you as such an age?"

She met it in all honesty. "Oh I won't pretend I don't miss him. Sometimes I see him every day. Our friendship's like that. Make what you will of it!" she whimsically smiled; a little flicker of the kind, occasional in her, that had more than once moved him to wonder what he might best make of *her*. "But he's perfectly right," she hastened to add, "and I would n't have him fail in any way at present for the world. I'd sooner not see him for three months. I begged him to be beautiful to them, and he fully feels it for himself."

Strether turned away under his quick perception; she was so odd a mixture of lucidity and mystery. She fell in at moments with the theory about her he most cherished, and she seemed at others to blow it into air. She spoke now as if her art were all an innocence, and then again as if her innocence were all an art. "Oh he's giving himself up, and he'll do so to the end. How can he but want, now that it's within reach, his full impression? — which is much more important, you know, than either yours or mine. But he's just soaking," Strether said as he came back; "he's going in conscientiously for a saturation. I'm bound to say he *is* very good."

"Ah," she quietly replied, "to whom do you say it?" And then more quietly still: "He's capable of anything."

Strether more than reaffirmed — "Oh he's excellent. I more and more like," he insisted, "to see him with them;" though the oddity of this tone between them grew sharper for him even while they spoke. It placed the young man so before them as the result of her interest and the product of her genius, acknowledged so her part in the phenomenon and made the phenomenon so rare, that more than ever yet he might have been on the very point of asking her for some more detailed account of the whole business than he had yet received from her. The occasion almost forced upon him some question as to how she had managed and as to the appearance such miracles presented from her own singularly close place of survey. The moment in fact however passed, giving way to more present history, and he continued simply to mark his appreciation of the happy truth. "It's a tremendous comfort to feel how one can trust him." And then again while for a little she said nothing — as if after all to *her* trust there might be a special limit: "I mean for making a good show to them."

"Yes," she thoughtfully returned — "but if they shut their eyes to it!"

Strether for an instant had his own thought. "Well perhaps that won't matter!"

"You mean because he probably — do what they will — won't like them?"

"Oh 'do what they will' —! They won't do much; especially if Sarah has n't more — well, more than one has yet made out — to give."

Madame de Vionnet weighed it. "Ah she has all her grace!" It was a statement over which, for a little, they could look at each other sufficiently straight, and though it produced no protest from Strether the effect was somehow as if he had treated it as a joke. "She may be persuasive and caressing with him; she may be eloquent beyond words. She may get hold of him," she wound up — "well, as neither you nor I have."

"Yes, she *may*" — and now Strether smiled. "But he has spent all his time each day with Jim. He's still showing Jim round."

She visibly wondered. "Then how about Jim?"

Strether took a turn before he answered. "Has n't he given you Jim? Has n't he before this 'done' him for you?" He was a little at a loss. "Does n't he tell you things?"

She hesitated. "No" — and their eyes once more gave and took. "Not as you do. You somehow make me see them — or at least feel them. And I have n't

asked too much," she added; "I've of late wanted
so not to worry him."

"Ah for that, so have I," he said with encouraging
assent; so that — as if she had answered everything
— they were briefly sociable on it. It threw him back
on his other thought, with which he took another
turn; stopping again, however, presently with something of a glow. "You see Jim's really immense. I
think it will be Jim who'll do it."

She wondered. "Get hold of him?"

"No — just the other thing. Counteract Sarah's
spell." And he showed now, our friend, how far he
had worked it out. "Jim's intensely cynical."

"Oh dear Jim!" Madame de Vionnet vaguely
smiled.

"Yes, literally — dear Jim! He's awful. What
he wants, heaven forgive him, is to help us."

"You mean" — she was eager — "help *me?*"

"Well, Chad and me in the first place. But he
throws you in too, though without as yet seeing you
much. Only, so far as he does see you — if you don't
mind — he sees you as awful."

"'Awful'?" — she wanted it all.

"A regular bad one — though of course of a tremendously superior kind. Dreadful, delightful, irresistible."

"Ah dear Jim! I should like to know him. I *must.*"

"Yes, naturally. But will it do? You may, you
know," Strether suggested, "disappoint him."

She was droll and humble about it. "I can but try.
But my wickedness then," she went on, "is my re-
commendation for him?"

BOOK NINTH

"Your wickedness and the charms with which, in such a degree as yours, he associates it. He understands, you see, that Chad and I have above all wanted to have a good time, and his view is simple and sharp. Nothing will persuade him — in the light, that is, of my behaviour — that I really did n't, quite as much as Chad, come over to have one before it was too late. He would n't have expected it of me; but men of my age, at Woollett — and especially the least likely ones — have been noted as liable to strange outbreaks, belated uncanny clutches at the unusual, the ideal. It 's an effect that a lifetime of Woollett has quite been observed as having; and I thus give it to you, in Jim's view, for what it 's worth. Now his wife and his mother-in-law," Strether continued to explain, "have, as in honour bound, no patience with such phenomena, late or early — which puts Jim, as against his relatives, on the other side. Besides," he added, "I don't think he really wants Chad back. If Chad does n't come — "

"He'll have " — Madame de Vionnet quite apprehended —"more of the free hand ?"

"Well, Chad's the bigger man."

"So he'll work now, *en dessous*, to keep him quiet ?"

"No — he won't 'work' at all, and he won't do anything *en dessous*. He's very decent and won't be a traitor in the camp. But he'll be amused with his own little view of our duplicity, he'll sniff up what he supposes to be Paris from morning till night, and he'll be, as to the rest, for Chad — well, just what he is."

She thought it over. "A warning ?"

He met it almost with glee. "You *are* as wonderful as everybody says!" And then to explain all he meant: "I drove him about for his first hour, and do you know what — all beautifully unconscious — he most put before me? Why that something like *that* is at bottom, as an improvement to his present state, as in fact the real redemption of it, what they think it may not be too late to make of our friend." With which, as, taking it in, she seemed, in her recurrent alarm, bravely to gaze at the possibility, he completed his statement. "But it *is* too late. Thanks to you!"

It drew from her again one of her indefinite reflexions. "Oh 'me' — after all!"

He stood before her so exhilarated by his demonstration that he could fairly be jocular. "Everything's comparative. You're better than *that*."

"You" — she could but answer him — "are better than anything." But she had another thought. "*Will* Mrs. Pocock come to me?"

"Oh yes — she'll do that. As soon, that is, as my friend Waymarsh — *her* friend now — leaves her leisure."

She showed an interest. "Is he so much her friend as that?"

"Why, did n't you see it all at the hotel?"

"Oh" — she was amused —"'all' is a good deal to say. I don't know — I forget. I lost myself in *her*."

"You were splendid," Strether returned — "but 'all' is n't a good deal to say: it's only a little. Yet it's charming so far as it goes. She wants a man to herself."

"And hasn't she got *you?*"

"Do you think she looked at me — or even at you — as if she had?" Strether easily dismissed that irony. "Every one, you see, must strike her as having somebody. You've got Chad — and Chad has got you."

"I see" — she made of it what she could. "And you've got Maria."

Well, he on his side accepted that. "I've got Maria. And Maria has got me. So it goes."

"But Mr. Jim — whom has he got?"

"Oh he has got — or it's as *if* he had — the whole place."

"But for Mr. Waymarsh" — she recalled — "isn't Miss Barrace before any one else?"

He shook his head. "Miss Barrace is a *raffinée,* and her amusement won't lose by Mrs. Pocock. It will gain rather — especially if Sarah triumphs and she comes in for a view of it."

"How well you know us!" Madame de Vionnet, at this, frankly sighed.

"No — it seems to me it's we that I know. I know Sarah — it's perhaps on that ground only that my feet are firm. Waymarsh will take her round while Chad takes Jim — and I shall be, I assure you, delighted for both of them. Sarah will have had what she requires — she will have paid her tribute to the ideal; and he will have done about the same. In Paris it's in the air — so what can one do less? If there's a point that, beyond any other, Sarah wants to make, it's that she didn't come out to be narrow. We shall feel at least that."

"Oh," she sighed, "the quantity we seem likely to 'feel'! But what becomes, in these conditions, of the girl?"

"Of Mamie—if we're all provided? Ah for that," said Strether, "you can trust Chad."

"To be, you mean, all right to her?"

"To pay her every attention as soon as he has polished off Jim. He wants what Jim can give him — and what Jim really won't — though he has had it all, and more than all, from me. He wants in short his own personal impression, and he'll get it — strong. But as soon as he has got it Mamie won't suffer."

"Oh Mamie must n't *suffer!*" Madame de Vionnet soothingly emphasised.

But Strether could reassure her. "Don't fear. As soon as he has done with Jim, Jim will fall to me. And then you'll see."

It was as if in a moment she saw already; yet she still waited. Then "Is she really quite charming?" she asked.

He had got up with his last words and gathered in his hat and gloves. "I don't know; I'm watching. I'm studying the case, as it were — and I dare say I shall be able to tell you."

She wondered. "Is it a case?"

"Yes — I think so. At any rate I shall see."

"But have n't you known her before?"

"Yes," he smiled — "but somehow at home she was n't a case. She has become one since." It was as if he made it out for himself. "She has become one here."

BOOK NINTH

"So very very soon?"

He measured it, laughing. "Not sooner than I did."

"And you became one — ?"

"Very very soon. The day I arrived."

Her intelligent eyes showed her thought of it. "Ah but the day you arrived you met Maria. Whom has Miss Pocock met?"

He paused again, but he brought it out. "Has n't she met Chad?"

"Certainly — but not for the first time. He's an old friend." At which Strether had a slow amused significant headshake that made her go on: "You mean that for *her* at least he's a new person — that she sees him as different?"

"She sees him as different."

"And how does she see him?"

Strether gave it up. "How can one tell how a deep little girl sees a deep young man?"

"Is every one so deep? Is she too?"

"So it strikes me — deeper than I thought. But wait a little — between us we'll make it out. You'll judge for that matter yourself."

Madame de Vionnet looked for the moment fairly bent on the chance. "Then she *will* come with her? —I mean Mamie with Mrs. Pocock?"

"Certainly. Her curiosity, if nothing else, will in any case work that. But leave it all to Chad."

"Ah," wailed Madame de Vionnet, turning away a little wearily, "the things I leave to Chad!"

The tone of it made him look at her with a kindness that showed his vision of her suspense. But he fell back on his confidence. "Oh well — trust him. Trust him all the way." He had indeed no sooner so spoken than the queer displacement of his point of view appeared again to come up for him in the very sound, which drew from him a short laugh, immediately checked. He became still more advisory. "When they do come give them plenty of Miss Jeanne. Let Mamie see her well."

She looked for a moment as if she placed them face to face. "For Mamie to hate her?"

He had another of his corrective headshakes. "Mamie won't. Trust *them*."

She looked at him hard, and then as if it were what she must always come back to: "It's *you* I trust. But I was sincere," she said, "at the hotel. I did, I do, want my child —"

"Well?" — Strether waited with deference while she appeared to hesitate as to how to put it.

"Well, to do what she can for me."

Strether for a little met her eyes on it; after which something that might have been unexpected to her came from him. "Poor little duck!"

Not more expected for himself indeed might well have been her echo of it. "Poor little duck! But she immensely wants herself," she said, "to see our friend's cousin."

"Is that what she thinks her?"

"It's what we call the young lady."

He thought again; then with a laugh: "Well, your daughter will help you."

And now at last he took leave of her, as he had been intending for five minutes. But she went part of the way with him, accompanying him out of the room and into the next and the next. Her noble old apartment offered a succession of three, the first two of which indeed, on entering, smaller than the last, but each with its faded and formal air, enlarged the office of the antechamber and enriched the sense of approach. Strether fancied them, liked them, and, passing through them with her more slowly now, met a sharp renewal of his original impression. He stopped, he looked back; the whole thing made a vista, which he found high melancholy and sweet — full, once more, of dim historic shades, of the faint far-away cannon-roar of the great Empire. It was doubtless half the projection of his mind, but his mind was a thing that, among old waxed parquets, pale shades of pink and green, pseudo-classic candelabra, he had always need-fully to reckon with. They could easily make him irrelevant. The oddity, the originality, the poetry — he did n't know what to call it — of Chad's con-nexion reaffirmed for him its romantic side. "They ought to see this, you know. They *must*."

"The Pococks?" — she looked about in depreca-tion; she seemed to see gaps he did n't.

"Mamie and Sarah — Mamie in particular."

"My shabby old place? But *their* things —!"

"Oh their things! You were talking of what will do something for you —"

"So that it strikes you," she broke in, "that my poor place may? Oh," she ruefully mused, "that *would* be desperate!"

"Do you know what I wish?" he went on. "I wish Mrs. Newsome herself could have a look."

She stared, missing a little his logic. "It would make a difference?"

Her tone was so earnest that as he continued to look about he laughed. "It might!"

"But you've told her, you tell me —"

"All about you? Yes, a wonderful story. But there's all the indescribable — what one gets only on the spot."

"Thank you!" she charmingly and sadly smiled.

"It's all about me here," he freely continued. "Mrs. Newsome feels things."

But she seemed doomed always to come back to doubt. "No one feels so much as *you*. No — not any one."

"So much the worse then for every one. It's very easy."

They were by this time in the antechamber, still alone together, as she had n't rung for a servant. The antechamber was high and square, grave and suggestive too, a little cold and slippery even in summer, and with a few old prints that were precious, Strether divined, on the walls. He stood in the middle, slightly lingering, vaguely directing his glasses, while, leaning against the door-post of the room, she gently pressed her cheek to the side of the recess. "*You* would have been a friend."

"I?" — it startled him a little.

"For the reason you say. You 're not stupid." And then abruptly, as if bringing it out were somehow founded on that fact: "We 're marrying Jeanne."

It affected him on the spot as a move in a game, and he was even then not without the sense that that wasn't the way Jeanne should be married. But he quickly showed his interest, though — as quickly afterwards struck him — with an absurd confusion of mind. "'You'? You and — a — not Chad?" Of course it was the child's father who made the 'we,' but to the child's father it would have cost him an effort to allude. Yet did n't it seem the next minute that Monsieur de Vionnet was after all not in question? — since she had gone on to say that it was indeed to Chad she referred and that he had been in the whole matter kindness itself.

"If I must tell you all, it is he himself who has put us in the way. I mean in the way of an opportunity that, so far as I can yet see, is all I could possibly have dreamed of. For all the trouble Monsieur de Vionnet will ever take!" It was the first time she had spoken to him of her husband, and he could n't have expressed how much more intimate with her it suddenly made him feel. It was n't much, in truth — there were other things in what she was saying that were far more; but it was as if, while they stood there together so easily in these cold chambers of the past, the single touch had shown the reach of her confidence. "But our friend," she asked, "has n't then told you?"

"He has told me nothing."

"Well, it has come with rather a rush — all in a very few days; and has n't moreover yet taken a form that permits an announcement. It's only for you — absolutely you alone — that I speak; I so want you to know." The sense he had so often had, since the first hour of his disembarkment, of being further and further "in," treated him again at this moment to another twinge; but in this wonderful way of her putting him in there continued to be something exquisitely remorseless. "Monsieur de Vionnet will accept what he *must* accept. He has proposed half a dozen things —each one more impossible than the other; and he would n't have found this if he lives to a hundred. Chad found it," she continued with her lighted, faintly flushed, her conscious confidential face, "in the quietest way in the world. Or rather it found *him* — for everything finds him; I mean finds him right. You 'll think we do such things strangely — but at my age," she smiled, "one has to accept one's conditions. Our young man's people had seen her; one of his sisters, a charming woman — we know all about them — had observed her somewhere with me. She had spoken to her brother — turned him on; and we were again observed, poor Jeanne and I, without our in the least knowing it. It was at the beginning of the winter; it went on for some time; it outlasted our absence; it began again on our return; and it luckily seems all right. The young man had met Chad, and he got a friend to approach him — as having a decent interest in us. Mr. Newsome looked well before he leaped; he kept beautifully quiet and satisfied himself fully; then only he spoke. It 's what has for some time past occupied us. It seems as if it were what would do; really, really all one could wish. There are only two or three points to be settled — they depend on her father. But this time I think we 're safe."

Strether, consciously gaping a little, had fairly hung upon her lips. "I hope so with all my heart."

128

BOOK NINTH

And then he permitted himself: "Does nothing depend on *her?*"

"Ah naturally; everything did. But she's pleased *comme tout.* She has been perfectly free; and he — our young friend — is really a combination. I quite adore him."

Strether just made sure. "You mean your future son-in-law?"

"Future if we all bring it off."

"Ah well," said Strether decorously, "I heartily hope you may." There seemed little else for him to say, though her communication had the oddest effect on him. Vaguely and confusedly he was troubled by it; feeling as if he had even himself been concerned in something deep and dim. He had allowed for depths, but these were greater: and it was as if, oppressively — indeed absurdly — he was responsible for what they had now thrown up to the surface. It was — through something ancient and cold in it — what he would have called the real thing. In short his hostess's news, though he could n't have explained why, was a sensible shock, and his oppression a weight he felt he must somehow or other immediately get rid of. There were too many connexions missing to make it tolerable he should do anything else. He was prepared to suffer — before his own inner tribunal — for Chad; he was prepared to suffer even for Madame de Vionnet. But he was n't prepared to suffer for the little girl. So now having said the proper thing, he wanted to get away. She held him an instant, however, with another appeal.

"Do I seem to you very awful?"

"Awful? Why so?" But he called it to himself, even as he spoke, his biggest insincerity yet.

"Our arrangements are so different from yours."

"Mine?" Oh he could dismiss that too! "I have n't any arrangements."

"Then you must accept mine; all the more that they're excellent. They're founded on a *vieille sagesse.* There will be much more, if all goes well, for you to hear and to know, and everything, believe me, for you to like. Don't be afraid; you'll be satisfied." Thus she could talk to him of what, of her innermost life — for that was what it came to — he must "accept"; thus she could extraordinarily speak as if in such an affair his being satisfied had an importance. It was all a wonder and made the whole case larger. He had struck himself at the hotel, before Sarah and Waymarsh, as being in her boat; but where on earth was he now? This question was in the air till her own lips quenched it with another. "And do you suppose *he* — who loves her so — would do anything reckless or cruel?"

He wondered what he supposed. "Do you mean your young man — ?"

"I mean yours. I mean Mr. Newsome." It flashed for Strether the next moment a finer light, and the light deepened as she went on. "He takes, thank God, the truest tenderest interest in her."

It deepened indeed. "Oh I'm sure of that!"

"You were talking," she said, "about one's trusting him. You see then how I do."

He waited a moment — it all came. "I see — I see." He felt he really did see.

BOOK NINTH

"He would n't hurt her for the world, nor — assuming she marries at all — risk anything that might make against her happiness. And — willingly, at least — he would never hurt *me*."

Her face, with what he had by this time grasped, told him more than her words; whether something had come into it, or whether he only read clearer, her whole story — what at least he then took for such — reached out to him from it. With the initiative she now attributed to Chad it all made a sense, and this sense — a light, a lead, was what had abruptly risen before him. He wanted, once more, to get off with these things; which was at last made easy, a servant having, for his assistance, on hearing voices in the hall, just come forward. All that Strether had made out was, while the man opened the door and impersonally waited, summed up in his last word. "I don't think, you know, Chad will tell me anything."

"No — perhaps not yet."

"And I won't as yet speak to him."

"Ah that's as you'll think best. You must judge."

She had finally given him her hand, which he held a moment. "How *much* I have to judge!"

"Everything," said Madame de Vionnet: a remark that was indeed — with the refined disguised suppressed passion of her face — what he most carried away.

II

So far as a direct approach was concerned Sarah
had neglected him, for the week now about to end,
with a civil consistency of chill that, giving him a
higher idea of her social resource, threw him back on
the general reflexion that a woman could always be
amazing. It indeed helped a little to console him that
he felt sure she had for the same period also left
Chad's curiosity hanging; though on the other hand,
for his personal relief, Chad could at least go through
the various motions — and he made them extraordinarily numerous — of seeing she had a good time.
There was n't a motion on which, in her presence,
poor Strether could so much as venture, and all he
could do when he was out of it was to walk over for a
talk with Maria. He walked over of course much less
than usual, but he found a special compensation in a
certain half-hour during which, toward the close of a
crowded empty expensive day, his several companions
seemed to him so disposed of as to give his forms and
usages a rest. He had been with them in the morning
and had nevertheless called on the Pococks in the
afternoon; but their whole group, he then found, had
dispersed after a fashion of which it would amuse
Miss Gostrey to hear. He was sorry again, gratefully
sorry she was so out of it — she who had really put
him in; but she had fortunately always her appetite
for news. The pure flame of the disinterested burned

in her cave of treasures as a lamp in a Byzantine
vault. It was just now, as happened, that for so fine a
sense as hers a near view would have begun to pay.
Within three days, precisely, the situation on which
he was to report had shown signs of an equilibrium;
the effect of his look in at the hotel was to confirm
this appearance. If the equilibrium might only pre-
vail! Sarah was out with Waymarsh, Mamie was out
with Chad, and Jim was out alone. Later on indeed
he himself was booked to Jim, was to take him that
evening to the Varieties — which Strether was careful to pronounce as Jim pronounced them.

Miss Gostrey drank it in. "What then to-night do
the others do?"

"Well, it has been arranged. Waymarsh takes
Sarah to dine at Bignon's."

She wondered. "And what do they do after?
They can't come straight home."

"No, they can't come straight home — at least
Sarah can't. It's their secret, but I think I've guessed
it." Then as she waited: "The circus."

It made her stare a moment longer, then laugh almost to extravagance. "There's no one like you!"

"Like *me*?" — he only wanted to understand.

"Like all of you together — like all of us: Woollett,
Milrose and their products. We're abysmal — but
may we never be less so! Mr. Newsome," she continued, "meanwhile takes Miss Pocock —?"

"Precisely — to the Français: to see what *you* took
Waymarsh and me to, a family-bill."

"Ah then may Mr. Chad enjoy it as *I* did!" But
she saw so much in things. "Do they spend their

evenings, your young people, like that, alone together?"

"Well, they're young people — but they're old friends."

"I see, I see. And do *they* dine — for a difference — at Brébant's?"

"Oh where they dine is their secret too. But I've my idea that it will be, very quietly, at Chad's own place."

"She'll come to him there alone?"

They looked at each other a moment. "He has known her from a child. Besides," said Strether with emphasis, "Mamie's remarkable. She's splendid."

She wondered. "Do you mean she expects to bring it off?"

"Getting hold of him? No — I think not."

"She doesn't want him enough? — or doesn't believe in her power?" On which as he said nothing she continued: "She finds she doesn't care for him?"

"No — I think she finds she does. But that's what I mean by so describing her. It's *if* she does that she's splendid. But we'll see," he wound up, "where she comes out."

"You seem to show me sufficiently," Miss Gostrey laughed, "where she goes in! But is her childhood's friend," she asked, "permitting himself recklessly to flirt with her?"

"No — not that. Chad's also splendid. They're *all* splendid!" he declared with a sudden strange sound of wistfulness and envy. "They're at least *happy*."

"Happy?" — it appeared, with their various difficulties, to surprise her.

"Well — I seem to myself among them the only one who is n't."

She demurred. "With your constant tribute to the ideal?"

He had a laugh at his tribute to the ideal, but he explained after a moment his impression. "I mean they're living. They're rushing about. I've already had my rushing. I'm waiting."

"But are n't you," she asked by way of cheer, "waiting with *me*?"

He looked at her in all kindness. "Yes — if it were n't for that!"

"And you help me to wait," she said. "However," she went on, "I've really something for you that will help you to wait and which you shall have in a minute. Only there's something more I want from you first. I revel in Sarah."

"So do I. If it were n't," he again amusedly sighed, "for *that* —!"

"Well, you owe more to women than any man I ever saw. We do seem to keep you going. Yet Sarah, as I see her, must be great."

"She *is*" — Strether fully assented : "great! Whatever happens, she won't, with these unforgettable days, have lived in vain."

Miss Gostrey had a pause. "You mean she has fallen in love?"

"I mean she wonders if she has n't — and it serves all her purpose."

135

"It has indeed," Maria laughed, "served women's purposes before!"

"Yes — for giving in. But I doubt if the idea — as an idea — has ever up to now answered so well for holding out. That's *her* tribute to the ideal — we each have our own. It's her romance — and it seems to me better on the whole than mine. To have it in Paris too," he explained — "on this classic ground, in this charged infectious air, with so sudden an intensity: well, it's more than she expected. She has had in short to recognise the breaking out for her of a real affinity — and with everything to enhance the drama."

Miss Gostrey followed. "Jim for instance?"

"Jim. Jim hugely enhances. Jim was made to enhance. And then Mrs. Waymarsh. It's the crowning touch — it supplies the colour. He's positively separated."

"And she herself unfortunately isn't — that supplies the colour too." Miss Gostrey was all there. But somehow —! "Is *he* in love?"

Strether looked at her a long time; then looked all about the room; then came a little nearer. "Will you never tell any one in the world as long as ever you live?"

"Never." It was charming.

"He thinks Sarah really is. But he has no fear," Strether hastened to add.

"Of her being affected by it?"

"Of *his* being. He likes it, but he knows she can hold out. He's helping her, he's floating her over, by kindness."

Maria rather funnily considered it. "Floating her over in champagne ? The kindness of dining her, nose to nose, at the hour when all Paris is crowding to profane delights, and in the — well, in the great temple, as one hears of it, of pleasure ?"

"That's just *it*, for both of them," Strether insisted —"and all of a supreme innocence. The Parisian place, the feverish hour, the putting before her of a hundred francs' worth of food and drink, which they'll scarcely touch — all that's the dear man's own romance; the expensive kind, expensive in francs and centimes, in which he abounds. And the circus afterwards — which is cheaper, but which he'll find some means of making as dear as possible — that's also *his* tribute to the ideal. It does for him. He'll see her through. They won't talk of anything worse than you and me."

"Well, we're bad enough perhaps, thank heaven," she laughed, "to upset them! Mr. Waymarsh at any rate is a hideous old coquette." And the next moment she had dropped everything for a different pursuit. "What you don't appear to know is that Jeanne de Vionnet has become engaged. She's to marry — it has been definitely arranged — young Monsieur de Montbron."

He fairly blushed. "Then — if you know it — it's 'out'?"

"Don't I often know things that are *not* out ? However," she said, "this will be out to-morrow. But I see I've counted too much on your possible ignorance. You've been before me, and I don't make you jump as I hoped."

He gave a gasp at her insight. "You never fail! I've *had* my jump. I had it when I first heard."

"Then if you knew why did n't you tell me as soon as you came in?"

"Because I had it from her as a thing not yet to be spoken of."

Miss Gostrey wondered. "From Madame de Vionnet herself?"

"As a probability — not quite a certainty: a good cause in which Chad has been working. So I've waited."

"You need wait no longer," she returned. "It reached me yesterday — roundabout and accidental, but by a person who had had it from one of the young man's own people — as a thing quite settled. I was only keeping it for you."

"You thought Chad would n't have told me?"

She hesitated. "Well, if he has n't —"

"He has n't. And yet the thing appears to have been practically his doing. So there we are."

"There we are!" Maria candidly echoed.

"That's why I jumped. I jumped," he continued to explain, "because it means, this disposition of the daughter, that there's now nothing else: nothing else but him and the mother."

"Still — it simplifies."

"It simplifies" — he fully concurred. "But that's precisely where we are. It marks a stage in his relation. The act is his answer to Mrs. Newsome's demonstration."

"It tells," Maria asked, "the worst?"

"The worst."

138

"But is the worst what he wants Sarah to know?"

"He does n't care for Sarah."

At which Miss Gostrey's eyebrows went up. "You mean she has already dished herself?"

Strether took a turn about; he had thought it out again and again before this, to the end; but the vista seemed each time longer. "He wants his good friend to know the best. I mean the measure of his attachment. She asked for a sign, and he thought of that one. There it is."

"A concession to her jealousy?"

Strether pulled up. "Yes — call it that. Make it lurid — for that makes my problem richer."

"Certainly, let us have it lurid — for I quite agree with you that we want none of our problems poor. But let us also have it clear. Can he, in the midst of such a preoccupation, or on the heels of it, have seriously cared for Jeanne? — cared, I mean, as a young man at liberty would have cared?"

Well, Strether had mastered it. "I think he can have thought it would be charming if he *could* care. It would be nicer."

"Nicer than being tied up to Marie?"

"Yes — than the discomfort of an attachment to a person he can never hope, short of a catastrophe, to marry. And he was quite right," said Strether. "It would certainly have been nicer. Even when a thing 's already nice there mostly *is* some other thing that would have been nicer — or as to which we wonder if it would n't. But his question was all the same a dream. He *could n't* care in that way. He *is* tied up to Marie. The relation is too special and has gone too

THE AMBASSADORS

far. It's the very basis, and his recent lively contribution toward establishing Jeanne in life has been his definite and final acknowledgement to Madame de Vionnet that he has ceased squirming. I doubt meanwhile," he went on, "if Sarah has at all directly attacked him."

His companion brooded. "But won't he wish for his own satisfaction to make his ground good to her?"

"No — he'll leave it to me, he'll leave everything to me. I 'sort of' feel" — he worked it out — "that the whole thing will come upon me. Yes, I shall have every inch and every ounce of it. I shall be *used* for it —!" And Strether lost himself in the prospect. Then he fancifully expressed the issue. "To the last drop of my blood."

Maria, however, roundly protested. "Ah you'll please keep a drop for *me*. I shall have a use for it!" — which she didn't however follow up. She had come back the next moment to another matter. "Mrs. Pocock, with her brother, is trusting only to her general charm?"

"So it would seem."

"And the charm's not working?"

Well, Strether put it otherwise, "She's sounding the note of home — which is the very best thing she can do."

"The best for Madame de Vionnet?"

"The best for home itself. The natural one; the right one."

"Right," Maria asked, "when it fails?"

Strether had a pause. "The difficulty's Jim. Jim's the note of home."

140

BOOK NINTH

She debated. "Ah surely not the note of Mrs. Newsome."

But he had it all. "The note of the home for which Mrs. Newsome wants him — the home of the business. Jim stands, with his little legs apart, at the door of *that* tent; and Jim *is*, frankly speaking, extremely awful."

Maria stared. "And you in, you poor thing, for your evening with him?"

"Oh he's all right for *me!*" Strether laughed. "Any one's good enough for *me*. But Sarah shouldn't, all the same, have brought him. She doesn't appreciate him."

His friend was amused with this statement of it. "Doesn't know, you mean, how bad he is?"

Strether shook his head with decision. "Not really."

She wondered. "Then doesn't Mrs. Newsome?"

It made him frankly do the same. "Well, no — since you ask me."

Maria rubbed it in. "Not really either?"

"Not at all. She rates him rather high." With which indeed, immediately, he took himself up. "Well, he *is* good too, in his way. It depends on what you want him for."

Miss Gostrey, however, wouldn't let it depend on anything — wouldn't have it, and wouldn't want him, at any price. "It suits my book," she said, "that he should be impossible; and it suits it still better," she more imaginatively added, "that Mrs. Newsome doesn't know he is."

Strether, in consequence, had to take it from her,

but he fell back on something else. "I'll tell you who does really know."

"Mr. Waymarsh? Never!"

"Never indeed. I'm not *always* thinking of Mr. Waymarsh; in fact I find now I never am." Then he mentioned the person as if there were a good deal in it. "Mamie."

"His own sister?" Oddly enough it but let her down. "What good will that do?"

"None perhaps. But there — as usual — we are!"

III

THERE they were yet again, accordingly, for two days
more; when Strether, on being, at Mrs. Pocock's
hotel, ushered into that lady's salon, found himself
at first assuming a mistake on the part of the servant
who had introduced him and retired. The occupants
had n't come in, for the room looked empty as only
a room can look in Paris, of a fine afternoon, when the
faint murmur of the huge collective life, carried on
out of doors, strays among scattered objects even as
a summer air idles in a lonely garden. Our friend
looked about and hesitated; observed, on the evidence
of a table charged with purchases and other matters,
that Sarah had become possessed — by no aid from
him — of the last number of the salmon-coloured
Revue; noted further that Mamie appeared to have
received a present of Fromentin's "Maîtres d'Autre-
fois" from Chad, who had written her name on the
cover; and pulled up at the sight of a heavy letter
addressed in a hand he knew. This letter, forwarded
by a banker and arriving in Mrs. Pocock's absence,
had been placed in evidence, and it drew from the
fact of its being unopened a sudden queer power to
intensify the reach of its author. It brought home to
him the scale on which Mrs. Newsome — for she had
been copious indeed this time — was writing to her
daughter while she kept *him* in durance; and it had
altogether such an effect upon him as made him for a

143

few minutes stand still and breathe low. In his own
room, at his own hotel, he had dozens of well-filled
envelopes superscribed in that character; and there
was actually something in the renewal of his interrupted vision of the character that played straight
into the so frequent question of whether he were n't
already disinherited beyond appeal. It was such an
assurance as the sharp downstrokes of her pen had
n't yet had occasion to give him; but they somehow
at the present crisis stood for a probable absoluteness
in any decree of the writer. He looked at Sarah's
name and address, in short, as if he had been looking
hard into her mother's face, and then turned from it
as if the face had declined to relax. But since it was
in a manner as if Mrs. Newsome were thereby all the
more, instead of the less, in the room, and were conscious, sharply and sorely conscious, of himself, so he
felt both held and hushed, summoned to stay at least
and take his punishment. By staying, accordingly,
he took it — creeping softly and vaguely about and
waiting for Sarah to come in. She *would* come in if
he stayed long enough, and he had now more than
ever the sense of her success in leaving him a prey to
anxiety. It was n't to be denied that she had had a
happy instinct, from the point of view of Woollett,
in placing him thus at the mercy of her own initiative.
It was very well to try to say he did n't care — that
she might break ground when she would, might never
break it at all if she would n't, and that he had no
confession whatever to wait upon her with: he
breathed from day to day an air that damnably required clearing, and there were moments when he

quite ached to precipitate that process. He could n't
doubt that, should she only oblige him by surprising
him just as he then was, a clarifying scene of some
sort would result from the concussion.

He humbly circulated in this spirit till he suddenly had a fresh arrest. Both the windows of the
room stood open to the balcony, but it was only
now that, in the glass of the leaf of one of them,
folded back, he caught a reflexion quickly recognised as the colour of a lady's dress. Somebody had
been then all the while on the balcony, and the person, whoever it might be, was so placed between the
windows as to be hidden from him; while on the other
hand the many sounds of the street had covered his
own entrance and movements. If the person were
Sarah he might on the spot therefore be served to his
taste. He might lead her by a move or two up to
the remedy for his vain tension; as to which, should
he get nothing else from it, he would at least have
the relief of pulling down the roof on their heads.
There was fortunately no one at hand to observe —
in respect to his valour — that even on this completed reasoning he still hung fire. He had been
waiting for Mrs. Pocock and the sound of the oracle;
but he had to gird himself afresh — which he did
in the embrasure of the window, neither advancing
nor retreating — before provoking the revelation. It
was apparently for Sarah to come more into view;
he was in that case there at her service. She did however, as meanwhile happened, come more into view;
only she luckily came at the last minute as a contra-
diction of Sarah. The occupant of the balcony was

after all quite another person, a person presented, on a second look, by a charming back and a slight shift of her position, as beautiful brilliant unconscious Mamie — Mamie alone at home, Mamie passing her time in her own innocent way, Mamie in short rather shabbily used, but Mamie absorbed interested and interesting. With her arms on the balustrade and her attention dropped to the street she allowed Strether to watch her, to consider several things, without her turning round.

But the oddity was that when he *had* so watched and considered he simply stepped back into the room without following up his advantage. He revolved there again for several minutes, quite as with something new to think of and as if the bearings of the possibility of Sarah had been superseded. For frankly, yes, it *had* bearings thus to find the girl in solitary possession. There was something in it that touched him to a point not to have been reckoned beforehand, something that softly but quite pressingly spoke to him, and that spoke the more each time he paused again at the edge of the balcony and saw her still unaware. Her companions were plainly scattered; Sarah would be off somewhere with Waymarsh and Chad off somewhere with Jim. Strether didn't at all mentally impute to Chad that he was with his "good friend"; he gave him the benefit of supposing him involved in appearances that, had he had to describe them — for instance to Maria — he would have conveniently qualified as more subtle. It came to him indeed the next thing that there was perhaps almost an excess of refinement in having

left Mamie in such weather up there alone; however she might in fact have extemporised, under the
charm of the Rue de Rivoli, a little makeshift Paris
of wonder and fancy. Our friend in any case now
recognised — and it was as if at the recognition
Mrs. Newsome's fixed intensity had suddenly, with
a deep audible grasp, grown thin and vague — that
day after day he had been conscious in respect to
his young lady of something odd and ambiguous,
yet something into which he could at last read a
meaning. It had been at the most, this mystery,
an obsession — oh an obsession agreeable; and it had
just now fallen into its place as at the touch of a
spring. It had represented the possibility between
them of some communication baffled by accident and
delay — the possibility even of some relation as yet
unacknowledged.

There was always their old relation, the fruit of
the Woollett years; but that — and it was what was
strangest — had nothing whatever in common with
what was now in the air. As a child, as a "bud,"
and then again as a flower of expansion, Mamie had
bloomed for him, freely, in the almost incessantly
open doorways of home; where he remembered her
as first very forward, as then very backward — for
he had carried on at one period, in Mrs. Newsome's
parlours (oh Mrs. Newsome's phases and his own!)
a course of English Literature re-enforced by exams
and teas — and once more, finally, as very much in
advance. But he had kept no great sense of points
of contact; it not being in the nature of things at
Woollett that the freshest of the buds should find her-

self in the same basket with the most withered of the winter apples. The child had given sharpness, above all, to his sense of the flight of time; it was but the day before yesterday that he had tripped up on her hoop, yet his experience of remarkable women — destined, it would seem, remarkably to grow — felt itself ready this afternoon, quite braced itself, to include her. She had in fine more to say to him than he had ever dreamed the pretty girl of the moment *could* have; and the proof of the circumstance was that, visibly, unmistakeably, she had been able to say it to no one else. It was something she could mention neither to her brother, to her sister-in-law nor to Chad; though he could just imagine that had she still been at home she might have brought it out, as a supreme tribute to age, authority and attitude, for Mrs. Newsome. It was moreover something in which they all took an interest; the strength of their interest was in truth just the reason of her prudence. All this then, for five minutes, was vivid to Strether, and it put before him that, poor child, she had now but her prudence to amuse her. That, for a pretty girl in Paris, struck him, with a rush, as a sorry state; so that under the impression he went out to her with a step as hypocritically alert, he was well aware, as if he had just come into the room. She turned with a start at his voice; preoccupied with him though she might be, she was just a scrap disappointed. "Oh I thought you were Mr. Bilham!"

The remark had been at first surprising and our friend's private thought, under the influence of it, temporarily blighted; yet we are able to add that he

presently recovered his inward tone and that many
a fresh flower of fancy was to bloom in the same air.
Little Bilham — since little Bilham was, somewhat
incongruously, expected — appeared behindhand; a
circumstance by which Strether was to profit. They
came back into the room together after a little, the
couple on the balcony, and amid its crimson-and-
gold elegance, with the others still absent, Strether
passed forty minutes that he appraised even at the
time as far, in the whole queer connexion, from his
idlest. Yes indeed, since he had the other day so
agreed with Maria about the inspiration of the lurid,
here was something for his problem that surely did n't
make it shrink and that was floated in upon him as
part of a sudden flood. He was doubtless not to know
till afterwards, on turning them over in thought, of
how many elements his impression was composed;
but he none the less felt, as he sat with the charming
girl, the signal growth of a confidence. For she *was*
charming, when all was said — and none the less
so for the visible habit and practice of freedom and
fluency. She was charming, he was aware, in spite
of the fact that if he had n't found her so he would
have found her something he should have been in
peril of expressing as "funny." Yes, she was funny,
wonderful Mamie, and without dreaming it; she was
bland, she was bridal — with never, that he could
make out as yet, a bridegroom to support it; she was
handsome and portly and easy and chatty, soft and
sweet and almost disconcertingly reassuring. She
was dressed, if we might so far discriminate, less as
a young lady than as an old one — had an old one

been supposable to Strether as so committed to vanity; the complexities of her hair missed moreover also the looseness of youth; and she had a mature manner of bending a little, as to encourage and reward, while she held neatly together in front of her a pair of strikingly polished hands: the combination of all of which kept up about her the glamour of her "receiving," placed her again perpetually between the windows and within sound of the ice-cream plates, suggested the enumeration of all the names, all the Mr. Brookses and Mr. Snookses, gregarious specimens of a single type, she was happy to "meet."

But if all this was where she was funny, and if what was funnier than the rest was the contrast between her beautiful benevolent patronage — such a hint of the polysyllabic as might make her something of a bore toward middle age — and her rather flat little voice, the voice, naturally, unaffectedly yet, of a girl of fifteen; so Strether, none the less, at the end of ten minutes, felt in her a quiet dignity that pulled things bravely together. If quiet dignity, almost more than matronly, with voluminous, too voluminous clothes, was the effect she proposed to produce, that was an ideal one could like in her when once one had got into relation. The great thing now for her visitor was that this was exactly what he had done; it made so extraordinary a mixture of the brief and crowded hour. It was the mark of a relation that he had begun so quickly to find himself sure she was, of all people, as might have been said, on the side and of the party of Mrs. Newsome's original ambassador. She was in *his* interest and not in Sarah's; and some sign of that was precisely what he had been feeling in her, these last days, as imminent. Finally placed, in Paris, in immediate presence of the situation and of the hero of it — by whom Strether was incapable of meaning any one but Chad — she had accomplished, and really in a manner all unexpected to herself, a change of base; deep still things had come to pass within her, and by the time she had grown sure of them Strether had become aware of the little drama. When she knew where she was, in short, he had made it out; and he made it out at present still better; though with never a direct word passing between them all the while on the subject of his own predicament. There had been at first, as he sat there with her, a moment during which he wondered if she meant to break ground in respect to his prime undertaking. That door stood so strangely ajar that he was half-prepared to be conscious, at any juncture, of her having, of any one's having, quite bounced in. But, friendly, familiar, light of touch and happy of tact, she exquisitely stayed out; so that it was for all the world as if to show she could deal with him without being reduced to — well, scarcely anything.

It fully came up for them then, by means of their talking of everything *but* Chad, that Mamie, unlike Sarah, unlike Jim, knew perfectly what had become of him. It fully came up that she had taken to the last fraction of an inch the measure of the change in him, and that she wanted Strether to know what a secret she proposed to make of it. They talked most conveniently — as if they had had no chance yet — about Woollett; and that had virtually the effect of

151

their keeping the secret more close. The hour took on for Strether, little by little, a queer sad sweetness of quality; he had such a revulsion in Mamie's favour and on behalf of her social value as might have come from remorse at some early injustice. She made him, as under the breath of some vague western whiff, homesick and freshly restless; he could really for the time have fancied himself stranded with her on a far shore, during an ominous calm, in a quaint community of shipwreck. Their little interview was like a picnic on a coral strand; they passed each other, with melancholy smiles and looks sufficiently allusive, such cupfuls of water as they had saved. Especially sharp in Strether meanwhile was the conviction that his companion really knew, as we have hinted, where she had come out. It was at a very particular place — only *that* she would never tell him; it would be above all what he should have to puzzle for himself. This was what he hoped for, because his interest in the girl would n't be complete without it. No more would the appreciation to which she was entitled — so assured was he that the more he saw of her process the more he should see of her pride. She saw, herself, everything; but she knew what she did n't want, and that it was that had helped her. What did n't she want? — there was a pleasure lost for her old friend in not yet knowing, as there would doubtless be a thrill in getting a glimpse. Gently and sociably she kept that dark to him, and it was as if she soothed and beguiled him in other ways to make up for it. She came out with her impression of Madame de Vionnet — of whom she had "heard so much"; she came out

with her impression of Jeanne, whom she had been
"dying to see": she brought it out with a blandness
by which her auditor was really stirred that she had
been with Sarah early that very afternoon, and after
dreadful delays caused by all sorts of things, mainly,
eternally, by the purchase of clothes — clothes that
unfortunately would n't be themselves eternal — to
call in the Rue de Bellechasse.

At the sound of these names Strether almost blushed
to feel that he could n't have sounded them first —
and yet could n't either have justified his squeam-
ishness. Mamie made them easy as he could n't
have begun to do, and yet it could only have cost her
more than he should ever have had to spend. It was
as friends of Chad's, friends special, distinguished,
desirable, enviable, that she spoke of them, and she
beautifully carried it off that much as she had heard
of them — though she did n't say how or where,
which was a touch of her own — she had found them
beyond her supposition. She abounded in praise of
them, and after the manner of Woollett — which
made the manner of Woollett a loveable thing again
to Strether. He had never so felt the true inwardness
of it as when his blooming companion pronounced
the elder of the ladies of the Rue de Bellechasse too
fascinating for words and declared of the younger
that she was perfectly ideal, a real little monster of
charm. "Nothing," she said of Jeanne, "ought ever
to happen to her — she's so awfully right as she is.
Another touch will spoil her — so she ought n't to be
touched."

"Ah but things, here in Paris," Strether observed,

"do happen to little girls." And then for the joke's and the occasion's sake: "Have n't you found that yourself?"

"That things happen —? Oh I'm not a little girl. I'm a big battered blowsy one. *I* don't care," Mamie laughed, "*what* happens."

Strether had a pause while he wondered if it might n't happen that he should give her the pleasure of learning that he found her nicer than he had really dreamed — a pause that ended when he had said to himself that, so far as it at all mattered for her, she had in fact perhaps already made this out. He risked accordingly a different question — though conscious, as soon as he had spoken, that he seemed to place it in relation to her last speech. "But that Mademoiselle de Vionnet is to be married — I suppose you've heard of *that*."

For all, he then found, he need fear! "Dear, yes; the gentleman was there: Monsieur de Montbron, whom Madame de Vionnet presented to us."

"And was he nice?"

Mamie bloomed and bridled with her best reception manner. "Any man's nice when he's in love."

It made Strether laugh. "But is Monsieur de Montbron in love — already — with *you?*"

"Oh that's not necessary — it's so much better he should be so with *her:* which, thank goodness, I lost no time in discovering for myself. He's perfectly gone — and I could n't have borne it for her if he had n't been. She's just too sweet."

Strether hesitated. "And through being in love too?"

154

On which with a smile that struck him as wonderful Mamie had a wonderful answer. "She does n't know if she is or not."

It made him again laugh out. "Oh but *you* do!"

She was willing to take it that way. "Oh yes, I know everything." And as she sat there rubbing her polished hands and making the best of it — only holding her elbows perhaps a little too much out — the momentary effect for Strether was that every one else, in all their affair, seemed stupid.

"Know that poor little Jeanne does n't know what's the matter with her?"

It was as near as they came to saying that she was probably in love with Chad; but it was quite near enough for what Strether wanted; which was to be confirmed in his certitude that, whether in love or not, she appealed to something large and easy in the girl before him. Mamie would be fat, too fat, at thirty; but she would always be the person who, at the present sharp hour, had been disinterestedly tender. "If I see a little more of her, as I hope I shall, I think she'll like me enough — for she seemed to like me to-day — to want me to tell her."

"And *shall* you?"

"Perfectly. I shall tell her the matter with her is that she wants only too much to do right. To do right for her, naturally," said Mamie, "is to please."

"Her mother, do you mean?"

"Her mother first."

Strether waited. "And then?"

"Well, 'then' — Mr. Newsome."

There was something really grand for him in the

serenity of this reference. "And last only Monsieur de Montbron?"

"Last only" — she good-humouredly kept it up.

Strether considered. "So that every one after all then will be suited?"

She had one of her few hesitations, but it was a question only of a moment; and it was her nearest approach to being explicit with him about what was between them. "I think I can speak for myself. *I* shall be."

It said indeed so much, told such a story of her being ready to help him, so committed to him that truth, in short, for such use as he might make of it toward those ends of his own with which, patiently and trustfully, she had nothing to do — it so fully achieved all this that he appeared to himself simply to meet it in its own spirit by the last frankness of admiration. Admiration was of itself almost accusatory, but nothing less would serve to show her how nearly he understood. He put out his hand for good-bye with a "Splendid, splendid, splendid!" And he left her, in her splendour, still waiting for little Bilham.

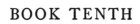

BOOK TENTH

I

STRETHER occupied beside little Bilham, three evenings after his interview with Mamie Pocock, the same
deep divan they had enjoyed together on the first
occasion of our friend's meeting Madame de Vionnet
and her daughter in the apartment of the Boulevard
Malesherbes, where his position affirmed itself again
as ministering to an easy exchange of impressions.
The present evening had a different stamp; if the
company was much more numerous, so, inevitably,
were the ideas set in motion. It was on the other
hand, however, now strongly marked that the talk-
ers moved, in respect to such matters, round an
inner, a protected circle. They knew at any rate
what really concerned them to-night, and Strether
had begun by keeping his companion close to it.
Only a few of Chad's guests had dined — that is
fifteen or twenty, a few compared with the large
concourse offered to sight by eleven o'clock; but number and mass, quantity and quality, light, fragrance,
sound, the overflow of hospitality meeting the high
tide of response, had all from the first pressed upon
Strether's consciousness, and he felt himself somehow part and parcel of the most festive scene, as
the term was, in which he had ever in his life been
engaged. He had perhaps seen, on Fourths of July
and on dear old domestic Commencements, more
people assembled, but he had never seen so many in

proportion to the space, or had at all events never known so great a promiscuity to show so markedly as picked. Numerous as was the company, it had still been made so by selection, and what was above all rare for Strether was that, by no fault of his own, he was in the secret of the principle that had worked. He had n't enquired, he had averted his head, but Chad had put him a pair of questions that themselves smoothed the ground. He had n't answered the questions, he had replied that they were the young man's own affair; and he had then seen perfectly that the latter's direction was already settled.

Chad had applied for counsel only by way of intimating that he knew what to do; and he had clearly never known it better than in now presenting to his sister the whole circle of his society. This was all in the sense and the spirit of the note struck by him on that lady's arrival; he had taken at the station itself a line that led him without a break, and that enabled him to lead the Pococks — though dazed a little, no doubt, breathless, no doubt, and bewildered — to the uttermost end of the passage accepted by them perforce as pleasant. He had made it for them violently pleasant and mercilessly full; the upshot of which was, to Strether's vision, that they had come all the way without discovering it to be really no passage at all. It was a brave blind alley, where to pass was impossible and where, unless they stuck fast, they would have — which was always awkward — publicly to back out. They were touching bottom assuredly tonight; the whole scene represented the terminus of the *cul-de-sac*. So could things go when there was a hand to keep them consistent— a hand that pulled the wire with a skill at which the elder man more and more marvelled. The elder man felt responsible, but he also felt successful, since what had taken place was simply the issue of his own contention, six weeks before, that they properly should wait to see what their friends would have really to say. He had determined Chad to wait, he had determined him to see; he was therefore not to quarrel with the time given up to the business. As much as ever, accordingly, now that a fortnight had elapsed, the situation created for Sarah, and against which she had raised no protest, was that of her having accommodated herself to her adventure as to a pleasure-party surrendered perhaps even somewhat in excess to bustle and to "pace." If her brother had been at any point the least bit open to criticism it might have been on the ground of his spicing the draught too highly and pouring the cup too full. Frankly treating the whole occasion of the presence of his relatives as an opportunity for amusement, he left it, no doubt, but scant margin as an opportunity for anything else. He suggested, invented, abounded — yet all the while with the loosest easiest rein. Strether, during his own weeks, had gained a sense of knowing Paris; but he saw it afresh, and with fresh emotion, in the form of the knowledge offered to his colleague.

A thousand unuttered thoughts hummed for him in the air of these observations; not the least frequent of which was that Sarah might well of a truth not quite know whither she was drifting. She was in no position not to appear to expect that Chad should treat her handsomely; yet she struck our friend as privately stiffening a little each time she missed the chance of marking the great *nuance*. The great *nuance* was in brief that of course her brother must treat her handsomely— she should like to see him not; but that treating her handsomely, none the less, was n't all in all— treating her handsomely buttered no parsnips; and that in fine there were moments when she felt the fixed eyes of their admirable absent mother fairly screw into the flat of her back. Strether, watching, after his habit, and overscoring with thought, positively had moments of his own in which he found himself sorry for her—occasions on which she affected him as a person seated in a runaway vehicle and turning over the question of a possible jump. *Would* she jump, could she, would *that* be a safe place?—this question, at such instants, sat for him in her lapse into pallor, her tight lips, her conscious eyes. It came back to the main point at issue: would she be, after all, to be squared? He believed on the whole she would jump; yet his alternations on this subject were the more especial stuff of his suspense. One thing remained well before him —a conviction that was in fact to gain sharpness from the impressions of this evening: that if she *should* gather in her skirts, close her eyes and quit the carriage while in motion, he would promptly enough become aware. She would alight from her headlong course more or less directly upon him; it would be appointed to him, unquestionably, to receive her entire weight. Signs and portents of the experience thus in reserve for him had, as it happened, multi-

plied even through the dazzle of Chad's party. It
was partly under the nervous consciousness of such
a prospect that, leaving almost every one in the two
other rooms, leaving those of the guests already known
to him as well as a mass of brilliant strangers of both
sexes and of several varieties of speech, he had desired
five quiet minutes with little Bilham, whom he always found soothing and even a little inspiring, and
to whom he had actually moreover something distinct
and important to say.

He had felt of old — for it already seemed long ago
— rather humiliated at discovering he could learn in
talk with a personage so much his junior the lesson of
a certain moral ease; but he had now got used to that
— whether or no the mixture of the fact with other
humiliations had made it indistinct, whether or no
directly from little Bilham's example, the example of
his being contentedly just the obscure and acute little
Bilham he was. It worked so for him, Strether seemed
to see; and our friend had at private hours a wan
smile over the fact that he himself, after so many more
years, was still in search of something that would
work. However, as we have said, it worked just now
for them equally to have found a corner a little apart.
What particularly kept it apart was the circumstance
that the music in the salon was admirable, with two
or three such singers as it was a privilege to hear in
private. Their presence gave a distinction to Chad's
entertainment, and the interest of calculating their
effect on Sarah was actually so sharp as to be almost
painful. Unmistakeably, in her single person, the motive of the composition and dressed in a splendour of

crimson which affected Strether as the sound of a fall through a skylight, she would now be in the forefront of the listening circle and committed by it up to her eyes. Those eyes during the wonderful dinner itself he had n't once met; having confessedly — perhaps a little pusillanimously — arranged with Chad that he should be on the same side of the table. But there was no use in having arrived now with little Bilham at an unprecedented point of intimacy unless he could pitch everything into the pot. "You who sat where you could see her, what does she make of it all? By which I mean on what terms does she take it?"

"Oh she takes it, I judge, as proving that the claim of his family is more than ever justified."

"She is n't then pleased with what he has to show?"

"On the contrary; she's pleased with it as with his capacity to do this kind of thing — more than she has been pleased with anything for a long time. But she wants him to show it *there*. He has no right to waste it on the likes of us."

Strether wondered. "She wants him to move the whole thing over?"

"The whole thing — with an important exception. Everything he has 'picked up' — and the way he knows how. She sees no difficulty in that. She'd run the show herself, and she'll make the handsome concession that Woollett would be on the whole in some ways the better for it. Not that it would n't be also in some ways the better for Woollett. The people there are just as good."

"Just as good as you and these others? Ah that may be. But such an occasion as this, whether or no,"

Strether said, "isn't the people. It's what has made the people possible."

"Well then," his friend replied, "there you are; I give you my impression for what it's worth. Mrs. Pocock has *seen,* and that's to-night how she sits there. If you were to have a glimpse of her face you'd understand me. She has made up her mind — to the sound of expensive music."

Strether took it freely in. "Ah then I shall have news of her."

"I don't want to frighten you, but I think that likely. However," little Bilham continued, "if I'm of the least use to you to hold on by — !"

"You're not of the least!" — and Strether laid an appreciative hand on him to say it. "No one's of the least." With which, to mark how gaily he could take it, he patted his companion's knee. "I must meet my fate alone, and I *shall* — oh you'll see! And yet," he pursued the next moment, "you *can* help me too. You once said to me" — he followed this further — "that you held Chad should marry. I did n't see then so well as I know now that you meant he should marry Miss Pocock. Do you still consider that he should? Because if you do" — he kept it up — "I want you immediately to change your mind. You can help me that way."

"Help you by thinking he should *not* marry?"

"Not marry at all events Mamie."

"And who then?"

"Ah," Strether returned, "that I'm not obliged to say. But Madame de Vionnet — I suggest — when he can."

165

"Oh!" said little Bilham with some sharpness.

"Oh precisely! But he need n't marry at all —
I'm at any rate not obliged to provide for it. Whereas
in your case I rather feel that I *am*."

Little Bilham was amused. "Obliged to provide
for my marrying?"

"Yes — after all I've done to you!"

The young man weighed it. "Have you done as
much as that?"

"Well," said Strether, thus challenged, "of course
I must remember what you've also done to *me*. We
may perhaps call it square. But all the same," he went
on, "I wish awfully you'd marry Mamie Pocock yourself."

Little Bilham laughed out. "Why it was only the
other night, in this very place, that you were proposing
to me a different union altogether."

"Mademoiselle de Vionnet?" Well, Strether easily confessed it. "That, I admit, was a vain image.
This is practical politics. I want to do something good
for both of you — I wish you each so well; and you
can see in a moment the trouble it will save me to
polish you off by the same stroke. She likes you, you
know. You console her. And she's splendid."

Little Bilham stared as a delicate appetite stares at
an overheaped plate. "What do I console her for?"

It just made his friend impatient. "Oh come, you
know!"

"And what proves for you that she likes me?"

"Why the fact that I found her three days ago
stopping at home alone all the golden afternoon on the
mere chance that you'd come to her, and hanging

over her balcony on that of seeing your cab drive up.
I don't know what you want more."

Little Bilham after a moment found it. "Only just
to know what proves to you that I like *her*."

"Oh if what I've just mentioned isn't enough to
make you do it, you're a stony-hearted little fiend.
Besides" — Strether encouraged his fancy's flight —
"you showed your inclination in the way you kept her
waiting, kept her on purpose to see if she cared enough
for you."

His companion paid his ingenuity the deference of
a pause. "I didn't keep her waiting. I came at the
hour. I wouldn't have kept her waiting for the
world," the young man honourably declared.

"Better still—then there you are!" And Strether,
charmed, held him the faster. "Even if you didn't do
her justice, moreover," he continued, "I should insist
on your immediately coming round to it. I want
awfully to have worked it. I want" — and our friend
spoke now with a yearning that was really earnest —
"at least to have done *that*."

"To have married me off — without a penny?"

"Well, I shan't live long; and I give you my word,
now and here, that I'll leave you every penny of my
own. I haven't many, unfortunately, but you shall
have them all. And Miss Pocock, I think, has a few.
I want," Strether went on, "to have been at least to
that extent constructive — even expiatory. I've been
sacrificing so to strange gods that I feel I want to put
on record, somehow, my fidelity — fundamentally
unchanged after all — to our own. I feel as if my
hands were embrued with the blood of monstrous

alien altars — of another faith altogether. There it
is — it's done." And then he further explained. "It
took hold of me because the idea of getting her quite
out of the way for Chad helps to clear my ground."

The young man, at this, bounced about, and it
brought them face to face in admitted amusement.
"You want me to marry as a convenience to Chad?"

"No," Strether debated — "*he* does n't care whether
you marry or not. It's as a convenience simply to
my own plan *for* him."

"'Simply'!" — and little Bilham's concurrence
was in itself a lively comment. "Thank you. But I
thought," he continued, "you had exactly *no* plan
'for' him."

"Well then call it my plan for myself — which may
be well, as you say, to have none. His situation, don't
you see? is reduced now to the bare facts one has to
recognise. Mamie does n't want him, and he does n't
want Mamie: so much as that these days have made
clear. It's a thread we can wind up and tuck in."

But little Bilham still questioned. "*You* can —
since you seem so much to want to. But why should
I?"

Poor Strether thought it over, but was obliged of
course to admit that his demonstration did superficially fail. "Seriously, there *is* no reason. It's my
affair — I must do it alone. I've only my fantastic
need of making my dose stiff."

Little Bilham wondered. "What do you call your
dose?"

"Why what I have to swallow. I want my conditions unmitigated."

BOOK TENTH

He had spoken in the tone of talk for talk's sake, and yet with an obscure truth lurking in the loose folds; a circumstance presently not without its effect on his young friend. Little Bilham's eyes rested on him a moment with some intensity; then suddenly, as if everything had cleared up, he gave a happy laugh. It seemed to say that if pretending, or even trying, or still even hoping, to be able to care for Mamie would be of use, he was all there for the job. "I'll do anything in the world for you!"

"Well," Strether smiled, "anything in the world is all I want. I don't know anything that pleased me in her more," he went on, "than the way that, on my finding her up there all alone, coming on her unawares and feeling greatly for her being so out of it, she knocked down my tall house of cards with her instant and cheerful allusion to the next young man. It was somehow so the note I needed — her staying at home to receive him."

"It was Chad of course," said little Bilham, "who asked the next young man — I like your name for me! — to call."

"So I supposed — all of which, thank God, is in our innocent and natural manners. But do you know," Strether asked, "if Chad knows — ?" And then as this interlocutor seemed at a loss: "Why where she has come out."

Little Bilham, at this, met his face with a conscious look; it was as if, more than anything yet, the allusion had penetrated. "Do you know yourself?"

Strether lightly shook his head. "There I stop. Oh, odd as it may appear to you, there *are* things I

169

don't know. I only got the sense from her of something very sharp, and yet very deep down, that she was keeping all to herself. That is I had begun with the belief that she *had* kept it to herself; but face to face with her there I soon made out that there was a person with whom she would have shared it. I had thought she possibly might with *me* — but I saw then that I was only half in her confidence. When, turning to me to greet me — for she was on the balcony and I had come in without her knowing it — she showed me she had been expecting *you* and was proportionately disappointed, I got hold of the tail of my conviction. Half an hour later I was in possession of all the rest of it. You know what has happened." He looked at his young friend hard — then he felt sure. "For all you say, you're up to your eyes. So there you are."

Little Bilham after an instant pulled half round. "I assure you she hasn't told me anything."

"Of course she hasn't. For what do you suggest that I suppose her to take you? But you've been with her every day, you've seen her freely, you've liked her greatly — I stick to that — and you've made your profit of it. You know what she has been through as well as you know that she has dined here to-night — which must have put her, by the way, through a good deal more."

The young man faced this blast; after which he pulled round the rest of the way. "I haven't in the least said she hasn't been nice to me. But she's proud."

"And quite properly. But not too proud for that."

"It's just her pride that has made her. Chad,"
little Bilham loyally went on, "has really been as kind
to her as possible. It's awkward for a man when a
girl's in love with him."

"Ah but she is n't — now."

Little Bilham sat staring before him; then he sprang
up as if his friend's penetration, recurrent and insist-
ent, made him really after all too nervous. "No —
she is n't now. It is n't in the least," he went on,
"Chad's fault. He's really all right. I mean he would
have been willing. But she came over with ideas.
Those she had got at home. They had been her
motive and support in joining her brother and his
wife. She was to *save* our friend."

"Ah like me, poor thing?" Strether also got to his
feet.

"Exactly — she had a bad moment. It was very
soon distinct to her, to pull her up, to let her down,
that, alas, he was, he *is*, saved. There's nothing left
for her to do."

"Not even to love him?"

"She would have loved him better as she originally
believed him."

Strether wondered. "Of course one asks one's self
what notion a little girl forms, where a young man's
in question, of such a history and such a state."

"Well, this little girl saw them, no doubt, as obscure, but she saw them practically as wrong. The
wrong for her *was* the obscure. Chad turns out at any
rate right and good and disconcerting, while what she
was all prepared for, primed and girded and wound
up for, was to deal with him as the general opposite."

"Yet was n't her whole point" — Strether weighed
it — "that he was to be, that he *could* be, made better,
redeemed?"

Little Bilham fixed it all a moment, and then with
a small headshake that diffused a tenderness: "She's
too late. Too late for the miracle."

"Yes" — his companion saw enough. "Still, if
the worst fault of his condition is that it may be all
there for her to profit by — ?"

"Oh she does n't want to 'profit,' in that flat way.
She does n't want to profit by another woman's work
— she wants the miracle to have been her own miracle.
That's what she's too late for."

Strether quite felt how it all fitted, yet there seemed
one loose piece. "I 'm bound to say, you know, that
she strikes one, on these lines, as fastidious — what
you call here *difficile.*"

Little Bilham tossed up his chin. "Of course she's
difficile — on any lines! What else in the world *are*
our Mamies — the real, the right ones?"

"I see, I see," our friend repeated, charmed by the
responsive wisdom he had ended by so richly ex-
tracting. "Mamie is one of the real and the right."

"The very thing itself."

"And what it comes to then," Strether went on,
"is that poor awful Chad is simply too good for her."

"Ah too good was what he was after all to be; but
it was she herself, and she herself only, who was to
have made him so."

It hung beautifully together, but with still a loose
end. "Would n't he do for her even if he should
after all break —"

"With his actual influence?" Oh little Bilham had for this enquiry the sharpest of all his controls. "How can he 'do' — on any terms whatever — when he's flagrantly spoiled?"

Strether could only meet the question with his passive, his receptive pleasure. "Well, thank goodness, *you're* not! *You* remain for her to save, and I come back, on so beautiful and full a demonstration, to my contention of just now — that of your showing distinct signs of her having already begun."

The most he could further say to himself — as his young friend turned away — was that the charge encountered for the moment no renewed denial. Little Bilham, taking his course back to the music, only shook his good-natured ears an instant, in the manner of a terrier who has got wet; while Strether relapsed into the sense — which had for him in these days most of comfort — that he was free to believe in anything that from hour to hour kept him going. He had positively motions and flutters of this conscious hour-to-hour kind, temporary surrenders to irony, to fancy, frequent instinctive snatches at the growing rose of observation, constantly stronger for him, as he felt, in scent and colour, and in which he could bury his nose even to wantonness. This last resource was offered him, for that matter, in the very form of his next clear perception — the vision of a prompt meeting, in the doorway of the room, between little Bilham and brilliant Miss Barrace, who was entering as Bilham withdrew. She had apparently put him a question, to which he had replied by turning to indicate his late interlocutor; toward whom, after an inter-

173

rogation further aided by a resort to that optical machinery which seemed, like her other ornaments, curious and archaic, the genial lady, suggesting more than ever for her fellow guest the old French print, the historic portrait, directed herself with an intention that Strether instantly met. He knew in advance the first note she would sound, and took in as she approached all her need of sounding it. Nothing yet had been so "wonderful" between them as the present occasion; and it was her special sense of this quality in occasions that she was there, as she was in most places, to feed. That sense had already been so well fed by the situation about them that she had quitted the other room, forsaken the music, dropped out of the play, abandoned, in a word, the stage itself, that she might stand a minute behind the scenes with Strether and so perhaps figure as one of the famous augurs replying, behind the oracle, to the wink of the other. Seated near him presently where little Bilham had sat, she replied in truth to many things; beginning as soon as he had said to her — what he hoped he said without fatuity — "All you ladies are extraordinarily kind to me."

She played her long handle, which shifted her observation; she saw in an instant all the absences that left them free. "How can we be anything else? But isn't that exactly your plight? 'We ladies' — oh we're nice, and you must be having enough of us! As one of us, you know, I don't pretend I'm crazy about us. But Miss Gostrey at least to-night has left you alone, hasn't she?" With which she again looked about as if Maria might still lurk.

"Oh yes," said Strether; "she's only sitting up for me at home." And then as this elicited from his companion her gay "Oh, oh, oh!" he explained that he meant sitting up in suspense and prayer. "We thought it on the whole better she should n't be present; and either way of course it's a terrible worry for her." He abounded in the sense of his appeal to the ladies, and they might take their choice of his doing so from humility or from pride. "Yet she inclines to believe I shall come out."

"Oh I incline to believe too you'll come out!" — Miss Barrace, with her laugh, was not to be behind. "Only the question's about *where*, is n't it? However," she happily continued, "if it's anywhere at all it must be very far on, must n't it? To do us justice, I think, you know," she laughed, "we do, among us all, want you rather far on. Yes, yes," she repeated in her quick droll way; "we want you very, *very* far on!" After which she wished to know why he had thought it better Maria should n't be present.

"Oh," he replied, "it was really her own idea. I should have wished it. But she dreads responsibility."

"And is n't that a new thing for her?"

"To dread it? No doubt — no doubt. But her nerve has given way."

Miss Barrace looked at him a moment. "She has too much at stake." Then less gravely: "Mine, luckily for me, holds out."

"Luckily for me too" — Strether came back to that. "My own is n't so firm, *my* appetite for responsibility is n't so sharp, as that I have n't felt the very principle of this occasion to be 'the more the merrier.' If we *are* so merry it's because Chad has understood so well."

"He has understood amazingly," said Miss Barrace.

"It's wonderful!" — Strether anticipated for her.

"It's wonderful!" she, to meet it, intensified; so that, face to face over it, they largely and recklessly laughed. But she presently added: "Oh I see the principle. If one did n't one would be lost. But when once one has got hold of it —"

"It's as simple as twice two! From the moment he had to do something —"

"A crowd" — she took him straight up — "was the only thing? Rather, rather: a rumpus of sound," she laughed, "or nothing. Mrs. Pocock's built in, or built out — whichever you call it; she's packed so tight she can't move. She's in splendid isolation" — Miss Barrace embroidered the theme.

Strether followed, but scrupulous of justice. "Yet with every one in the place successively introduced to her."

"Wonderfully — but just so that it does build her out. She's bricked up, she's buried alive!"

Strether seemed for a moment to look at it; but it brought him to a sigh. "Oh but she's not dead! It will take more than this to kill her."

His companion had a pause that might have been for pity. "No, I can't pretend I think she's finished — or that it's for more than to-night." She remained pensive as if with the same compunction. "It's only up to her chin." Then again for the fun of it: "She can breathe."

176

"She can breathe!" — he echoed it in the same spirit. "And do you know," he went on, "what's really all this time happening to me? — through the beauty of music, the gaiety of voices, the uproar in short of our revel and the felicity of your wit? The sound of Mrs. Pocock's respiration drowns for me, I assure you, every other. It's literally all I hear."

She focussed him with her clink of chains. "Well —!" she breathed ever so kindly.

"Well, what?"

"She *is* free from her chin up," she mused; "and that *will* be enough for her."

"It will be enough for me!" Strether ruefully laughed. "Waymarsh has really," he then asked, "brought her to see you?"

"Yes — but that's the worst of it. I could do you no good. And yet I tried hard."

Strether wondered. "And how did you try?"

"Why I did n't speak of you."

"I see. That was better."

"Then what would have been worse? For speaking or silent," she lightly wailed, "I somehow 'compromise.' And it has never been any one but you."

"That shows" — he was magnanimous — "that it's something not in you, but in one's self. It's *my* fault."

She was silent a little. "No, it's Mr. Waymarsh's. It's the fault of his having brought her."

"Ah then," said Strether good-naturedly, "why *did* he bring her?"

"He could n't afford not to."

"Oh you were a trophy — one of the spoils of conquest? But why in that case, since you do 'compromise' — "

"Don't I compromise *him* as well? I do compromise him as well," Miss Barrace smiled. "I compromise him as hard as I can. But for Mr. Waymarsh it is n't fatal. It's — so far as his wonderful relation with Mrs. Pocock is concerned — favourable." And then, as he still seemed slightly at sea: "The man who had succeeded with *me*, don't you see? For her to get him from me was such an added incentive."

Strether saw, but as if his path was still strewn with surprises. "It's 'from' you then that she has got him?"

She was amused at his momentary muddle. "You can fancy my fight! She believes in her triumph. I think it has been part of her joy."

"Oh her joy!" Strether sceptically murmured.

"Well, she thinks she has had her own way. And what's to-night for her but a kind of apotheosis? Her frock's really good."

"Good enough to go to heaven in? For after a real apotheosis," Strether went on, "there's nothing *but* heaven. For Sarah there's only to-morrow."

"And you mean that she won't find to-morrow heavenly?"

"Well, I mean that I somehow feel to-night — on her behalf — too good to be true. She has had her cake; that is she's in the act now of having it, of swallowing the largest and sweetest piece. There won't be another left for her. Certainly *I* have n't one. It can only, at the best, be Chad." He continued to make it out as for their common entertainment. "He

178

may have one, as it were, up his sleeve; yet it's borne in upon me that if he had —"

"He would n't"— she quite understood —"have taken all *this* trouble? I dare say not, and, if I may be quite free and dreadful, I very much hope he won't take any more. Of course I won't pretend now," she added, "not to know what it's a question of."

"Oh every one must know now," poor Strether thoughtfully admitted; "and it's strange enough and funny enough that one should feel everybody here at this very moment to be knowing and watching and waiting."

"Yes — is n't it indeed funny?" Miss Barrace quite rose to it. "That's the way we *are* in Paris." She was always pleased with a new contribution to that queerness. "It's wonderful! But, you know," she declared, "it all depends on you. I don't want to turn the knife in your vitals, but that's naturally what you just now meant by our all being on top of you. We know you as the hero of the drama, and we're gathered to see what you'll do."

Strether looked at her a moment with a light perhaps slightly obscured. "I think that must be why the hero has taken refuge in this corner. He's scared at his heroism — he shrinks from his part."

"Ah but we nevertheless believe he'll play it. That's why," Miss Barrace kindly went on, "we take such an interest in you. We feel you'll come up to the scratch." And then as he seemed perhaps not quite to take fire: "Don't let him do it."

"Don't let Chad go?"

"Yes, keep hold of him. With all this"— and she

179

indicated the general tribute — "he has done enough. We love him here — he's charming."

"It's beautiful," said Strether, "the way you all can simplify when you will."

But she gave it to him back. "It's nothing to the way *you* will when you must."

He winced at it as at the very voice of prophecy, and it kept him a moment quiet. He detained her, however, on her appearing about to leave him alone in the rather cold clearance their talk had made. "There positively is n't a sign of a hero to-night; the hero's dodging and shirking, the hero's ashamed. Therefore, you know, I think, what you must all *really* be occupied with is the heroine."

Miss Barrace took a minute. "The heroine?"

"The heroine. I've treated her," said Strether, "not a bit like a hero. Oh," he sighed, "I don't do it well!"

She eased him off. "You do it as you can." And then after another hesitation: "I think she's satisfied."

But he remained compunctious. "I have n't been near her. I have n't looked at her."

"Ah then you've lost a good deal!"

He showed he knew it. "She's more wonderful than ever?"

"Than ever. With Mr. Pocock."

Strether wondered. "Madame de Vionnet — with Jim?"

"Madame de Vionnet — with 'Jim.'" Miss Barrace was historic.

"And what's she doing with him?"

"Ah you must ask *him!*"

Strether's face lighted again at the prospect. "It *will* be amusing to do so." Yet he continued to wonder. "But she must have some idea."

"Of course she has — she has twenty ideas. She has in the first place," said Miss Barrace, swinging a little her tortoise-shell, "that of doing her part. Her part is to help *you.*"

It came out as nothing had come yet; links were missing and connexions unnamed, but it was suddenly as if they were at the heart of their subject. "Yes; how much more she does it," Strether gravely reflected, "than I help *her!*" It all came over him as with the near presence of the beauty, the grace, the intense, dissimulated spirit with which he had, as he said, been putting off contact. "*She* has courage."

"Ah she has courage!" Miss Barrace quite agreed; and it was as if for a moment they saw the quantity in each other's face.

But indeed the whole thing was present. "How much she must care!"

"Ah there it is. She does care. But it isn't, is it," Miss Barrace considerately added, "as if you had ever had any doubt of that?"

Strether seemed suddenly to like to feel that he really never had. "Why of course it's the whole point."

"Voilà!" Miss Barrace smiled.

"It's why one came out," Strether went on. "And it's why one has stayed so long. And it's also" — he abounded — "why one's going home. It's why, it's why —"

"It's why everything!" she concurred. "It's why she might be to-night — for all she looks and shows, and for all your friend 'Jim' does — about twenty years old. That's another of her ideas; to be for him, and to be quite easily and charmingly, as young as a little girl."

Strether assisted at his distance. "'For him'? For Chad — ?"

"For Chad, in a manner, naturally, always. But in particular to-night for Mr. Pocock." And then as her friend still stared: "Yes, it *is* of a bravery! But that's what she has: her high sense of duty." It was more than sufficiently before them. "When Mr. Newsome has his hands so embarrassed with his sister—"

"It's quite the least" — Strether filled it out — "that she should take his sister's husband? Certainly — quite the least. So she has taken him."

"She has taken him." It was all Miss Barrace had meant.

Still it remained enough. "It must be funny."

"Oh it *is* funny." That of course essentially went with it.

But it brought them back. "How indeed then she must care!" In answer to which Strether's entertainer dropped a comprehensive "Ah!" expressive perhaps of some impatience for the time he took to get used to it. She herself had got used to it long before.

II

WHEN one morning within the week he perceived the whole thing to be really at last upon him Strether's immediate feeling was all relief. He had known this morning that something was about to happen — known it, in a moment, by Waymarsh's manner when Waymarsh appeared before him during his brief consumption of coffee and a roll in the small slippery *salle-à-manger* so associated with rich rumination. Strether had taken there of late various lonely and absent-minded meals; he communed there, even at the end of June, with a suspected chill, the air of old shivers mixed with old savours, the air in which so many of his impressions had perversely matured; the place meanwhile renewing its message to him by the very circumstance of his single state. He now sat there, for the most part, to sigh softly, while he vaguely tilted his carafe, over the vision of how much better Waymarsh was occupied. That was really his success by the common measure — to have led this companion so on and on. He remembered how at first there had been scarce a squatting-place he could beguile him into passing; the actual outcome of which at last was that there was scarce one that could arrest him in his rush. His rush — as Strether vividly and amusedly figured it — continued to be all with Sarah, and contained perhaps moreover the word of the whole enigma, whipping up in its fine full-flavoured froth the very principle, for good or for ill, of his own, of Strether's destiny. It might after all, to the end, only be that they had united to save him, and indeed, so far as Waymarsh was concerned, that *had* to be the spring of action. Strether was glad at all events, in connexion with the case, that the saving he required was not more scant; so constituted a luxury was it in certain lights just to lurk there out of the full glare. He had moments of quite seriously wondering whether Waymarsh would n't in fact, thanks to old friendship and a conceivable indulgence, make about as good terms for him as he might make for himself. They would n't be the same terms of course; but they might have the advantage that he himself probably should be able to make none at all.

He was never in the morning very late, but Waymarsh had already been out, and, after a peep into the dim refectory, he presented himself with much less than usual of his large looseness. He had made sure, through the expanse of glass exposed to the court, that they would be alone; and there was now in fact that about him that pretty well took up the room. He was dressed in the garments of summer; and save that his white waistcoat was redundant and bulging these things favoured, they determined, his expression. He wore a straw hat such as his friend had n't yet seen in Paris, and he showed a buttonhole freshly adorned with a magnificent rose. Strether read on the instant his story — how, astir for the previous hour, the sprinkled newness of the day, so pleasant at that season in Paris, he was fairly panting with the pulse of adventure and had been with Mrs.

Pocock, unmistakeably, to the Marché aux Fleurs. Strether really knew in this vision of him a joy that was akin to envy; so reversed as he stood there did their old positions seem; so comparatively doleful now showed, by the sharp turn of the wheel, the posture of the pilgrim from Woollett. He wondered, this pilgrim, if he had originally looked to Waymarsh so brave and well, so remarkably launched, as it was at present the latter's privilege to appear. He recalled that his friend had remarked to him even at Chester that his aspect belied his plea of prostration; but there certainly could n't have been, for an issue, an aspect less concerned than Waymarsh's with the menace of decay. Strether had at any rate never resembled a Southern planter of the great days — which was the image picturesquely suggested by the happy relation between the fuliginous face and the wide panama of his visitor. This type, it further amused him to guess, had been, on Waymarsh's part, the object of Sarah's care; he was convinced that her taste had not been a stranger to the conception and purchase of the hat, any more than her fine fingers had been guiltless of the bestowal of the rose. It came to him in the current of thought, as things so oddly did come, that *he* had never risen with the lark to attend a brilliant woman to the Marché aux Fleurs; this could be fastened on him in connexion neither with Miss Gostrey nor with Madame de Vionnet; the practice of getting up early for adventures could indeed in no manner be fastened on him. It came to him in fact that just here was his usual case: he was for ever missing things through his general genius for missing them, while others were for ever picking them up through a contrary bent. And it was others who looked abstemious and he who looked greedy; it was he somehow who finally paid, and it was others who mainly partook. Yes, he should go to the scaffold yet for he would n't know quite whom. He almost, for that matter, felt on the scaffold now and really quite enjoying it. It worked out as *because* he was anxious there — it worked out as for this reason that Waymarsh was so blooming. It was *his* trip for health, for a change, that proved the success — which was just what Strether, planning and exerting himself, had desired it should be. That truth already sat full-blown on his companion's lips; benevolence breathed from them as with the warmth of active exercise, and also a little as with the bustle of haste.

"Mrs. Pocock, whom I left a quarter of an hour ago at her hotel, has asked me to mention to you that she would like to find you at home here in about another hour. She wants to see you; she has something to say — or considers, I believe, that you may have: so that I asked her myself why she should n't come right round. She has n't *been* round yet — to see our place; and I took upon myself to say that I was sure you 'd be glad to have her. The thing 's therefore, you see, to keep right here till she comes."

The announcement was sociably, even though, after Waymarsh's wont, somewhat solemnly made; but Strether quickly felt other things in it than these light features. It was the first approach, from that quarter, to admitted consciousness; it quickened his pulse; it simply meant at last that he should have but

186

himself to thank if he did n't know where he was. He had finished his breakfast; he pushed it away and was on his feet. There were plenty of elements of surprise, but only one of doubt. "The thing's for *you* to keep here too?" Waymarsh had been slightly ambiguous.

He was n't ambiguous, however, after this enquiry; and Strether's understanding had probably never before opened so wide and effective a mouth as it was to open during the next five minutes. It was no part of his friend's wish, as appeared, to help to receive Mrs. Pocock; he quite understood the spirit in which she was to present herself, but his connexion with her visit was limited to his having — well, as he might say — perhaps a little promoted it. He had thought, and had let her know it, that Strether possibly would think she might have been round before. At any rate, as turned out, she had been wanting herself, quite a while, to come. "I told her," said Waymarsh, "that it would have been a bright idea if she had only carried it out before."

Strether pronounced it so bright as to be almost dazzling. "But why *has n't* she carried it out before? She has seen me every day — she had only to name her hour. I 've been waiting and waiting."

"Well, I told her you had. And she has been waiting too." It was, in the oddest way in the world, on the showing of this tone, a genial new pressing coaxing Waymarsh; a Waymarsh conscious with a different consciousness from any he had yet betrayed, and actually rendered by it almost insinuating. He lacked only time for full persuasion, and Strether was to see in a moment why. Meantime, however, our friend perceived, he was announcing a step of some magnanimity on Mrs. Pocock's part, so that he could deprecate a sharp question. It was his own high purpose in fact to have smoothed sharp questions to rest. He looked his old comrade very straight in the eyes, and he had never conveyed to him in so mute a manner so much kind confidence and so much good advice. Everything that was between them was again in his face, but matured and shelved and finally disposed of. "At any rate," he added, "she's coming now."

Considering how many pieces had to fit themselves, it all fell, in Strether's brain, into a close rapid order. He saw on the spot what had happened, and what probably would yet; and it was all funny enough. It was perhaps just this freedom of appreciation that wound him up to his flare of high spirits. "What is she coming *for?*— to kill me?"

"She's coming to be very *very* kind to you, and you must let me say that I greatly hope you'll not be less so to herself."

This was spoken by Waymarsh with much gravity of admonition, and as Strether stood there he knew he had but to make a movement to take the attitude of a man gracefully receiving a present. The present was that of the opportunity dear old Waymarsh had flattered himself he had divined in him the slight soreness of not having yet thoroughly enjoyed; so he had brought it to him thus, as on a little silver break-fast-tray, familiarly though delicately— without oppressive pomp; and he was to bend and smile and acknowledge, was to take and use and be grateful. He was not—that was the beauty of it—to be asked to deflect too much from his dignity. No wonder the old boy bloomed in this bland air of his own distillation. Strether felt for a moment as if Sarah were actually walking up and down outside. Was n't she hanging about the porte-cochère while her friend thus summarily opened a way? Strether would meet her but to take it, and everything would be for the best in the best of possible worlds. He had never so much known what any one meant as, in the light of this demonstration, he knew what Mrs. Newsome did. It had reached Waymarsh from Sarah, but it had reached Sarah from her mother, and there was no break in the chain by which it reached *him*. "Has anything particular happened," he asked after a minute—"so suddenly to determine her? Has she heard anything unexpected from home?"

Waymarsh, on this, it seemed to him, looked at him harder than ever. "'Unexpected'?" He had a brief hesitation; then, however, he was firm. "We're leaving Paris."

"Leaving? That *is* sudden."

Waymarsh showed a different opinion. "Less so than it may seem. The purpose of Mrs. Pocock's visit is to explain to you in fact that it's *not*."

Strether did n't at all know if he had really an advantage— anything that would practically count as one; but he enjoyed for the moment— as for the first time in his life— the sense of so carrying it off. He wondered— it was amusing— if he felt as the impudent feel. "I shall take great pleasure, I assure you,

189

in any explanation. I shall be delighted to receive Sarah."

The sombre glow just darkened in his comrade's eyes; but he was struck with the way it died out again. It was too mixed with another consciousness— it was too smothered, as might be said, in flowers. He really for the time regretted it— poor dear old sombre glow! Something straight and simple, something heavy and empty, had been eclipsed in its company; something by which he had best known his friend. Waymarsh would n't *be* his friend, somehow, without the occasional ornament of the sacred rage, and the right to the sacred rage— inestimably precious for Strether's charity— he also seemed in a manner, and at Mrs. Pocock's elbow, to have forfeited. Strether remembered the occasion early in their stay when on that very spot he had come out with his earnest, his ominous "Quit it!"— and, so remembering, felt it hang by a hair that he did n't himself now utter the same note. Waymarsh was having a good time— this was the truth that was embarrassing for him, and he was having it then and there, he was having it in Europe, he was having it under the very protection of circumstances of which he did n't in the least approve; all of which placed him in a false position, with no issue possible— none at least by the grand manner. It was practically in the manner of any one— it was all but in poor Strether's own— that instead of taking anything up he merely made the most of having to be himself explanatory. "I'm not leaving for the United States direct. Mr. and Mrs. Pocock and Miss Mamie are thinking of a little trip before their own return, and we've been talking for some days past of our joining forces. We've settled it that we do join and that we sail together the end of next month. But we start to-morrow for Switzerland. Mrs. Pocock wants some scenery. She has n't had much yet."

He was brave in his way too, keeping nothing back, confessing all there was, and only leaving Strether to make certain connexions. "Is what Mrs. Newsome had cabled her daughter an injunction to break off short?"

The grand manner indeed at this just raised its head a little. "I know nothing about Mrs. Newsome's cables."

Their eyes met on it with some intensity — during the few seconds of which something happened quite out of proportion to the time. It happened that Strether, looking thus at his friend, did n't take his answer for truth — and that something more again occurred in consequence of *that*. Yes — Waymarsh just *did* know about Mrs. Newsome's cables: to what other end than that had they dined together at Bignon's? Strether almost felt for the instant that it was to Mrs. Newsome herself the dinner had been given; and, for that matter, quite felt how she must have known about it and, as he might think, protected and consecrated it. He had a quick blurred view of daily cables, questions, answers, signals: clear enough was his vision of the expense that, when so wound up, the lady at home was prepared to incur. Vivid not less was his memory of what, during his long observation of her, some of her attainments of that high pitch had cost her. Distinctly she was at the highest now, and Waymarsh, who imagined himself an independent performer, was really, forcing his fine old natural voice, an overstrained accompanist. The whole reference of his errand seemed to mark her for Strether as by this time consentingly familiar to him, and nothing yet had so despoiled her of a special shade of consideration. "You don't know," he asked, "whether Sarah has been directed from home to try me on the matter of my also going to Switzerland?"

"I know," said Waymarsh as manfully as possible, "nothing whatever about her private affairs; though I believe her to be acting in conformity with things that have my highest respect." It was as manful as possible, but it was still the false note — as it had to be to convey so sorry a statement. He knew everything, Strether more and more felt, that he thus disclaimed, and his little punishment was just in this doom to a second fib. What falser position — given the man — could the most vindictive mind impose? He ended by squeezing through a passage in which three months before he would certainly have stuck fast. "Mrs. Pocock will probably be ready herself to answer any enquiry you may put to her. But," he continued, "*but* —!" He faltered on it.

"But what? Don't put her too many?"

Waymarsh looked large, but the harm was done; he couldn't, do what he would, help looking rosy. "Don't do anything you'll be sorry for."

It was an attenuation, Strether guessed, of something else that had been on his lips; it was a sudden drop to directness, and was thereby the voice of sincerity. He had fallen to the supplicating note, and that immediately, for our friend, made a difference and reinstated him. They were in communication as they had been, that first morning, in Sarah's salon and in her presence and Madame de Vionnet's; and the same recognition of a great good will was again, after all, possible. Only the amount of response Waymarsh had then taken for granted was doubled, decupled now. This came out when he presently said: "Of course I need n't assure you *I* hope you 'll come with us." Then it was that his implications and expectations loomed up for Strether as almost pathetically gross.

The latter patted his shoulder while he thanked him, giving the go-by to the question of joining the Pococks; he expressed the joy he felt at seeing him go forth again so brave and free, and he in fact almost took leave of him on the spot. "I shall see you again of course before you go; but I 'm meanwhile much obliged to you for arranging so conveniently for what you 've told me. I shall walk up and down in the court there — dear little old court which we 've each bepaced so, this last couple of months, to the tune of our flights and our drops, our hesitations and our plunges: I shall hang about there, all impatience and excitement, please let Sarah know, till she graciously presents herself. Leave me with her without fear," he laughed; "I assure you I shan't hurt her. I don't think either she 'll hurt *me:* I 'm in a situation in which damage was some time ago discounted. Besides, *that* is n't what worries you — but don't, don't explain! We 're all right as we are: which was

the degree of success our adventure was pledged to
for each of us. We were n't, it seemed, all right as
we were before; and we 've got over the ground, all
things considered, quickly. I hope you 'll have a
lovely time in the Alps."

Waymarsh fairly looked up at him as from the foot
of them. "I don't know as I *ought* really to go."

It was the conscience of Milrose in the very voice
of Milrose, but, oh it was feeble and flat! Strether
suddenly felt quite ashamed for him; he breathed
a greater boldness. "*Let* yourself, on the contrary,
go — in all agreeable directions. These are precious
hours — at our age they may n't recur. Don't have
it to say to yourself at Milrose, next winter, that you
had n't courage for them." And then as his comrade queerly stared: "Live up to Mrs. Pocock."

"Live up to her?"

"You 're a great help to her."

Waymarsh looked at it as at one of the uncom-
fortable things that were certainly true and that it was
yet ironical to say. "It 's more then than you are."

"That 's exactly your own chance and advantage.
Besides," said Strether, "I do in my way contribute.
I know what I 'm about."

Waymarsh had kept on his great panama, and,
as he now stood nearer the door, his last look beneath the shade of it had turned again to darkness
and warning. "So do I! See here, Strether."

"I know what you 're going to say. 'Quit this'?"

"Quit this!" But it lacked its old intensity; nothing of it remained; it went out of the room with
him.

III

ALMOST the first thing, strangely enough, that, about an hour later, Strether found himself doing in Sarah's presence was to remark articulately on this failure, in their friend, of what had been superficially his great distinction. It was as if — he alluded of course to the grand manner — the dear man had sacrificed it to some other advantage; which would be of course only for himself to measure. It might be simply that he was physically so much more sound than on his first coming out; this was all prosaic, comparatively cheerful and vulgar. And fortunately, if one came to that, his improvement in health was really itself grander than any manner it could be conceived as having cost him. "You yourself alone, dear Sarah" — Strether took the plunge — "have done him, it strikes me, in these three weeks, as much good as all the rest of his time together."

It was a plunge because somehow the range of reference was, in the conditions, "funny," and made funnier still by Sarah's attitude, by the turn the occasion had, with her appearance, so sensibly taken. Her appearance was really indeed funnier than anything else — the spirit in which he felt her to be there as soon as she *was* there, the shade of obscurity that cleared up for him as soon as he was seated with her in the small *salon de lecture* that had, for the most part, in all the weeks, witnessed the wane of his early vivacity of discussion with Waymarsh. It was an immense thing, quite a tremendous thing, for her to have come: this truth opened out to him in spite of his having already arrived for himself at a fairly vivid view of it. He had done exactly what he had given Waymarsh his word for — had walked and re-walked the court while he awaited her advent; acquiring in this exercise an amount of light that affected him at the time as flooding the scene. She had decided upon the step in order to give him the benefit of a doubt, in order to be able to say to her mother that she had, even to abjectness, smoothed the way for him. The doubt had been as to whether he might n't take her as not having smoothed it — and the admonition had possibly come from Waymarsh's more detached spirit. Waymarsh had at any rate, certainly, thrown his weight into the scale — he had pointed to the importance of depriving their friend of a grievance. She had done justice to the plea, and it was to set herself right with a high ideal that she actually sat there in her state. Her calculation was sharp in the immobility with which she held her tall parasol-stick upright and at arm's length, quite as if she had struck the place to plant her flag; in the separate precautions she took not to show as nervous; in the aggressive repose in which she did quite nothing but wait for him. Doubt ceased to be possible from the moment he had taken in that she had arrived with no proposal whatever; that her concern was simply to show what she had come to receive. She had come to receive his submission, and Waymarsh was to have made it plain to him that she would expect nothing less. He saw fifty things, her host, at this convenient stage; but one of those he most saw was that their anxious friend had n't quite had the hand required of him. Waymarsh *had*, however, uttered the request that she might find him mild, and while hanging about the court before her arrival he had turned over with zeal the different ways in which he could be so. The difficulty was that if he was mild he was n't, for her purpose, conscious. If she wished him conscious — as everything about her cried aloud that she did — she must accordingly be at costs to make him so. Conscious he *was*, for himself — but only of too many things; so she must choose the one she required.

Practically, however, it at last got itself named, and when once that had happened they were quite at the centre of their situation. One thing had really done as well as another; when Strether had spoken of Waymarsh's leaving him, and that had necessarily brought on a reference to Mrs. Pocock's similar intention, the jump was but short to supreme lucidity. Light became indeed after that so intense that Strether would doubtless have but half made out, in the prodigious glare, by which of the two the issue had been in fact precipitated. It was, in their contracted quarters, as much there between them as if it had been something suddenly spilled with a crash and a splash on the floor. The form of his submission was to be an engagement to acquit himself within the twenty-four hours. "He'll go in a moment if you give him the word — he assures me on his honour he'll do that":

this came in its order, out of its order, in respect to Chad, after the crash had occurred. It came repeatedly during the time taken by Strether to feel that he was even more fixed in his rigour than he had supposed — the time he was not above adding to a little by telling her that such a way of putting it on her brother's part left him sufficiently surprised. She was n't at all funny at last — she was really fine; and he felt easily where she was strong — strong for herself. It had n't yet so come home to him that she was nobly and appointedly officious. She was acting in interests grander and clearer than that of her poor little personal, poor little Parisian equilibrium, and all his consciousness of her mother's moral pressure profited by this proof of its sustaining force. She would be held up; she would be strengthened; he need n't in the least be anxious for her. What would once more have been distinct to him had he tried to make it so was that, as Mrs. Newsome was essentially all moral pressure, the presence of this element was almost identical with her own presence. It was n't perhaps that he felt he was dealing with her straight, but it was certainly as if she had been dealing straight with *him*. She was reaching him somehow by the lengthened arm of the spirit, and he was having to that extent to take her into account; but he was n't reaching her in turn, not making her take *him;* he was only reaching Sarah, who appeared to take so little of him. "Something has clearly passed between you and Chad," he presently said, "that I think I ought to know something more about. Does he put it all," he smiled, "on me?"

"Did you come out," she asked, "to put it all on *him?*"

But he replied to this no further than, after an instant, by saying: "Oh it's all right. Chad I mean's all right in having said to you — well anything he may have said. I'll *take* it all — what he does put on me. Only I must see him before I see you again."

She hesitated, but she brought it out. "Is it absolutely necessary you should see me again?"

"Certainly, if I'm to give you any definite word about anything."

"Is it your idea then," she returned, "that I shall keep on meeting you only to be exposed to fresh humiliation?"

He fixed her a longer time. "Are your instructions from Mrs. Newsome that you shall, even at the worst, absolutely and irretrievably break with me?"

"My instructions from Mrs. Newsome are, if you please, my affair. You know perfectly what your own were, and you can judge for yourself of what it can do for you to have made what you have of them. You can perfectly see, at any rate, I'll go so far as to say, that if I wish not to expose myself I must wish still less to expose *her.*" She had already said more than she had quite expected; but, though she had also pulled up, the colour in her face showed him he should from one moment to the other have it all. He now indeed felt the high importance of his having it. "What is your conduct," she broke out as if to explain — "what is your conduct but an outrage to women like *us?* I mean your acting as if there can be a doubt — as between us and such another — of his duty?"

199

He thought a moment. It was rather much to deal with at once; not only the question itself, but the sore abysses it revealed. "Of course they're totally different kinds of duty."

"And do you pretend that he has any at all — to such another?"

"Do you mean to Madame de Vionnet?" He uttered the name not to affront her, but yet again to gain time — time that he needed for taking in something still other and larger than her demand of a moment before. It wasn't at once that he could see all that was in her actual challenge; but when he did he found himself just checking a low vague sound, a sound which was perhaps the nearest approach his vocal chords had ever known to a growl. Everything Mrs. Pocock had failed to give a sign of recognising in Chad as a particular part of a transformation — everything that had lent intention to this particular failure — affected him as gathered into a large loose bundle and thrown, in her words, into his face. The missile made him to that extent catch his breath; which however he presently recovered. "Why when a woman's at once so charming and so beneficent—"

"You can sacrifice mothers and sisters to her without a blush, and can make them cross the ocean on purpose to feel the more, and take from you the straighter, *how* you do it?"

Yes, she had taken him up as short and as sharply as that; but he tried not to flounder in her grasp. "I don't think there's anything I've done in any such calculated way as you describe. Everything has come

as a sort of indistinguishable part of everything else.
Your coming out belonged closely to my having come
before you, and my having come was a result of our
general state of mind. Our general state of mind had
proceeded, on its side, from our queer ignorance, our
queer misconceptions and confusions — from which,
since then, an inexorable tide of light seems to have
floated us into our perhaps still queerer knowledge.
Don't you *like* your brother as he is," he went on,
"and have n't you given your mother an intelligible
account of all that that comes to ?"

It put to her also, doubtless, his own tone, too many
things; this at least would have been the case had n't
his final challenge directly helped her. Everything, at
the stage they had reached, directly helped her, because everything betrayed in him such a basis of intention. He saw — the odd way things came out ! —
that he would have been held less monstrous had he
only been a little wilder. What exposed him was just
his poor old trick of quiet inwardness, what exposed
him was his *thinking* such offence. He had n't in the
least however the desire to irritate that Sarah imputed
to him, and he could only at last temporise, for the
moment, with her indignant view. She was altogether
more inflamed than he had expected, and he would
probably understand this better when he should learn
what had occurred for her with Chad. Till then her
view of his particular blackness, her clear surprise at
his not clutching the pole she held out, must pass as
extravagant. "I leave you to flatter yourself," she
returned, "that what you speak of is what *you 've*
beautifully done. When a thing has been already

described in such a lovely way — !" But she caught herself up, and her comment on his description rang out sufficiently loud. "Do you consider her even an apology for a decent woman?"

Ah there it was at last! She put the matter more crudely than, for his own mixed purposes, he had yet had to do; but essentially it was all one matter. It was so much — so much; and she treated it, poor lady, as so little. He grew conscious, as he was now apt to do, of a strange smile, and the next moment he found himself talking like Miss Barrace. "She has struck me from the first as wonderful. I've been thinking too moreover that, after all, she would probably have represented even for yourself something rather new and rather good."

He was to have given Mrs. Pocock with this, however, but her best opportunity for a sound of derision. "Rather new? I hope so with all my heart!"

"I mean," he explained, "that she might have affected you by her exquisite amiability — a real revelation, it has seemed to myself; her high rarity, her distinction of every sort."

He had been, with these words, consciously a little "precious"; but he had had to be — he could n't give her the truth of the case without them; and it seemed to him moreover now that he did n't care. He had at all events not served his cause, for she sprang at its exposed side. "A 'revelation' — to me: I've come to such a woman for a revelation? You talk to me about 'distinction' — you, you who've had your privilege? — when the most distinguished woman we shall either of us have seen in this world sits there insulted, in her loneliness, by your incredible comparison!"

Strether forbore, with an effort, from straying; but he looked all about him. "Does your mother herself make the point that she sits insulted?"

Sarah's answer came so straight, so "pat," as might have been said, that he felt on the instant its origin. "She has confided to my judgement and my tenderness the expression of her personal sense of everything, and the assertion of her personal dignity."

They were the very words of the lady of Woollett — he would have known them in a thousand; her parting charge to her child. Mrs. Pocock accordingly spoke to this extent by book, and the fact immensely moved him. "If she does really feel as you say it's of course very very dreadful. I've given sufficient proof, one would have thought," he added, "of my deep admiration for Mrs. Newsome."

"And pray what proof would one have thought you'd *call* sufficient? That of thinking this person here so far superior to her?"

He wondered again; he waited. "Ah dear Sarah, you must *leave* me this person here!"

In his desire to avoid all vulgar retorts, to show how, even perversely, he clung to his rag of reason, he had softly almost wailed this plea. Yet he knew it to be perhaps the most positive declaration he had ever made in his life, and his visitor's reception of it virtually gave it that importance. "That's exactly what I'm delighted to do. God knows *we* don't want her! You take good care not to meet," she observed in a still higher key, "my question about their life.

If you do consider it a thing one can even *speak* of, I congratulate you on your taste!"

The life she alluded to was of course Chad's and Madame de Vionnet's, which she thus bracketed together in a way that made him wince a little; there being nothing for him but to take home her full intention. It was none the less his inconsequence that while he had himself been enjoying for weeks the view of the brilliant woman's specific action, he just suffered from any characterisation of it by other lips. "I think tremendously well of her, at the same time that I seem to feel her 'life' to be really none of my business. It's my business, that is, only so far as Chad's own life is affected by it; and what has happened, don't you see? is that Chad's has been affected so beautifully. The proof of the pudding's in the eating" — he tried, with no great success, to help it out with a touch of pleasantry, while she let him go on as if to sink and sink. He went on however well enough, as well as he could do without fresh counsel; he indeed should n't stand quite firm, he felt, till he should have re-established his communications with Chad. Still, he could always speak for the woman he had so definitely promised to "save." This was n't quite for her the air of salvation; but as that chill fairly deepened what did it become but a reminder that one might at the worst perish *with* her? And it was simple enough — it was rudimentary: not, not to give her away. "I find in her more merits than you would probably have patience with my counting over. And do you know," he enquired, "the effect you produce on me by alluding to her in such terms? It's as if you had some motive in not recognising all she has done for your brother, and so shut your eyes to each side of the matter, in order, whichever side comes up, to get rid of the other. I don't, you must allow me to say, see how you can with any pretence to candour get rid of the side nearest you."

"Near me — *that* sort of thing?" And Sarah gave a jerk back of her head that well might have nullified any active proximity.

It kept her friend himself at his distance, and he respected for a moment the interval. Then with a last persuasive effort he bridged it. "You don't, on your honour, appreciate Chad's fortunate development?"

"Fortunate?" she echoed again. And indeed she was prepared. "I call it hideous."

Her departure had been for some minutes marked as imminent, and she was already at the door that stood open to the court, from the threshold of which she delivered herself of this judgement. It rang out so loud as to produce for the time the hush of everything else. Strether quite, as an effect of it, breathed less bravely; he could acknowledge it, but simply enough. "Oh if you think *that* — !"

"Then all's at an end? So much the better. I do think that!" She passed out as she spoke and took her way straight across the court, beyond which, separated from them by the deep arch of the porte-cochère, the low victoria that had conveyed her from her own hotel was drawn up. She made for it with decision, and the manner of her break, the sharp shaft of her rejoinder, had an intensity by which Strether was at first kept in arrest. She had let fly at him as from a stretched cord, and it took him a minute to recover from the sense of being pierced. It was not the penetration of surprise; it was that, much more, of certainty; his case being put for him as he had as yet only put it to himself. She was away at any rate; she had distanced him — with rather a grand spring, an effect of pride and ease, after all; she had got into her carriage before he could overtake her, and the vehicle was already in motion. He stopped halfway; he stood there in the court only seeing her go and noting that she gave him no other look. The way he had put it to himself was that all quite *might* be at an end. Each of her movements, in this resolute rupture, re-affirmed, re-enforced that idea. Sarah passed out of sight in the sunny street while, planted there in the centre of the comparatively grey court, he continued merely to look before him. It probably *was* all at an end.

BOOK ELEVENTH

I

HE went late that evening to the Boulevard Malesherbes, having his impression that it would be vain to
go early, and having also, more than once in the
course of the day, made enquiries of the concierge.
Chad had n't come in and had left no intimation; he
had affairs, apparently, at this juncture — as it occurred to Strether he so well might have — that kept
him long abroad. Our friend asked once for him at
the hotel in the Rue de Rivoli, but the only contribution offered there was the fact that every one was out.
It was with the idea that he would have to come home
to sleep that Strether went up to his rooms, from
which however he was still absent, though, from the
balcony, a few moments later, his visitor heard eleven
o'clock strike. Chad's servant had by this time answered for his reappearance; he *had*, the visitor
learned, come quickly in to dress for dinner and vanish
again. Strether spent an hour in waiting for him —
an hour full of strange suggestions, persuasions, re-
cognitions; one of those that he was to recall, at the
end of his adventure, as the particular handful that
most had counted. The mellowest lamplight and the
easiest chair had been placed at his disposal by Baptiste, subtlest of servants; the novel half-uncut, the
novel lemon-coloured and tender, with the ivory knife
athwart it like the dagger in a contadina's hair, had
been pushed within the soft circle — a circle which,
for some reason, affected Strether as softer still after

the same Baptiste had remarked that in the absence of a further need of anything by Monsieur he would betake himself to bed. The night was hot and heavy and the single lamp sufficient; the great flare of the lighted city, rising high, spending itself afar, played up from the Boulevard and, through the vague vista of the successive rooms, brought objects into view and added to their dignity. Strether found himself in possession as he never yet had been; he had been there alone, had turned over books and prints, had invoked, in Chad's absence, the spirit of the place, but never at the witching hour and never with a relish quite so like a pang.

He spent a long time on the balcony; he hung over it as he had seen little Bilham hang the day of his first approach, as he had seen Mamie hang over her own the day little Bilham himself might have seen her from below; he passed back into the rooms, the three that occupied the front and that communicated by wide doors; and, while he circulated and rested, tried to recover the impression that they had made on him three months before, to catch again the voice in which they had seemed then to speak to him. That voice, he had to note, failed audibly to sound; which he took as the proof of all the change in himself. He had heard, of old, only what he *could* then hear; what he could do now was to think of three months ago as a point in the far past. All voices had grown thicker and meant more things; they crowded on him as he moved about — it was the way they sounded together that would n't let him be still. He felt, strangely, as sad as if he had come for some wrong, and yet as excited as if he had

come for some freedom. But the freedom was what
was most in the place and the hour; it was the freedom
that most brought him round again to the youth of
his own that he had long ago missed. He could have
explained little enough to-day either why he had
missed it or why, after years and years, he should care
that he had; the main truth of the actual appeal of
everything was none the less that everything represented the substance of his loss, put it within reach,
within touch, made it, to a degree it had never been,
an affair of the senses. That was what it became for
him at this singular time, the youth he had long ago
missed — a queer concrete presence, full of mystery,
yet full of reality, which he could handle, taste, smell,
the deep breathing of which he could positively hear.
It was in the outside air as well as within; it was in
the long watch, from the balcony, in the summer
night, of the wide late life of Paris, the unceasing soft
quick rumble, below, of the little lighted carriages
that, in the press, always suggested the gamblers he
had seen of old at Monte Carlo pushing up to the
tables. This image was before him when he at last
became aware that Chad was behind.

"She tells me you put it all on *me*" — he had arrived after this promptly enough at that information;
which expressed the case however quite as the young
man appeared willing for the moment to leave it.
Other things, with this advantage of their virtually
having the night before them, came up for them, and
had, as well, the odd effect of making the occasion,
instead of hurried and feverish, one of the largest,
loosest and easiest to which Strether's whole adventure

was to have treated him. He had been pursuing Chad from an early hour and had overtaken him only now; but now the delay was repaired by their being so exceptionally confronted. They had foregathered enough of course in all the various times; they had again and again, since that first night at the theatre, been face to face over their question; but they had never been so alone together as they were actually alone — their talk had n't yet been so supremely for themselves. And if many things moreover passed before them, none passed more distinctly for Strether than that striking truth about Chad of which he had been so often moved to take note: the truth that everything came happily back with him to his knowing how to live. It had been seated in his pleased smile — a smile that pleased exactly in the right degree — as his visitor turned round, on the balcony, to greet his advent; his visitor in fact felt on the spot that there was nothing their meeting would so much do as bear witness to that facility. He surrendered himself accordingly to so approved a gift; for what was the meaning of the facility but that others *did* surrender themselves? He did n't want, luckily, to prevent Chad from living; but he was quite aware that even if he had he would himself have thoroughly gone to pieces. It was in truth essentially by bringing down his personal life to a function all subsidiary to the young man's own that he held together. And the great point, above all, the sign of how completely Chad possessed the knowledge in question, was that one thus became, not only with a proper cheerfulness, but with wild native impulses, the feeder of his stream. Their talk had accordingly not lasted three minutes without Strether's feeling basis enough for the excitement in which he had waited. This overflow fairly deepened, wastefully abounded, as he observed the smallness of anything corresponding to it on the part of his friend. That was exactly this friend's happy case; he "put out" his excitement, or whatever other emotion the matter involved, as he put out his washing; than which no arrangement could make more for domestic order. It was quite for Strether himself in short to feel a personal analogy with the laundress bringing home the triumphs of the mangle.

When he had reported on Sarah's visit, which he did very fully, Chad answered his question with perfect candour. "I positively referred her to you — told her she must absolutely see you. This was last night, and it all took place in teri minutes. It was our first free talk — really the first time she had tackled me. She knew I also knew what her line had been with yourself; knew moreover how little you had been doing to make anything difficult for her. So I spoke for you frankly — assured her you were all at her service. I assured her *I* was too," the young man continued; "and I pointed out how she could perfectly, at any time, have got at me. Her difficulty has been simply her not finding the moment she fancied."

"Her difficulty," Strether returned, "has been simply that she finds she's afraid of you. She's not afraid of *me*, Sarah, one little scrap; and it was just because she has seen how I can fidget when I give my mind to it that she has felt her best chance, rightly enough, to be in making me as uneasy as possible. I think she's at bottom as pleased to *have* you put it on me as you yourself can possibly be to put it."

"But what in the world, my dear man," Chad enquired in objection to this luminosity, "have I done to make Sally afraid?"

"You've been 'wonderful, wonderful,' as we say — we poor people who watch the play from the pit; and that's what has, admirably, made her. Made her all the more effectually that she could see you did n't set about it on purpose — I mean set about affecting her as with fear."

Chad cast a pleasant backward glance over his possibilities of motive. "I 've only wanted to be kind and friendly, to be decent and attentive — and I still only want to be."

Strether smiled at his comfortable clearness. "Well, there can certainly be no way for it better than by my taking the onus. It reduces your personal friction and your personal offence to almost nothing."

Ah but Chad, with his completer conception of the friendly, would n't quite have this! They had remained on the balcony, where, after their day of great and premature heat, the midnight air was delicious; and they leaned back in turn against the balustrade, all in harmony with the chairs and the flower-pots, the cigarettes and the starlight. "The onus is n't *really* yours — after our agreeing so to wait together and judge together. That was all my answer to Sally," Chad pursued — "that we have been, that we are, just judging together."

"I 'm not afraid of the burden," Strether explained; "I have n't come in the least that you should take it off me. I've come very much, it seems to me, to double up my fore legs in the manner of the camel when he gets down on his knees to make his back convenient. But I've supposed you all this while to have been doing a lot of special and private judging — about which I have n't troubled you; and I've only wished to have your conclusion first from you. I don't ask more than that; I'm quite ready to take it as it has come."

Chad turned up his face to the sky with a slow puff of his smoke. "Well, I've seen."

Strether waited a little. "I've left you wholly alone; have n't, I think I may say, since the first hour or two — when I merely preached patience — so much as breathed on you."

"Oh you've been awfully good!"

"We've both been good then — we've played the game. We've given them the most liberal conditions."

"Ah," said Chad, "splendid conditions! It was open to them, open to them " — he seemed to make it out, as he smoked, with his eyes still on the stars. He might in quiet sport have been reading their horoscope. Strether wondered meanwhile what had been open to them, and he finally let him have it. "It was open to them simply to let me alone; to have made up their minds, on really seeing me for themselves, that I could go on well enough as I was."

Strether assented to this proposition with full lucidity, his companion's plural pronoun, which stood all for Mrs. Newsome and her daughter, having no ambiguity for him. There was nothing, apparently, to stand for Mamie and Jim; and this added to our friend's sense of Chad's knowing what he thought. "But they've made up their minds to the opposite — that you *can't* go on as you are."

"No," Chad continued in the same way; "they won't have it for a minute."

Strether on his side also reflectively smoked. It was as if their high place really represented some moral elevation from which they could look down on their recent past. "There never was the smallest chance, do you know, that they *would* have it for a moment."

"Of course not — no real chance. But if they were willing to think there was —!"

"They were n't willing." Strether had worked it all out. "It was n't for you they came out, but for me. It was n't to see for themselves what you're doing, but what I'm doing. The first branch of their curiosity was inevitably destined, under my culpable delay, to give way to the second; and it's on the second that, if I may use the expression and you don't mind my marking the invidious fact, they've been of late exclusively perched. When Sarah sailed it was me, in other words, they were after."

Chad took it in both with intelligence and with indulgence. "It *is* rather a business then — what I've let you in for!"

Strether had again a brief pause; which ended in a reply that seemed to dispose once for all of this element of compunction. Chad was to treat it, at any rate, so far as they were again together, as having done so. "I was 'in' when you found me."

"Ah but it was you," the young man laughed, "who found *me*."

"I only found you out. It was you who found me in. It was all in the day's work for them, at all events, that they should come. And they've greatly enjoyed it," Strether declared.

"Well, I've tried to make them," said Chad.

His companion did himself presently the same justice. "So have I. I tried even this very morning — while Mrs. Pocock was with me. She enjoys for instance, almost as much as anything else, not being, as I've said, afraid of me; and I think I gave her help in that."

Chad took a deeper interest. "Was she very very nasty?"

Strether debated. "Well, she was the most important thing — she was definite. She was — at last — crystalline. And I felt no remorse. I saw that they must have come."

"Oh I wanted to see them for myself; so that if it were only for *that* —!" Chad's own remorse was as small.

This appeared almost all Strether wanted. "Is n't your having seen them for yourself then *the* thing, beyond all others, that has come of their visit?"

Chad looked as if he thought it nice of his old friend to put it so. "Don't you count it as anything that you're dished — if you *are* dished? Are you, my dear man, dished?"

It sounded as if he were asking if he had caught cold or hurt his foot, and Strether for a minute but smoked and smoked. "I want to see her again. I must see her."

"Of course you must." Then Chad hesitated. "Do you mean — a — Mother herself?"

"Oh your mother — that will depend."

It was as if Mrs. Newsome had somehow been placed by the words very far off. Chad however endeavoured in spite of this to reach the place. "What do you mean it will depend on?"

Strether, for all answer, gave him a longish look. "I was speaking of Sarah. I must positively — though she quite cast me off — see *her* again. I can't part with her that way."

"Then she was awfully unpleasant?"

Again Strether exhaled. "She was what she had to be. I mean that from the moment they're not delighted they can only be — well what I admit she was. We gave them," he went on, "their chance to be delighted, and they've walked up to it, and looked all round it, and not taken it."

"You can bring a horse to water —!" Chad suggested.

"Precisely. And the tune to which this morning Sarah was n't delighted — the tune to which, to adopt your metaphor, she refused to drink — leaves us on that side nothing more to hope."

Chad had a pause, and then as if consolingly: "It was never of course really the least on the cards that they would be 'delighted.'"

"Well, I don't know, after all," Strether mused. "I've had to come as far round. However" — he shook it off — "it's doubtless *my* performance that's absurd."

"There are certainly moments," said Chad, "when

you seem to me too good to be true. Yet if you are true," he added, "that seems to be all that need concern me."

"I'm true, but I'm incredible. I'm fantastic and ridiculous — I don't explain myself even *to* myself. How can they then," Strether asked, "understand me? So I don't quarrel with them."

"I see. They quarrel," said Chad rather comfortably, "with *us*." Strether noted once more the comfort, but his young friend had already gone on. "I should feel greatly ashamed, all the same, if I didn't put it before you again that you ought to think, after all, tremendously well. I mean before giving up beyond recall —" With which insistence, as from a certain delicacy, dropped.

Ah but Strether wanted it. "Say it all, say it all."

"Well, at your age, and with what — when all's said and done — Mother might do for you and be for you."

Chad had said it all, from his natural scruple, only to that extent; so that Strether after an instant himself took a hand. "My absence of an assured future. The little I have to show toward the power to take care of myself. The way, the wonderful way, she would certainly take care of me. Her fortune, her kindness, and the constant miracle of her having been disposed to go even so far. Of course, of course" — he summed it up. "There are those sharp facts."

Chad had meanwhile thought of another still. "And don't you really care — ?"

His friend slowly turned round to him. "Will you go?"

"I'll go if you'll say you now consider I should. You know," he went on, "I was ready six weeks ago."

"Ah," said Strether, "that was when you did n't know *I* was n't! You're ready at present because you do know it."

"That may be," Chad returned; "but all the same I'm sincere. You talk about taking the whole thing on your shoulders, but in what light do you regard me that you think me capable of letting you pay?" Strether patted his arm, as they stood together against the parapet, reassuringly — seeming to wish to contend that he *had* the wherewithal; but it was again round this question of purchase and price that the young man's sense of fairness continued to hover. "What it literally comes to for you, if you'll pardon my putting it so, is that you give up money. Possibly a good deal of money."

"Oh," Strether laughed, "if it were only just enough you'd still be justified in putting it so! But I've on my side to remind you too that *you* give up money; and more than 'possibly' — quite certainly, as I should suppose — a good deal."

"True enough; but I've got a certain quantity," Chad returned after a moment. "Whereas you, my dear man, you —"

"I can't be at all said" — Strether took him up — "to have a 'quantity' certain or uncertain? Very true. Still, I shan't starve."

"Oh you must n't *starve!*" Chad pacifically emphasised; and so, in the pleasant conditions, they continued to talk; though there was, for that matter, a pause in which the younger companion might have been taken as weighing again the delicacy of his then and there promising the elder some provision against the possibility just mentioned. This, however, he presumably thought best not to do, for at the end of another minute they had moved in quite a different direction. Strether had broken in by returning to the subject of Chad's passage with Sarah and enquiring if they had arrived, in the event, at anything in the nature of a "scene." To this Chad replied that they had on the contrary kept tremendously polite; adding moreover that Sally was after all not the woman to have made the mistake of not being. "Her hands are a good deal tied, you see. I got so, from the first," he sagaciously observed, "the start of her."

"You mean she has taken so much from you?"

"Well, I could n't of course in common decency give less: only she had n't expected, I think, that I'd give her nearly so much. And she began to take it before she knew it."

"And she began to like it," said Strether, "as soon as she began to take it!"

"Yes, she has liked it — also more than she expected." After which Chad observed: "But she does n't like *me*. In fact she hates me."

Strether's interest grew. "Then why does she want you at home?"

"Because when you hate you want to triumph, and if she should get me neatly stuck there she *would* triumph."

Strether followed afresh, but looking as he went. "Certainly — in a manner. But it would scarce be a

221

triumph worth having if, once entangled, feeling her dislike and possibly conscious in time of a certain quantity of your own, you should on the spot make yourself unpleasant to her."

"Ah," said Chad, "she can bear *me* — could bear me at least at home. It's my being there that would be her triumph. She hates me in Paris."

"She hates in other words — "

"Yes, *that's* it!" — Chad had quickly understood this understanding; which formed on the part of each as near an approach as they had yet made to naming Madame de Vionnet. The limitations of their distinctness did n't, however, prevent its fairly lingering in the air that it was this lady Mrs. Pocock hated. It added one more touch moreover to their established recognition of the rare intimacy of Chad's association with her. He had never yet more twitched away the last light veil from this phenomenon than in presenting himself as confounded and submerged in the feeling she had created at Woollett. "And I'll tell you who hates me too," he immediately went on.

Strether knew as immediately whom he meant, but with as prompt a protest. "Ah no! Mamie does n't hate — well," he caught himself in time — "anybody at all. Mamie's beautiful."

Chad shook his head. "That's just why I mind it. She certainly does n't like me."

"How much do you mind it? What would you do for her?"

"Well, I'd like her if she'd like me. Really, really," Chad declared.

It gave his companion a moment's pause. "You

asked me just now if I don't, as you said, 'care' about a certain person. You rather tempt me therefore to put the question in my turn. Don't *you* care about a certain other person?"

Chad looked at him hard in the lamplight of the window. "The difference is that I don't want to."

Strether wondered. "'Don't want' to?"

"I try not to — that is I *have* tried. I've done my best. You can't be surprised," the young man easily went on, "when you yourself set me on it. I was indeed," he added, "already on it a little; but you set me harder. It was six weeks ago that I thought I had come out."

Strether took it well in. "But you have n't come out!"

"I don't know — it's what I *want* to know," said Chad. "And if I could have sufficiently wanted — by myself — to go back, I think I might have found out."

"Possibly" — Strether considered. "But all you were able to achieve was to want to want to! And even then," he pursued, "only till our friends there came. Do you want to want to still?" As with a sound half-dolorous, half-droll and all vague and equivocal, Chad buried his face for a little in his hands, rubbing it in a whimsical way that amounted to an evasion, he brought it out more sharply : "*Do* you?"

Chad kept for a time his attitude, but at last he looked up, and then abruptly, "Jim *is* a damned dose!" he declared.

"Oh I don't ask you to abuse or describe or in any way pronounce on your relatives; I simply put it to you once more whether you're *now* ready. You say you've 'seen.' Is what you've seen that you can't resist?"

Chad gave him a strange smile — the nearest approach he had ever shown to a troubled one. "Can't you make me *not* resist?"

"What it comes to," Strether went on very gravely now and as if he had n't heard him, "what it comes to is that more has been done for you, I think, than I've ever seen done — attempted perhaps, but never so successfully done — by one human being for another."

"Oh an immense deal certainly" — Chad did it full justice. "And you yourself are adding to it."

It was without heeding this either that his visitor continued. "And our friends there won't have it."

"No, they simply won't."

"They demand you on the basis, as it were, of repudiation and ingratitude; and what has been the matter with me," Strether went on, "is that I have n't seen my way to working with you for repudiation."

Chad appreciated this. "Then as you have n't seen yours you naturally have n't seen mine. There it is." After which he proceeded, with a certain abruptness, to a sharp interrogation. "*Now* do you say she does n't hate me?"

Strether hesitated. "'She' — ?"

"Yes — Mother. We called it Sarah, but it comes to the same thing."

"Ah," Strether objected, "not to the same thing as her hating *you.*"

On which — though as if for an instant it had hung fire — Chad remarkably replied: "Well, if they hate my good friend, *that* comes to the same thing."

BOOK ELEVENTH

It had a note of inevitable truth that made Strether take it as enough, feel he wanted nothing more. The young man spoke in it for his "good friend" more than he had ever yet directly spoken, confessed to such deep identities between them as he might play with the idea of working free from, but which at a given moment could still draw him down like a whirlpool. And meanwhile he had gone on. "Their hating you too moreover — that also comes to a good deal."

"Ah," said Strether, "your mother does n't."

Chad, however, loyally stuck to it — loyally, that is, to Strether. "She will if you don't look out."

"Well, I do look out. I am, after all, looking out. That 's just why," our friend explained, "I want to see her again."

It drew from Chad again the same question. "To see Mother?"

"To see — for the present — Sarah."

"Ah then there you are! And what I don't for the life of me make out," Chad pursued with resigned perplexity, "is what you *gain* by it."

Oh it would have taken his companion too long to say! "That 's because you have, I verily believe, no imagination. You 've other qualities. But no imagination, don't you see? at all."

"I dare say. I do see." It was an idea in which Chad showed interest. "But have n't you yourself rather too much?"

"Oh *rather* — !" So that after an instant, under this reproach and as if it were at last a fact really to escape from, Strether made his move for departure.

II

ONE of the features of the restless afternoon passed by him after Mrs. Pocock's visit was an hour spent, shortly before dinner, with Maria Gostrey, whom of late, in spite of so sustained a call on his attention from other quarters, he had by no means neglected. And that he was still not neglecting her will appear from the fact that he was with her again at the same hour on the very morrow — with no less fine a consciousness moreover of being able to hold her ear. It continued inveterately to occur, for that matter, that whenever he had taken one of his greater turns he came back to where she so faithfully awaited him. None of these excursions had on the whole been livelier than the pair of incidents — the fruit of the short interval since his previous visit — on which he had now to report to her. He had seen Chad Newsome late the night before, and he had had that morning, as a sequel to this conversation, a second interview with Sarah. "But they're all off," he said, "at last."

It puzzled her a moment. "All? — Mr. Newsome with them?"

"Ah not yet! Sarah and Jim and Mamie. But Waymarsh with them — for Sarah. It's too beautiful," Strether continued; "I find I don't get over that — it's always a fresh joy. But it's a fresh joy too," he added, "that — well, what do you think? Little Bilham also goes. But he of course goes for Mamie."

Miss Gostrey wondered. "'For' her? Do you mean they're already engaged?"

"Well," said Strether, "say then for *me*. He'll do anything for me; just as I will, for that matter — anything I can — for him. Or for Mamie either. *She'll* do anything for me."

Miss Gostrey gave a comprehensive sigh. "The way you reduce people to subjection!"

"It's certainly, on one side, wonderful. But it's quite equalled, on another, by the way I don't. I haven't reduced Sarah, since yesterday; though I've succeeded in seeing her again, as I'll presently tell you. The others however are really all right. Mamie, by that blessed law of ours, absolutely must have a young man."

"But what must poor Mr. Bilham have? Do you mean they'll *marry* for you?"

"I mean that, by the same blessed law, it won't matter a grain if they don't — I shan't have in the least to worry."

She saw as usual what he meant. "And Mr. Jim? — who goes for him?"

"Oh," Strether had to admit, "I could n't manage *that*. He's thrown, as usual, on the world; the world which, after all, by his account — for he has prodigious adventures — seems very good to him. He fortunately — 'over here,' as he says — finds the world everywhere; and his most prodigious adventure of all," he went on, "has been of course of the last few days."

Miss Gostrey, already knowing, instantly made the connexion. "He has seen Marie de Vionnet again?"

"He went, all by himself, the day after Chad's party — did n't I tell you ? — to tea with her. By her invitation — all alone."

"Quite like yourself!" Maria smiled.

"Oh but he's more wonderful about her than I am!" And then as his friend showed how she could believe it, filling it out, fitting it on to old memories of the wonderful woman: "What I should have liked to manage would have been *her* going."

"To Switzerland with the party?"

"For Jim — and for symmetry. If it had been workable moreover for a fortnight she'd have gone. She's ready" — he followed up his renewed vision of her — "for anything."

Miss Gostrey went with him a minute. "She's too perfect!"

"She *will*, I think," he pursued, "go to-night to the station."

"To see him off?"

"With Chad — marvellously — as part of their general attention. And she does it" — it kept before him — "with a light, light grace, a free, free gaiety, that may well softly bewilder Mr. Pocock."

It kept her so before him that his companion had after an instant a friendly comment. "As in short it has softly bewildered a saner man. Are you really in love with her?" Maria threw off.

"It's of no importance I should know," he replied. "It matters so little — has nothing to do, practically, with either of us."

"All the same" — Maria continued to smile —

"they go, the five, as I understand you, and you and Madame de Vionnet stay."

"Oh and Chad." To which Strether added: "And you."

"Ah 'me'!" — she gave a small impatient wail again, in which something of the unreconciled seemed suddenly to break out. "*I* don't stay, it somehow seems to me, much to my advantage. In the presence of all you cause to pass before me I've a tremendous sense of privation."

Strether hesitated. "But your privation, your keeping out of everything, has been — has n't it? — by your own choice."

"Oh yes; it has been necessary — that is it has been better for you. What I mean is only that I seem to have ceased to serve you."

"How can you tell that?" he asked. "You don't know how you serve me. When you cease — "

"Well?" she said as he dropped.

"Well, I'll *let* you know. Be quiet till then."

She thought a moment. "Then you positively like me to stay?"

"Don't I treat you as if I did?"

"You're certainly very kind to me. But that," said Maria, "is for myself. It's getting late, as you see, and Paris turning rather hot and dusty. People are scattering, and some of them, in other places, want me. But if you want me here —!"

She had spoken as resigned to his word, but he had of a sudden a still sharper sense than he would have expected of desiring not to lose her. "I want you here."

THE AMBASSADORS

She took it as if the words were all she had wished; as if they brought her, gave her something that was the compensation of her case. "Thank you," she simply answered. And then as he looked at her a little harder, "Thank you very much," she repeated.

It had broken as with a slight arrest into the current of their talk, and it held him a moment longer. "Why, two months, or whatever the time was, ago, did you so suddenly dash off? The reason you afterwards gave me for having kept away three weeks was n't the real one."

She recalled. "I never supposed you believed it was. Yet," she continued, "if you did n't guess it that was just what helped you."

He looked away from her on this; he indulged, so far as space permitted, in one of his slow absences. "I've often thought of it, but never to feel that I could guess it. And you see the consideration with which I've treated you in never asking till now."

"Now then why *do* you ask?"

"To show you how I miss you when you're not here, and what it does for me."

"It does n't seem to have done," she laughed, "all it might! However," she added, "if you've really never guessed the truth I'll tell it you."

"I've never guessed it," Strether declared.

"Never?"

"Never."

"Well then I dashed off, as you say, so as not to have the confusion of being there if Marie de Vionnet should tell you anything to my detriment."

He looked as if he considerably doubted. "You

230

even then would have had to face it on your return."

"Oh if I had found reason to believe it something
very bad I'd have left you altogether."

"So then," he continued, "it was only on guessing
she had been on the whole merciful that you ventured
back?"

Maria kept it together. "I owe her thanks. Whatever her temptation she didn't separate us. That's
one of my reasons," she went on, "for admiring her
so."

"Let it pass then," said Strether, "for one of mine
as well. But what would have been her temptation?"

"What are ever the temptations of women?"

He thought — but hadn't, naturally, to think too
long. "Men?"

"She would have had you, with it, more for herself.
But she saw she could have you without it."

"Oh 'have' me!" Strether a trifle ambiguously
sighed. "*You*," he handsomely declared, "would
have had me at any rate *with* it."

"Oh 'have' you!" — she echoed it as he had done.
"I do have you, however," she less ironically said,
"from the moment you express a wish."

He stopped before her, full of the disposition. "I'll
express fifty."

Which indeed begot in her, with a certain inconsequence, a return of her small wail. "Ah there you
are!"

There, if it were so, he continued for the rest of the
time to be, and it was as if to show her how she could
still serve him that, coming back to the departure of

the Pococks, he gave her the view, vivid with a hundred more touches than we can reproduce, of what had happened for him that morning. He had had ten minutes with Sarah at her hotel, ten minutes reconquered, by irresistible pressure, from the time over which he had already described her to Miss Gostrey as having, at the end of their interview on his own premises, passed the great sponge of the future. He had caught her by not announcing himself, had found her in her sitting-room with a dressmaker and a *lingère* whose accounts she appeared to have been more or less ingenuously settling and who soon withdrew. Then he had explained to her how he had succeeded, late the night before, in keeping his promise of seeing Chad. "I told her I'd take it all."

"You'd 'take' it?"

"Why if he does n't go."

Maria waited. "And who takes it if he does?" she enquired with a certain grimness of gaiety.

"Well," said Strether, "I think I take, in any event, everything."

"By which I suppose you mean," his companion brought out after a moment, "that you definitely understand you now lose everything."

He stood before her again. "It does come perhaps to the same thing. But Chad, now that he has seen, does n't really want it."

She could believe that, but she made, as always, for clearness. "Still, what, after all, *has* he seen?"

"What they want of him. And it's enough."

"It contrasts so unfavourably with what Madame de Vionnet wants?"

232

"It contrasts — just so; all round, and tremendously."

"Therefore, perhaps, most of all with what *you*
want?"

"Oh," said Strether, "what I want is a thing I've
ceased to measure or even to understand."

But his friend none the less went on. "Do you want
Mrs. Newsome — after such a way of treating you?"

It was a straighter mode of dealing with this lady
than they had as yet — such was their high form —
permitted themselves; but it seemed not wholly for
this that he delayed a moment. "I dare say it has
been, after all, the only way she could have imagined."

"And does that make you want her any more?"

"I've tremendously disappointed her," Strether
thought it worth while to mention.

"Of course you have. That's rudimentary; that
was plain to us long ago. But is n't it almost as plain,"
Maria went on, "that you 've even yet your straight
remedy? Really drag him away, as I believe you still
can, and you 'd cease to have to count with her disappointment."

"Ah then," he laughed, "I should have to count
with yours!"

But this barely struck her now. "What, in that
case, should you call counting? You have n't come
out where you are, I think, to please *me*."

"Oh," he insisted, "that too, you know, has been
part of it. I can't separate — it 's all one; and that 's
perhaps why, as I say, I don't understand." But he
was ready to declare again that this did n't in the
least matter; all the more that, as he affirmed, he

had n't really as yet "come out." "She gives me after all, on its coming to the pinch, a last mercy, another chance. They don't sail, you see, for five or six weeks more, and they have n't — she admits that — expected Chad would take part in their tour. It's still open to him to join them, at the last, at Liverpool."

Miss Gostrey considered. "How in the world is it 'open' unless you open it? How can he join them at Liverpool if he but sinks deeper into his situation here?"

"He has given her — as I explained to you that she let me know yesterday — his word of honour to do as I say."

Maria stared. "But if you say nothing!"

Well, he as usual walked about on it. "I did say something this morning. I gave her my answer — the word I had promised her after hearing from himself what *he* had promised. What she demanded of me yesterday, you'll remember, was the engagement then and there to make him take up this vow."

"Well then," Miss Gostrey enquired, "was the purpose of your visit to her only to decline?"

"No; it was to ask, odd as that may seem to you, for another delay."

"Ah that's weak!"

"Precisely!" She had spoken with impatience, but, so far as that at least, he knew where he was. "If I *am* weak I want to find it out. If I don't find it out I shall have the comfort, the little glory, of thinking I'm strong."

"It's all the comfort, I judge," she returned, "that you *will* have!"

234

BOOK ELEVENTH

"At any rate," he said, "it will have been a month more. Paris may grow, from day to day, hot and dusty, as you say; but there are other things that are hotter and dustier. I'm not afraid to stay on; the summer here must be amusing in a wild — if it is n't a tame — way of its own; the place at no time more picturesque. I think I shall like it. And then," he benevolently smiled for her, "there will be always you."

"Oh," she objected, "it won't be as a part of the picturesqueness that I shall stay, for I shall be the plainest thing about you. You may, you see, at any rate," she pursued, "have nobody else. Madame de Vionnet may very well be going off, may n't she? — and Mr. Newsome by the same stroke: unless indeed you've had an assurance from them to the contrary. So that if your idea's to stay for them" — it was her duty to suggest it — "you may be left in the lurch. Of course if they do stay" — she kept it up — "they would be part of the picturesqueness. Or else indeed you might join them somewhere."

Strether seemed to face it as if it were a happy thought; but the next moment he spoke more critically. "Do you mean that they'll probably go off together?"

She just considered. "I think it will be treating you quite without ceremony if they do; though after all," she added, "it would be difficult to see now quite what degree of ceremony properly meets your case."

"Of course," Strether conceded, "my attitude toward them is extraordinary."

"Just so; so that one may ask one's self what style of proceeding on their own part can altogether match it. The attitude of their own that won't pale in its light they've doubtless still to work out. The really handsome thing perhaps," she presently threw off, "*would* be for them to withdraw into more secluded conditions, offering at the same time to share them with you." He looked at her, on this, as if some generous irritation — all in his interest — had suddenly again flickered in her; and what she next said indeed half-explained it. "Don't really be afraid to tell me if what now holds you *is* the pleasant prospect of the empty town, with plenty of seats in the shade, cool drinks, deserted museums, drives to the Bois in the evening, and our wonderful woman all to yourself." And she kept it up still more. "The handsomest thing of *all*, when one makes it out, would, I dare say, be that Mr. Chad should for a while go off by himself. It's a pity, from that point of view," she wound up, "that he does n't pay his mother a visit. It would at least occupy your interval." The thought in fact held her a moment. "Why does n't he pay his mother a visit? Even a week, at this good moment, would do."

"My dear lady," Strether replied — and he had it even to himself surprisingly ready — "my dear lady, his mother has paid *him* a visit. Mrs. Newsome has been with him, this month, with an intensity that I'm sure he has thoroughly felt; he has lavishly entertained her, and she has let him have her thanks. Do you suggest he shall go back for more of them?"

Well, she succeeded after a little in shaking it off.

"I see. It's what you don't suggest — what you have n't suggested. And you know."

"So would you, my dear," he kindly said, "if you had so much as seen her."

"As seen Mrs. Newsome?"

"No, Sarah — which, both for Chad and for myself, has served all the purpose."

"And served it in a manner," she responsively mused, "so extraordinary!"

"Well, you see," he partly explained, "what it comes to is that she's all cold thought — which Sarah could serve to us cold without its really losing anything. So it is that we know what she thinks of us."

Maria had followed, but she had an arrest. "What I've never made out, if you come to that, is what you think — I mean you personally — of *her*. Don't you so much, when all's said, as care a little?"

"That," he answered with no loss of promptness, "is what even Chad himself asked me last night. He asked me if I don't mind the loss — well, the loss of an opulent future. Which moreover," he hastened to add, "was a perfectly natural question."

"I call your attention, all the same," said Miss Gostrey, "to the fact that I don't ask it. What I venture to ask is whether it's to Mrs. Newsome herself that you're indifferent."

"I have n't been so" — he spoke with all assurance. "I've been the very opposite. I've been, from the first moment, preoccupied with the impression everything might be making on her — quite oppressed, haunted, tormented by it. I've been interested *only* in her seeing what I've seen. And I've been as disappointed in her refusal to see it as she has been in what has appeared to her the perversity of my insistence."

"Do you mean that she has shocked you as you've shocked her?"

Strether weighed it. "I'm probably not so shockable. But on the other hand I've gone much further to meet her. She, on her side, has n't budged an inch."

"So that you're now at last" — Maria pointed the moral — "in the sad stage of recriminations."

"No — it's only to you I speak. I've been like a lamb to Sarah. I've only put my back to the wall. It's to *that* one naturally staggers when one has been violently pushed there."

She watched him a moment. "Thrown over?"

"Well, as I feel I've landed somewhere I think I must have been thrown."

She turned it over, but as hoping to clarify much rather than to harmonise. "The thing is that I suppose you've been disappointing —"

"Quite from the very first of my arrival? I dare say. I admit I was surprising even to myself."

"And then of course," Maria went on, "I had much to do with it."

"With my being surprising —?"

"That will do," she laughed, "if you're too delicate to call it *my* being! Naturally," she added, "you came over more or less for surprises."

"Naturally!" — he valued the reminder.

"But they were to have been all for you" — she

continued to piece it out — "and none of them for *her*."

Once more he stopped before her as if she had touched the point. "That's just her difficulty — that she doesn't admit surprises. It's a fact that, I think, describes and represents her; and it falls in with what I tell you — that she's all, as I've called it, fine cold thought. She had, to her own mind, worked the whole thing out in advance, and worked it out for me as well as for herself. Whenever she has done that, you see, there's no room left; no margin, as it were, for any alteration. She's filled as full, packed as tight, as she'll hold, and if you wish to get anything more or different either out or in — "

"You've got to make over altogether the woman herself?"

"What it comes to," said Strether, "is that you've got morally and intellectually to get rid of her."

"Which would appear," Maria returned, "to be practically what you've done."

But her friend threw back his head. "I haven't touched her. She won't *be* touched. I see it now as I've never done; and she hangs together with a perfection of her own," he went on, "that does suggest a kind of wrong in *any* change of her composition. It was at any rate," he wound up, "the woman herself, as you call her, the whole moral and intellectual being or block, that Sarah brought me over to take or to leave."

It turned Miss Gostrey to deeper thought. "Fancy having to take at the point of the bayonet a whole moral and intellectual being or block!"

"It was in fact," said Strether, "what, at home, I *had* done. But somehow over there I did n't quite know it."

"One never does, I suppose," Miss Gostrey concurred, "realise in advance, in such a case, the size, as you may say, of the block. Little by little it looms up. It has been looming for you more and more till at last you see it all."

"I see it all," he absently echoed, while his eyes might have been fixing some particularly large iceberg in a cool blue northern sea. "It's magnificent!" he then rather oddly exclaimed.

But his friend, who was used to this kind of inconsequence in him, kept the thread. "There's nothing so magnificent — for making others feel you — as to have no imagination."

It brought him straight round. "Ah there you are! It's what I said last night to Chad. That he himself, I mean, has none."

"Then it would appear," Maria suggested, "that he has, after all, something in common with his mother."

"He has in common that he makes one, as you say, 'feel' him. And yet," he added, as if the question were interesting, "one feels others too, even when they have plenty."

Miss Gostrey continued suggestive. "Madame de Vionnet?"

"*She* has plenty."

"Certainly — she had quantities of old. But there are different ways of making one's self felt."

"Yes, it comes, no doubt, to that. You now —"

He was benevolently going on, but she would n't
have it. "Oh I *don't* make myself felt; so my quantity need n't be settled. Yours, you know," she said,
"is monstrous. No one has ever had so much."

It struck him for a moment. "That's what Chad
also thinks."

"There *you* are then — though it is n't for him to
complain of it!"

"Oh he does n't complain of it," said Strether.

"That's all that would be wanting! But apropos
of what," Maria went on, "did the question come
up?"

"Well, of his asking me what it is I gain."

She had a pause. "Then as I've asked you too it
settles *my* case. Oh you *have*," she repeated, "treasures of imagination."

But he had been for an instant thinking away from
this, and he came up in another place. "And yet
Mrs. Newsome — it's a thing to remember — *has*
imagined, did, that is, imagine, and apparently still
does, horrors about what I should have found. I was
booked, by her vision — extraordinarily intense, after
all — to find them; and that I did n't, that I could n't,
that, as she evidently felt, I would n't — this evidently did n't at all, as they say, 'suit' her book. It
was more than she could bear. That was her disappointment."

"You mean you were to have found Chad himself
horrible?"

"I was to have found the woman."

"Horrible?"

"Found her as she imagined her." And Strether

241

paused as if for his own expression of it he could add no touch to that picture.

His companion had meanwhile thought. "She imagined stupidly — so it comes to the same thing."

"Stupidly? Oh!" said Strether.

But she insisted. "She imagined meanly."

He had it, however, better. "It couldn't but be ignorantly."

"Well, intensity with ignorance — what do you want worse?"

This question might have held him, but he let it pass. "Sarah isn't ignorant — now; she keeps up the theory of the horrible."

"Ah but she's intense — and that by itself will do sometimes as well. If it doesn't do, in this case, at any rate, to deny that Marie's charming, it will do at least to deny that she's good."

"What I claim is that she's good for Chad."

"You don't claim" — she seemed to like it clear — "that she's good for *you*."

But he continued without heeding. "That's what I wanted them to come out for — to see for themselves if she's bad for him."

"And now that they've done so they won't admit that she's good even for anything?"

"They do think," Strether presently admitted, "that she's on the whole about as bad for me. But they're consistent of course, inasmuch as they've their clear view of what's good for both of us."

"For you, to begin with" — Maria, all responsive, confined the question for the moment — "to eliminate from your existence and if possible even from your memory the dreadful creature that *I* must gruesomely shadow forth for them, even more than to eliminate the distincter evil — thereby a little less portentous — of the person whose confederate you 've suffered yourself to become. However, that's comparatively simple. You can easily, at the worst, after all, give me up."

"I can easily at the worst, after all, give you up." The irony was so obvious that it needed no care. "I can easily at the worst, after all, even forget you."

"Call that then workable. But Mr. Newsome has much more to forget. How can *he* do it?"

"Ah there again we are! That's just what I was to have made him do; just where I was to have worked with him and helped."

She took it in silence and without attenuation — as if perhaps from very familiarity with the facts; and her thought made a connexion without showing the links. "Do you remember how we used to talk at Chester and in London about my seeing you through?" She spoke as of far-off things and as if they had spent weeks at the places she named.

"It's just what you *are* doing."

"Ah but the worst — since you 've left such a margin — may be still to come. You may yet break down."

"Yes, I may yet break down. But will you take me — ?"

He had hesitated, and she waited. "Take you — ?"

"For as long as I can bear it."

She also debated. "Mr. Newsome and Madame de Vionnet may, as we were saying, leave town. How long do you think you can bear it without them?"

Strether's reply to this was at first another question. "Do you mean in order to get away from me?"

Her answer had an abruptness. "Don't find me rude if I say I should think they'd want to!"

He looked at her hard again — seemed even for an instant to have an intensity of thought under which his colour changed. But he smiled. "You mean after what they've done to me?"

"After what *she* has."

At this, however, with a laugh, he was all right again. "Ah but she has n't done it yet!"

III

HE had taken the train a few days after this from a station — as well as *to* a station — selected almost at random; such days, whatever should happen, were numbered, and he had gone forth under the impulse — artless enough, no doubt — to give the whole of one of them to that French ruralism, with its cool special green, into which he had hitherto looked only through the little oblong window of the picture-frame. It had been as yet for the most part but a land of fancy for him — the background of fiction, the medium of art, the nursery of letters; practically as distant as Greece, but practically also well-nigh as consecrated. Romance could weave itself, for Strether's sense, out of elements mild enough; and even after what he had, as he felt, lately "been through," he could thrill a little at the chance of seeing something somewhere that would remind him of a certain small Lambinet that had charmed him, long years before, at a Boston dealer's and that he had quite absurdly never forgotten. It had been offered, he remembered, at a price he had been instructed to believe the lowest ever named for a Lambinet, a price he had never felt so poor as on having to recognise, all the same, as beyond a dream of possibility. He had dreamed — had turned and twisted possibilities for an hour: it had been the only adventure of his life in connexion with the purchase of a work of art. The adventure, it will be perceived, was modest; but the memory, beyond all reason and by some accident of association, was sweet. The little Lambinet abode with him as the picture he *would* have bought — the particular production that had made him for the moment overstep the modesty of nature. He was quite aware that if he were to see it again he should perhaps have a drop or a shock, and he never found himself wishing that the wheel of time would turn it up again, just as he had seen it in the maroon-coloured, sky-lighted inner shrine of Tremont Street. It would be a different thing, however, to see the remembered mixture resolved back into its elements — to assist at the restoration to nature of the whole far-away hour: the dusty day in Boston, the background of the Fitchburg Depot, of the maroon-coloured sanctum, the special-green vision, the ridiculous price, the poplars, the willows, the rushes, the river, the sunny silvery sky, the shady woody horizon.

He observed in respect to his train almost no condition save that it should stop a few times after getting out of the *banlieue;* he threw himself on the general amiability of the day for the hint of where to alight. His theory of his excursion was that he could alight anywhere — not nearer Paris than an hour's run — on catching a suggestion of the particular note required. It made its sign, the suggestion — weather, air, light, colour and his mood all favouring — at the end of some eighty minutes; the train pulled up just at the right spot, and he found himself getting out as securely as if to keep an appointment. It will be felt of him that he could amuse himself, at his age, with very small things if it be again noted that his appoint-

ment was only with a superseded Boston fashion. He
had n't gone far without the quick confidence that it
would be quite sufficiently kept. The oblong gilt
frame disposed its enclosing lines; the poplars and
willows, the reeds and river — a river of which he
did n't know, and did n't want to know, the name —
fell into a composition, full of felicity, within them;
the sky was silver and turquoise and varnish; the village on the left was white and the church on the right
was grey; it was all there, in short — it was what he
wanted: it was Tremont Street, it was France, it was
Lambinet. Moreover he was freely walking about in
it. He did this last, for an hour, to his heart's content,
making for the shady woody horizon and boring so
deep into his impression and his idleness that he might
fairly have got through them again and reached the
maroon-coloured wall. It was a wonder, no doubt,
that the taste of idleness for him should n't need more
time to sweeten; but it had in fact taken the few previous days; it had been sweetening in truth ever since
the retreat of the Pococks. He walked and walked as
if to show himself how little he had now to do; he had
nothing to do but turn off to some hillside where he
might stretch himself and hear the poplars rustle,
and whence — in the course of an afternoon so spent,
an afternoon richly suffused too with the sense of a
book in his pocket — he should sufficiently command
the scene to be able to pick out just the right little rus-
tic inn for an experiment in respect to dinner. There
was a train back to Paris at 9.20, and he saw himself
partaking, at the close of the day, with the enhance-
ments of a coarse white cloth and a sanded floor, of

something fried and felicitous, washed down with
authentic wine; after which he might, as he liked,
either stroll back to his station in the gloaming or propose for the local *carriole* and converse with his driver,
a driver who naturally would n't fail of a stiff clean
blouse, of a knitted nightcap and of the genius of response — who, in fine, would sit on the shafts, tell
him what the French people were thinking, and remind him, as indeed the whole episode would inci-
dentally do, of Maupassant. Strether heard his lips,
for the first time in French air, as this vision assumed
consistency, emit sounds of expressive intention without fear of his company. He had been afraid of Chad
and of Maria and of Madame de Vionnet; he had been
most of all afraid of Waymarsh, in whose presence, so
far as they had mixed together in the light of the
town, he had never without somehow paying for it
aired either his vocabulary or his accent. He usually
paid for it by meeting immediately afterwards Waymarsh's eye.

Such were the liberties with which his fancy played
after he had turned off to the hillside that did really
and truly, as well as most amiably, await him beneath
the poplars, the hillside that made him feel, for a mur-
murous couple of hours, how happy had been his
thought. He had the sense of success, of a finer harmony in things; nothing but what had turned out as
yet according to his plan. It most of all came home to
him, as he lay on his back on the grass, that Sarah had
really gone, that his tension was really relaxed; the
peace diffused in these ideas might be delusive, but it
hung about him none the less for the time. It fairly,

for half an hour, sent him to sleep; he pulled his straw hat over his eyes — he had bought it the day before with a reminiscence of Waymarsh's — and lost himself anew in Lambinet. It was as if he had found out he was tired — tired not from his walk, but from that inward exercise which had known, on the whole, for three months, so little intermission. That was it — when once they were off he had dropped; this moreover was what he had dropped to, and now he was touching bottom. He was kept luxuriously quiet, soothed and amused by the consciousness of what he had found at the end of his descent. It was very much what he had told Maria Gostrey he should like to stay on for, the hugely-distributed Paris of summer, alternately dazzling and dusky, with a weight lifted for him off its columns and cornices and with shade and air in the flutter of awnings as wide as avenues. It was present to him without attenuation that, reaching out, the day after making the remark, for some proof of his freedom, he had gone that very afternoon to see Madame de Vionnet. He had gone again the next day but one, and the effect of the two visits, the after-sense of the couple of hours spent with her, was almost that of fulness and frequency. The brave intention of frequency, so great with him from the moment of his finding himself unjustly suspected at Woollett, had remained rather theoretic, and one of the things he could muse about under his poplars was the source of the special shyness that had still made him careful. He had surely got rid of it now, this special shyness; what had become of it if it had n't precisely, within the week, rubbed off?

249

It struck him now in fact as sufficiently plain that if he had still been careful he had been so for a reason. He had really feared, in his behaviour, a lapse from good faith; if there was a danger of one's liking such a woman too much one's best safety was in waiting at least till one had the right to do so. In the light of the last few days the danger was fairly vivid; so that it was proportionately fortunate that the right was likewise established. It seemed to our friend that he had on each occasion profited to the utmost by the latter: how could he have done so more, he at all events asked himself, than in having immediately let her know that, if it was all the same to her, he preferred not to talk about anything tiresome? He had never in his life so sacrificed an armful of high interests as in that remark; he had never so prepared the way for the comparatively frivolous as in addressing it to Madame de Vionnet's intelligence. It had n't been till later that he quite recalled how in conjuring away everything but the pleasant he had conjured away almost all they had hitherto talked about; it was not till later even that he remembered how, with their new tone, they had n't so much as mentioned the name of Chad himself. One of the things that most lingered with him on his hillside was this delightful facility, with such a woman, of arriving at a new tone; he thought, as he lay on his back, of all the tones she might make possible if one were to try her, and at any rate of the probability that one could trust her to fit them to occasions. He had wanted her to feel that, as he was disinterested now, so she herself should be, and she had showed she felt it, and he had showed he was grateful, and it had been for all the world as if he were calling for the first time. They had had other, but irrelevant, meetings; it was quite as if, had they sooner known how much they *really* had in common, there were quantities of comparatively dull matters they might have skipped. Well, they were skipping them now, even to graceful gratitude, even to handsome "Don't mention it!" — and it was amazing what could still come up without reference to what had been going on between them. It might have been, on analysis, nothing more than Shakespeare and the musical glasses; but it had served all the purpose of his appearing to have said to her: "Don't like me, if it's a question of liking me, for anything obvious and clumsy that I've, as they call it, 'done' for you: like me — well, like me, hang it, for anything else you choose. So, by the same propriety, don't be for me simply the person I've come to know through my awkward connexion with Chad — was ever anything, by the way, *more* awkward? Be for me, please, with all your admirable tact and trust, just whatever I may show you it's a present pleasure to me to think you." It had been a large indication to meet; but if she had n't met it what *had* she done, and how had their time together slipped along so smoothly, mild but not slow, and melting, liquefying, into his happy illusion of idleness? He could recognise on the other hand that he had probably not been without reason, in his prior, his restricted state, for keeping an eye on his liability to lapse from good faith.

He really continued in the picture — that being for himself his situation — all the rest of this rambling day; so that the charm was still, was indeed more than ever upon him when, toward six o'clock, he found himself amicably engaged with a stout white-capped deep-voiced woman at the door of the *auberge* of the biggest village, a village that affected him as a thing of whiteness, blueness and crookedness, set in coppery green, and that had the river flowing behind or before it — one could n't say which; at the bottom, in particular, of the inn-garden. He had had other adventures before this; had kept along the height, after shaking off slumber; had admired, had almost coveted, another small old church, all steep roof and dim slate-colour without and all whitewash and paper flowers within; had lost his way and had found it again; had conversed with rustics who struck him perhaps a little more as men of the world than he had expected; had acquired at a bound a fearless facility in French; had had, as the afternoon waned, a watery *bock*, all pale and Parisian, in the café of the furthest village, which was not the biggest; and had meanwhile not once overstepped the oblong gilt frame. The frame had drawn itself out for him, as much as you please; but that was just his luck. He had finally come down again to the valley, to keep within touch of stations and trains, turning his face to the quarter from which he had started; and thus it was that he had at last pulled up before the hostess of the Cheval Blanc, who met him, with a rough readiness that was like the clatter of sabots over stones, on their common ground of a *côtelette de veau à l'oseille* and a subsequent lift. He had walked many miles and did n't know he was tired; but he still knew he was amused, and even that, though he had been alone all day, he had never yet so struck himself as engaged with others and in midstream of his drama. It might have passed for finished, his drama, with its catastrophe all but reached: it had, however, none the less been vivid again for him as he thus gave it its fuller chance. He had only had to be at last well out of it to feel it, oddly enough, still going on.

For this had been all day at bottom the spell of the picture — that it was essentially more than anything else a scene and a stage, that the very air of the play was in the rustle of the willows and the tone of the sky. The play and the characters had, without his knowing it till now, peopled all his space for him, and it seemed somehow quite happy that they should offer themselves, in the conditions so supplied, with a kind of inevitability. It was as if the conditions made them not only inevitable, but so much more nearly natural and right as that they were at least easier, pleasanter, to put up with. The conditions had nowhere so asserted their difference from those of Woollett as they appeared to him to assert it in the little court of the Cheval Blanc while he arranged with his hostess for a comfortable climax. They were few and simple, scant and humble, but they were *the thing*, as he would have called it, even to a greater degree than Madame de Vionnet's old high salon where the ghost of the Empire walked. "The" thing was the thing that implied the greatest number of other things of the sort he had had to tackle; and it was queer of course, but so it was — the implication here was complete. Not a single one of his observations but somehow fell into a place

in it; not a breath of the cooler evening that was n't
somehow a syllable of the text. The text was simply,
when condensed, that in *these* places such things were,
and that if it was in them one elected to move about
one had to make one's account with what one lighted
on. Meanwhile at all events it was enough that they
did affect one — so far as the village aspect was concerned — as whiteness, crookedness and blueness set
in coppery green; there being positively, for that matter, an outer wall of the White Horse that was painted
the most improbable shade. That was part of the
amusement — as if to show that the fun was harm-
less; just as it was enough, further, that the picture
and the play seemed supremely to melt together in the
good woman's broad sketch of what she could do for
her visitor's appetite. He felt in short a confidence,
and it was general, and it was all he wanted to feel. It
suffered no shock even on her mentioning that she had
in fact just laid the cloth for two persons who, unlike
Monsieur, had arrived by the river — in a boat of
their own; who had asked her, half an hour before,
what she could do for them, and had then paddled
away to look at something a little further up — from
which promenade they would presently return. Monsieur might meanwhile, if he liked, pass into the
garden, such as it was, where she would serve him,
should he wish it — for there were tables and benches
in plenty — a "bitter" before his repast. Here she
would also report to him on the possibility of a conveyance to his station, and here at any rate he would
have the *agrément* of the river.

It may be mentioned without delay that Monsieur

had the *agrément* of everything, and in particular, for the next twenty twenty minutes, of a small and primitive pavilion that, at the garden's edge, almost overhung the water, testifying, in its somewhat battered state, to much fond frequentation. It consisted of little more than a platform, slightly raised, with a couple of benches and a table, a protecting rail and a projecting roof; but it raked the full grey-blue stream, which, taking a turn a short distance above, passed out of sight to reappear much higher up; and it was clearly in esteemed requisition for Sundays and other feasts. Strether sat there and, though hungry, felt at peace; the confidence that had so gathered for him deepened with the lap of the water, the ripple of the surface, the rustle of the reeds on the opposite bank, the faint diffused coolness and the slight rock of a couple of small boats attached to a rough landing-place hard by. The valley on the further side was all copper-green level and glazed pearly sky, a sky hatched across with screens of trimmed trees, which looked flat, like espaliers; and though the rest of the village straggled away in the near quarter the view had an emptiness that made one of the boats suggestive. Such a river set one afloat almost before one could take up the oars — the idle play of which would be moreover the aid to the full impression. This perception went so far as to bring him to his feet; but that movement, in turn, made him feel afresh that he was tired, and while he leaned against a post and continued to look out he saw something that gave him a sharper arrest.

IV

WHAT he saw was exactly the right thing — a boat advancing round the bend and containing a man who held the paddles and a lady, at the stern, with a pink parasol. It was suddenly as if these figures, or something like them, had been wanted in the picture, had been wanted more or less all day, and had now drifted into sight, with the slow current, on purpose to fill up the measure. They came slowly, floating down, evidently directed to the landing-place near their spectator and presenting themselves to him not less clearly as the two persons for whom his hostess was already preparing a meal. For two very happy persons he found himself straightway taking them — a young man in shirt-sleeves, a young woman easy and fair, who had pulled pleasantly up from some other place and, being acquainted with the neighbourhood, had known what this particular retreat could offer them. The air quite thickened, at their approach, with further intimations; the intimation that they were expert, familiar, frequent — that this would n't at all events be the first time. They knew how to do it, he vaguely felt — and it made them but the more idyllic, though at the very moment of the impression, as happened, their boat seemed to have begun to drift wide, the oarsman letting it go. It had by this time none the less come much nearer — near enough for Strether to dream the lady in the stern had for some

256

reason taken account of his being there to watch
them. She had remarked on it sharply, yet her companion had n't turned round; it was in fact almost as
if our friend had felt her bid him keep still. She had
taken in something as a result of which their course
had wavered, and it continued to waver while they
just stood off. This little effect was sudden and rapid,
so rapid that Strether's sense of it was separate only
for an instant from a sharp start of his own. He too
had within the minute taken in something, taken in
that he knew the lady whose parasol, shifting as if to
hide her face, made so fine a pink point in the shining
scene. It was too prodigious, a chance in a million,
but, if he knew the lady, the gentleman, who still presented his back and kept off, the gentleman, the coat-
less hero of the idyll, who had responded to her start,
was, to match the marvel, none other than Chad.

Chad and Madame de Vionnet were then like himself taking a day in the country — though it was as
queer as fiction, as farce, that their country could happen to be exactly his; and she had been the first at
recognition, the first to feel, across the water, the
shock — for it appeared to come to that — of their
wonderful accident. Strether became aware, with
this, of what was taking place — that her recognition
had been even stranger for the pair in the boat, that
her immediate impulse had been to control it, and
that she was quickly and intensely debating with Chad
the risk of betrayal. He saw they would show nothing
if they could feel sure he had n't made them out; so
that he had before him for a few seconds his own hesitation. It was a sharp fantastic crisis that had popped

up as if in a dream, and it had had only to last the few seconds to make him feel it as quite horrible. They were thus, on either side, *trying* the other side, and all for some reason that broke the stillness like some unprovoked harsh note. It seemed to him again, within the limit, that he had but one thing to do — to settle their common question by some sign of surprise and joy. He hereupon gave large play to these things, agitating his hat and his stick and loudly calling out — a demonstration that brought him relief as soon as he had seen it answered. The boat, in mid-stream, still went a little wild — which seemed natural, however, while Chad turned round, half springing up; and his good friend, after blankness and wonder, began gaily to wave her parasol. Chad dropped afresh to his paddles and the boat headed round, amazement and pleasantry filling the air meanwhile, and relief, as Strether continued to fancy, superseding mere violence. Our friend went down to the water under this odd impression as of violence averted — the violence of their having "cut" him, out there in the eye of nature, on the assumption that he would n't know it. He awaited them with a face from which he was conscious of not being able quite to banish this idea that they would have gone on, not seeing and not knowing, missing their dinner and disappointing their hostess, had he himself taken a line to match. That at least was what darkened his vision for the moment. Afterwards, after they had bumped at the landing-place and he had assisted their getting ashore, everything found itself sponged over by the mere miracle of the encounter.

BOOK ELEVENTH

They could so much better at last, on either side, treat it as a wild extravagance of hazard, that the situation was made elastic by the amount of explanation called into play. Why indeed — apart from oddity — the situation should have been really stiff was a question naturally not practical at the moment, and in fact, so far as we are concerned, a question tackled, later on and in private, only by Strether himself. He was to reflect later on and in private that it was mainly *he* who had explained — as he had had moreover comparatively little difficulty in doing. He was to have at all events meanwhile the worrying thought of their perhaps secretly suspecting him of having plotted this coincidence, taking such pains as might be to give it the semblance of an accident. That possibility — as their imputation — did n't of course bear looking into for an instant; yet the whole incident was so manifestly, arrange it as they would, an awkward one, that he could scarce keep disclaimers in respect to his own presence from rising to his lips. Disclaimers of intention would have been as tactless as his presence was practically gross; and the narrowest escape they either of them had was his lucky escape, in the event, from making any. Nothing of the sort, so far as surface and sound were involved, was even in question; surface and sound all made for their common ridiculous good fortune, for the general *invraisemblance* of the occasion, for the charming chance that they had, the others, in passing, ordered some food to be ready, the charming chance that he had himself not eaten, the charming chance, even more, that their little plans, their hours, their train, in short, from *là-*

259

bas, would all match for their return together to Paris. The chance that was most charming of all, the chance that drew from Madame de Vionnet her clearest, gayest "*Comme cela se trouve !*" was the announcement made to Strether after they were seated at table, the word given him by their hostess in respect to his carriage for the station, on which he might now count. It settled the matter for his friends as well; the conveyance — it *was* all too lucky! — would serve for them; and nothing was more delightful than his being in a position to make the train so definite. It might have been, for themselves — to hear Madame de Vionnet — almost unnaturally vague, a detail left to be fixed; though Strether indeed was afterwards to remember that Chad had promptly enough intervened to forestall this appearance, laughing at his companion's flightiness and making the point that he had, after all, in spite of the bedazzlement of a day out with her, known what he was about.

Strether was to remember afterwards further that this had had for him the effect of forming Chad's almost sole intervention; and indeed he was to remember further still, in subsequent meditation, many things that, as it were, fitted together. Another of them was for instance that the wonderful woman's overflow of surprise and amusement was wholly into French, which she struck him as speaking with an unprecedented command of idiomatic turns, but in which she got, as he might have said, somewhat away from him, taking all at once little brilliant jumps that he could but lamely match. The question of his own French had never come up for them; it was the one thing she would n't have permitted — it belonged, for a person who had been through much, to mere boredom; but the present result was odd, fairly veiling her identity, shifting her back into a mere voluble class or race to the intense audibility of which he was by this time inured. When she spoke the charming slightly strange English he best knew her by he seemed to feel her as a creature, among all the millions, with a language quite to herself, the real monopoly of a special shade of speech, beautifully easy for her, yet of a colour and a cadence that were both inimitable and matters of accident. She came back to these things after they had shaken down in the inn-parlour and knew, as it were, what was to become of them; it was inevitable that loud ejaculation over the prodigy of their convergence should at last wear itself out. Then it was that his impression took fuller form — the impression, destined only to deepen, to complete itself, that they had something to put a face upon, to carry off and make the best of, and that it was she who, admirably on the whole, was doing this. It was familiar to him of course that they had something to put a face upon; their friendship, their connexion, took any amount of explaining — that would have been made familiar by his twenty minutes with Mrs. Pocock if it had n't already been so. Yet his theory, as we know, had bountifully been that the facts were specifically none of his business, and were, over and above, so far as one had to do with them, intrinsically beautiful; and this might have prepared him for anything, as well as rendered him proof against mystification. When he reached home that night, however, he knew he had been, at bottom, neither prepared nor proof; and since we have spoken of what he was, after his return, to recall and interpret, it may as well immediately be said that his real experience of these few hours put on, in that belated vision — for he scarce went to bed till morning — the aspect that is most to our purpose.

He then knew more or less how he had been affected — he but half knew at the time. There had been plenty to affect him even after, as has been said, they had shaken down; for his consciousness, though muffled, had its sharpest moments during this passage, a marked drop into innocent friendly Bohemia. They then had put their elbows on the table, deploring the premature end of their two or three dishes; which they had tried to make up with another bottle while Chad joked a little spasmodically, perhaps even a little irrelevantly, with the hostess. What it all came to had been that fiction and fable *were*, inevitably, in the air, and not as a simple term of comparison, but as a result of things said; also that they were blinking it, all round, and that they yet need n't, so much as that, have blinked it — though indeed if they had n't Strether did n't quite see what else they could have done. Strether did n't quite see *that* even at an hour or two past midnight, even when he had, at his hotel, for a long time, without a light and without undressing, sat back on his bedroom sofa and stared straight before him. He was, at that point of vantage, in full possession, to make of it all what he could. He kept making of it that there had been simply a *lie* in the charming affair — a lie on which one could now, de-

tached and deliberate, perfectly put one's finger. It
was with the lie that they had eaten and drunk and
talked and laughed, that they had waited for their
carriole rather impatiently, and had then got into the
vehicle and, sensibly subsiding, driven their three or
four miles through the darkening summer night. The
eating and drinking, which had been a resource, had
had the effect of having served its turn; the talk and
laughter had done as much; and it was during their
somewhat tedious progress to the station, during the
waits there, the further delays, their submission to
fatigue, their silences in the dim compartment of the
much-stopping train, that he prepared himself for reflexions to come. It had been a performance, Madame
de Vionnet's manner, and though it had to that degree
faltered toward the end, as through her ceasing to believe in it, as if she had asked herself, or Chad had
found a moment surreptitiously to ask her, what after
all was the use, a performance it had none the less
quite handsomely remained, with the final fact about
it that it was on the whole easier to keep up than to
abandon.

From the point of view of presence of mind it had
been very wonderful indeed, wonderful for readiness,
for beautiful assurance, for the way her decision was
taken on the spot, without time to confer with Chad,
without time for anything. Their only conference
could have been the brief instants in the boat before
they confessed to recognising the spectator on the
bank, for they had n't been alone together a moment
since and must have communicated all in silence. It
was a part of the deep impression for Strether, and

not the least of the deep interest, that they *could* so
communicate — that Chad in particular could let her
know he left it to her. He habitually left things to
others, as Strether was so well aware, and it in fact
came over our friend in these meditations that there
had been as yet no such vivid illustration of his
famous knowing how to live. It was as if he had
humoured her to the extent of letting her lie without
correction — almost as if, really, he would be coming
round in the morning to set the matter, as between
Strether and himself, right. Of course he could n't
quite come; it was a case in which a man was obliged
to accept the woman's version, even when fantastic;
if she had, with more flurry than she cared to show,
elected, as the phrase was, to represent that they had
left Paris that morning, and with no design but of
getting back within the day — if she had so sized-up,
in the Woollett phrase, their necessity, she knew best
her own measure. There were things, all the same, it
was impossible to blink and which made this measure
an odd one — the too evident fact for instance that
she had n't started out for the day dressed and hatted
and shod, and even, for that matter, pink parasol'd, as
she had been in the boat. From what did the drop in
her assurance proceed as the tension increased —
from what did this slightly baffled ingenuity spring
but from her consciousness of not presenting, as night
closed in, with not so much as a shawl to wrap her
round, an appearance that matched her story? She
admitted that she was cold, but only to blame her
imprudence, which Chad suffered her to give such account of as she might. Her shawl and Chad's overcoat

and her other garments, and his, those they had each worn the day before, were at the place, best known to themselves — a quiet retreat enough, no doubt — at which they had been spending the twenty-four hours, to which they had fully meant to return that evening, from which they had so remarkably swum into Strether's ken, and the tacit repudiation of which had been thus the essence of her comedy. Strether saw how she had perceived in a flash that they could n't quite look to going back there under his nose; though, honestly, as he gouged deeper into the matter, he was somewhat surprised, as Chad likewise had perhaps been, at the uprising of this scruple. He seemed even to divine that she had entertained it rather for Chad than for herself, and that, as the young man had lacked the chance to enlighten her, she had had to go on with it, he meanwhile mistaking her motive.

He was rather glad, none the less, that they had in point of fact not parted at the Cheval Blanc, that he had n't been reduced to giving them his blessing for an idyllic retreat down the river. He had had in the actual case to make-believe more than he liked, but this was nothing, it struck him, to what the other event would have required. Could he, literally, quite have faced the other event ? Would he have been capable of making the best of it with them ? This was what he was trying to do now; but with the advantage of his being able to give more time to it a good deal counteracted by his sense of what, over and above the central fact itself, he had to swallow. It was the quantity of make-believe involved and so vividly exemplified that most disagreed with his spiritual stomach. He moved,

however, from the consideration of that quantity —
to say nothing of the consciousness of that organ —
back to the other feature of the show, the deep, deep
truth of the intimacy revealed. That was what, in his
vain vigil, he oftenest reverted to: intimacy, at such
a point, was *like* that — and what in the world else
would one have wished it to be like? It was all very
well for him to feel the pity of its being so much like
lying; he almost blushed, in the dark, for the way he
had dressed the possibility in vagueness, as a little girl
might have dressed her doll. He had made them —
and by no fault of their own — momentarily pull it
for him, the possibility, out of this vagueness; and
must he not therefore take it now as they had had
simply, with whatever thin attenuations, to give it to
him? The very question, it may be added, made him
feel lonely and cold. There was the element of the
awkward all round, but Chad and Madame de Vionnet had at least the comfort that they could talk it over
together. With whom could *he* talk of such things?
— unless indeed always, at almost any stage, with
Maria? He foresaw that Miss Gostrey would come
again into requisition on the morrow; though it
was n't to be denied that he was already a little afraid
of her "What on earth — that 's what I want to know
now — had you then supposed?" He recognised at
last that he had really been trying all along to suppose nothing. Verily, verily, his labour had been lost.
He found himself supposing innumerable and wonderful things.

BOOK TWELFTH

I

STRETHER could n't have said he had during the previous hours definitely expected it; yet when, later on, that morning — though no later indeed than for his coming forth at ten o'clock — he saw the concierge produce, on his approach, a *petit bleu* delivered since his letters had been sent up, he recognised the appearance as the first symptom of a sequel. He then knew he had been thinking of some early sign from Chad as more likely, after all, than not; and this would be precisely the early sign. He took it so for granted that he opened the *petit bleu* just where he had stopped, in the pleasant cool draught of the porte-cochere — only curious to see where the young man would, at such a juncture, break out. His curiosity, however, was more than gratified; the small missive, whose gummed edge he had detached without attention to the address, not being from the young man at all, but from the person whom the case gave him on the spot as still more worth while. Worth while or not, he went round to the nearest telegraph-office, the big one on the Boulevard, with a directness that almost confessed to a fear of the danger of delay. He might have been thinking that if he did n't go before he could think he would n't perhaps go at all. He at any rate kept, in the lower side-pocket of his morning coat, a very deliberate hand on his blue missive, crumpling it up rather tenderly than harshly. He wrote a reply, on the Boulevard, also in the form of a *petit bleu* — which was quickly done, under pressure of the place, inasmuch as, like Madame de Vionnet's own communication, it consisted of the fewest words. She had asked him if he could do her the very great kindness of coming to see her that evening at half-past nine, and he answered, as if nothing were easier, that he would present himself at the hour she named. She had added a line of postscript, to the effect that she would come to him elsewhere and at his own hour if he preferred; but he took no notice of this, feeling that if he saw her at all half the value of it would be in seeing her where he had already seen her best. He might n't see her at all; that was one of the reflexions he made after writing and before he dropped his closed card into the box; he might n't see any one at all any more at all; he might make an end as well now as ever, leaving things as they were, since he was doubtless not to leave them better, and taking his way home so far as should appear that a home remained to him. This alternative was for a few minutes so sharp that if he at last did deposit his missive it was perhaps because the pressure of the place had an effect.

There was none other, however, than the common and constant pressure, familiar to our friend under the rubric of *Postes et Télégraphes* — the something in the air of these establishments; the vibration of the vast strange life of the town, the influence of the types, the performers concocting their messages; the little prompt Paris women, arranging, pretexting goodness knew what, driving the dreadful needle-pointed public pen at the dreadful sand-strewn public table: implements that symbolised for Strether's too interpretative innocence something more acute in manners, more sinister in morals, more fierce in the national life. After he had put in his paper he had ranged himself, he was really amused to think, on the side of the fierce, the sinister, the acute. He was carrying on a correspondence, across the great city, quite in the key of the *Postes et Télégraphes* in general; and it was fairly as if the acceptance of that fact had come from something in his state that sorted with the occupation of his neighbours. He was mixed up with the typical tale of Paris, and so were they, poor things — how could they all together help being? They were no worse than he, in short, and he no worse than they — if, queerly enough, no better; and at all events he had settled his hash, so that he went out to begin, from that moment, his day of waiting. The great settlement was, as he felt, in his preference for seeing his correspondent in her own best conditions. *That* was part of the typical tale, the part most significant in respect to himself. He liked the place she lived in, the picture that each time squared itself, large and high and clear, around her: every occasion of seeing it was a pleasure of a different shade. Yet what precisely was he doing with shades of pleasure now, and why had n't he properly and logically compelled her to commit herself to whatever of disadvantage and penalty the situation might throw up? He might have proposed, as for Sarah Pocock, the cold hospitality of his own *salon de lecture,* in which the chill of Sarah's visit seemed still to abide and shades of pleasure were dim; he might have suggested a stone bench in the dusty Tuileries or a penny chair at the back part of the Champs Elysées. These things would have been a trifle stern, and sternness alone now would n't be sinister. An instinct in him cast about for some form of discipline in which they might meet — some awkwardness they would suffer from, some danger, or at least some grave inconvenience, they would incur. This would give a sense — which the spirit required, rather ached and sighed in the absence of — that somebody was paying something somewhere and somehow, that they were at least not all floating together on the silver stream of impunity. Just instead of that to go and see her late in the evening, as if, for all the world — well, as if he were as much in the swim as anybody else : this had as little as possible in common with the penal form.

Even when he had felt that objection melt away, however, the practical difference was small; the long stretch of his interval took the colour it would, and if he lived on thus with the sinister from hour to hour it proved an easier thing than one might have supposed in advance. He reverted in thought to his old tradition, the one he had been brought up on and which even so many years of life had but little worn away; the notion that the state of the wrongdoer, or at least this person's happiness, presented some special difficulty. What struck him now rather was the ease of it—for nothing in truth appeared easier. It was an ease he himself fairly tasted of for the rest of the day; giving himself quite up; not so much as trying to dress it out, in any particular whatever, as a difficulty; not after all going to see Maria — which would have been in a manner a result of such dressing; only idling, lounging, smoking, sitting in the shade, drinking lemonade and consuming ices. The day had turned to heat and eventual thunder, and he now and again went back to his hotel to find that Chad had n't been there. He had n't yet struck himself, since leaving Woollett, so much as a loafer, though there had been times when he believed himself touching bottom. This was a deeper depth than any, and with no foresight, scarcely with a care, as to what he should bring up. He almost wondered if he did n't *look* demoralised and disreputable; he had the fanciful vision, as he sat and smoked, of some accidental, some motived, return of the Pococks, who would be passing along the Boulevard and would catch this view of him. They would have distinctly, on his appearance, every ground for scandal. But fate failed to administer even that sternness; the Pococks never passed and Chad made no sign. Strether meanwhile continued to hold off from Miss Gostrey, keeping her till to-morrow; so that by evening his irresponsibility, his impunity, his luxury, had become — there was no other word for them — immense.

Between nine and ten, at last, in the high clear picture — he was moving in these days, as in a gallery, from clever canvas to clever canvas — he drew a long breath: it was so presented to him from the first that the spell of his luxury would n't be broken. He would n't have, that is, to become responsible — this was admirably in the air: she had sent for

273

him precisely to let him feel it, so that he might go on with the comfort (comfort already established, had n't it been ?) of regarding his ordeal, the ordeal of the weeks of Sarah's stay and of their climax, as safely traversed and left behind him. Did n't she just wish to assure him that *she* now took it all and so kept it; that he was absolutely not to worry any more, was only to rest on his laurels and continue generously to help her ? The light in her beautiful formal room was dim, though it would do, as everything would always do; the hot night had kept out lamps, but there was a pair of clusters of candles that glimmered over the chimney-piece like the tall tapers of an altar. The windows were all open, their redundant hangings swaying a little, and he heard once more, from the empty court, the small plash of the fountain. From beyond this, and as from a great distance — beyond the court, beyond the *corps de logis* forming the front — came, as if excited and exciting, the vague voice of Paris. Strether had all along been subject to sudden gusts of fancy in connexion with such matters as these — odd starts of the historic sense, suppositions and divinations with no warrant but their intensity. Thus and so, on the eve of the great recorded dates, the days and nights of revolution, the sounds had come in, the omens, the beginnings broken out. They were the smell of revolution, the smell of the public temper — or perhaps simply the smell of blood.

It was at present queer beyond words, "subtle," he would have risked saying, that such suggestions should keep crossing the scene; but it was doubtless

the effect of the thunder in the air, which had hung
about all day without release. His hostess was dressed
as for thunderous times, and it fell in with the kind
of imagination we have just attributed to him that
she should be in simplest coolest white, of a character
so old-fashioned, if he were not mistaken, that Madame Roland must on the scaffold have worn something like it. This effect was enhanced by a small
black fichu or scarf, of crape or gauze, disposed
quaintly round her bosom and now completing as
by a mystic touch the pathetic, the noble analogy.
Poor Strether in fact scarce knew what analogy was
evoked for him as the charming woman, receiving
him and making him, as she could do such things, at
once familiarly and gravely welcome, moved over
her great room with her image almost repeated in its
polished floor, which had been fully bared for summer. The associations of the place, all felt again;
the gleam here and there, in the subdued light, of glass
and gilt and parquet, with the quietness of her own
note as the centre — these things were at first as delicate as if they had been ghostly, and he was sure in
a moment that, whatever he should find he had come
for, it would n't be for an impression that had pre-
viously failed him. That conviction held him from
the outset, and, seeming singularly to simplify, certi-
fied to him that the objects about would help him,
would really help them both. No, he might never
see them again — this was only too probably the last
time; and he should certainly see nothing in the least
degree like them. He should soon be going to where
such things were not, and it would be a small mercy

for memory, for fancy, to have, in that stress, a loaf on the shelf. He knew in advance he should look back on the perception actually sharpest with him as on the view of something old, old, old, the oldest thing he had ever personally touched; and he also knew, even while he took his companion in as the feature among features, that memory and fancy could n't help being enlisted for her. She might intend what she would, but this was beyond anything she could intend, with things from far back — tyrannies of history, facts of type, values, as the painters said, of expression — all working for her and giving her the supreme chance, the chance of the happy, the really luxurious few, the chance, on a great occasion, to be natural and simple. She had never, with him, been more so; or if it was the perfection of art it would never — and that came to the same thing — be proved against her.

What was truly wonderful was her way of differing so from time to time without detriment to her simplicity. Caprices, he was sure she felt, were before anything else bad manners, and that judgement in her was by itself a thing making more for safety of intercourse than anything that in his various own past intercourses he had had to reckon on. If therefore her presence was now quite other than the one she had shown him the night before, there was nothing of violence in the change — it was all harmony and reason. It gave him a mild deep person, whereas he had had on the occasion to which their interview was a direct reference a person committed to movement and surface and abounding in them; but she was in either character more remarkable for nothing than for her bridging of intervals, and this now fell in with what he understood he was to leave to her. The only thing was that, if he was to leave it *all* to her, why exactly had she sent for him ? He had had, vaguely, in advance, his explanation, his view of the probability of her wishing to set something right, to deal in some way with the fraud so lately practised on his presumed credulity. Would she attempt to carry it further or would she blot it out ? Would she throw over it some more or less happy colour; or would she do nothing about it at all ? He perceived soon enough at least that, however reasonable she might be, she was n't vulgarly confused, and it herewith pressed upon him that their eminent "lie," Chad's and hers, was simply after all such an inevitable tribute to good taste as he could n't have wished them not to render. Away from them, during his vigil, he had seemed to wince at the amount of comedy involved; whereas in his present posture he could only ask himself how he should enjoy any attempt from her to take the comedy back. He should n't enjoy it at all; but, once more and yet once more, he could trust her. That is he could trust her to make deception right. As she presented things the ugliness — goodness knew why — went out of them; none the less too that she could present them, with an art of her own, by not so much as touching them. She let the matter, at all events, lie where it was — where the previous twenty-four hours had placed it; appearing merely to circle about it respectfully, tenderly, almost piously, while she took up another question.

She knew she had n't really thrown dust in his eyes; this, the previous night, before they separated, had practically passed between them; and, as she had sent for him to see what the difference thus made for him might amount to, so he was conscious at the end of five minutes that he had been tried and tested. She had settled with Chad after he left them that she would, for her satisfaction, assure herself of this quantity, and Chad had, as usual, let her have her way. Chad was always letting people have their way when he felt that it would somehow turn his wheel for him; it somehow always did turn his wheel. Strether felt, oddly enough, before these facts, freshly and con-sentingly passive; they again so rubbed it into him that the couple thus fixing his attention were intimate, that his intervention had absolutely aided and intens-ified their intimacy, and that in fine he must accept the consequence of that. He had absolutely become, himself, with his perceptions and his mistakes, his concessions and his reserves, the droll mixture, as it must seem to them, of his braveries and his fears, the general spectacle of his art and his innocence, almost an added link and certainly a common price-less ground for them to meet upon. It was as if he had been hearing their very tone when she brought out a reference that was comparatively straight. "The last twice that you 've been here, you know, I never asked you," she said with an abrupt transition — they had been pretending before this to talk simply of the charm of yesterday and of the interest of the country they had seen. The effort was confessedly vain; not for such talk had she invited him; and her impatient reminder was of their having done for it all the needful on his coming to her after Sarah's flight. What she had n't asked him then was to state to her where and how he stood for her; she had been resting on Chad's report of their midnight hour together in the Boulevard Malesherbes. The thing therefore she at present desired was ushered in by this recall of the two occasions on which, disinterested and merciful, she had n't worried him. To-night truly she *would* worry him, and this was her appeal to him to let her risk it. He was n't to mind if she bored him a little: she had behaved, after all — had n't she ? — so awfully, awfully well.

II

"Oh, you're all right, you're all right," he almost impatiently declared; his impatience being moreover not for her pressure, but for her scruple. More and more distinct to him was the tune to which she would have had the matter out with Chad; more and more vivid for him the idea that she had been nervous as to what he might be able to "stand." Yes, it had been a question if he had "stood" what the scene on the river had given him, and, though the young man had doubtless opined in favour of his recuperation, her own last word must have been that she should feel easier in seeing for herself. That was it, unmistakeably; she *was* seeing for herself. What he could stand was thus, in these moments, in the balance for Strether, who reflected, as he became fully aware of it, that he must properly brace himself. He wanted fully to appear to stand all he might; and there was a certain command of the situation for him in this very wish not to look too much at sea. She was ready with everything, but so, sufficiently, was he; that is he was at one point the more prepared of the two, inasmuch as, for all her cleverness, she could n't produce on the spot — and it was surprising — an account of the motive of her note. He had the advantage that his pronouncing her "all right" gave him for an enquiry. "May I ask, delighted as I've been to come,

if you've wished to say something special?" He
spoke as if she might have seen he had been waiting
for it — not indeed with discomfort, but with natural
interest. Then he saw that she was a little taken
aback, was even surprised herself at the detail she
had neglected — the only one ever yet; having somehow assumed he would know, would recognise, would
leave some things not to be said. She looked at him,
however, an instant as if to convey that if he wanted
them *all* —!

"Selfish and vulgar — that's what I must seem to
you. You've done everything for me, and here I am
as if I were asking for more. But it is n't," she went
on, "because I 'm afraid — though I *am* of course
afraid, as a woman in my position always is. I mean
it is n't because one lives in terror — it is n't because
of that one is selfish, for I 'm ready to give you my
word to-night that I don't care; don't care what still
may happen and what I may lose. I don't ask you to
raise your little finger for me again, nor do I wish so
much as to mention to you what we've talked of before, either my danger or my safety, or his mother, or
his sister, or the girl he may marry, or the fortune
he may make or miss, or the right or the wrong, of
any kind, he may do. If after the help one has had
from you one can't either take care of one's self or
simply hold one's tongue, one must renounce all
claim to be an object of interest. It's in the name of
what I *do* care about that I 've tried still to keep hold
of you. How can I be indifferent," she asked, "to
how I appear to you?" And as he found himself unable immediately to say: "Why, if you 're going, *need*

you, after all? Is it impossible you should stay on
— so that one may n't lose you?"

"Impossible I should live with you here instead of
going home?"

"Not 'with' us, if you object to that, but near enough
to us, somewhere, for us to see you — well," she
beautifully brought out, "when we feel we *must*. How
shall we not sometimes feel it? I 've wanted to see
you often when I could n't," she pursued, "all these
last weeks. How shan't I then miss you now, with
the sense of your being gone forever?" Then as if
the straightness of this appeal, taking him unpre-
pared, had visibly left him wondering: "Where *is*
your 'home' moreover now — what has become of
it? I 've made a change in your life, I know I have;
I 've upset everything in your mind as well; in your
sense of — what shall I call it? — all the decencies
and possibilities. It gives me a kind of detestation—"
She pulled up short.

Oh but he wanted to hear. "Detestation of
what?"

"Of everything — of life."

"Ah that 's too much," he laughed — "or too
little!"

"Too little, precisely" — she was eager. "What I
hate is myself — when I think that one has to take
so much, to be happy, out of the lives of others, and
that one is n't happy even then. One does it to cheat
one's self and to stop one's mouth — but that 's only
at the best for a little. The wretched self is always
there, always making one somehow a fresh anxiety.
What it comes to is that it 's not, that it 's never, a

happiness, any happiness at all, to *take*. The only safe thing is to give. It's what plays you least false." Interesting, touching, strikingly sincere as she let these things come from her, she yet puzzled and troubled him — so fine was the quaver of her quietness. He felt what he had felt before with her, that there was always more behind what she showed, and more and more again behind that. "You know so, at least," she added, "where you are!"

"*You* ought to know it indeed then; for isn't what you've been giving exactly what has brought us together this way? You've been making, as I've so fully let you know I've felt," Strether said, "the most precious present I've ever seen made, and if you can't sit down peacefully on that performance you *are*, no doubt, born to torment yourself. But you ought," he wound up, "to be easy."

"And not trouble you any more, no doubt — not thrust on you even the wonder and the beauty of what I've done; only let you regard our business as over, and well over, and see you depart in a peace that matches my own? No doubt, no doubt, no doubt," she nervously repeated — "all the more that I don't really pretend I believe you couldn't, for yourself, *not* have done what you have. I don't pretend you feel yourself victimised, for this evidently is the way you live, and it's what — we're agreed — is the best way. Yes, as you say," she continued after a moment, "I ought to be easy and rest on my work. Well then here am I doing so. I *am* easy. You'll have it for your last impression. When is it you say you go?" she asked with a quick change.

He took some time to reply — his last impression was more and more so mixed a one. It produced in him a vague disappointment, a drop that was deeper even than the fall of his elation the previous night. The good of what he had done, if he had done so much, was n't there to enliven him quite to the point that would have been ideal for a grand gay finale. Women were thus endlessly absorbent, and to deal with them was to walk on water. What was at bottom the matter with her, embroider as she might and disclaim as she might — what was at bottom the matter with her was simply Chad himself. It was of Chad she was after all renewedly afraid; the strange strength of her passion was the very strength of her fear; she clung to *him*, Lambert Strether, as to a source of safety she had tested, and, generous graceful truthful as she might try to be, exquisite as she was, she dreaded the term of his being within reach. With this sharpest perception yet, it was like a chill in the air to him, it was almost appalling, that a creature so fine could be, by mysterious forces, a creature so exploited. For at the end of all things they *were* mysterious: she had but made Chad what he was — so why could she think she had made him infinite ? She had made him better, she had made him best, she had made him anything one would; but it came to our friend with supreme queerness that he was none the less only Chad. Strether had the sense that *he*, a little, had made him too; his high appreciation had, as it were, consecrated her work. The work, however admirable, was nevertheless of the strict human order, and in short it was marvellous that the compan-

ion of mere earthly joys, of comforts, aberrations
(however one classed them) within the common experience, should be so transcendently prized. It might
have made Strether hot or shy, as such secrets of
others brought home sometimes do make us; but
he was held there by something so hard that it was
fairly grim. This was not the discomposure of last
night; that had quite passed — such discomposures
were a detail; the real coercion was to see a man in-
effably adored. There it was again — it took women,
it took women; if to deal with them was to walk on
water what wonder that the water rose? And it had
never surely risen higher than round this woman.
He presently found himself taking a long look from
her, and the next thing he knew he had uttered all
his thought. "You're afraid for your life!"

It drew out her long look, and he soon enough saw
why. A spasm came into her face, the tears she had
already been unable to hide overflowed at first in
silence, and then, as the sound suddenly comes from
a child, quickened to gasps, to sobs. She sat and
covered her face with her hands, giving up all attempt at a manner. "It's how you see me, it's how
you see me" — she caught her breath with it —
"and it's as I *am*, and as I must take myself, and of
course it's no matter." Her emotion was at first so
incoherent that he could only stand there at a loss,
stand with his sense of having upset her, though of
having done it by the truth. He had to listen to her in
a silence that he made no immediate effort to atten-
uate, feeling her doubly woeful amid all her dim diffused elegance; consenting to it as he had consented

285

to the rest, and even conscious of some vague inward irony in the presence of such a fine free range of bliss and bale. He could n't say it was *not* no matter; for he was serving her to the end, he now knew, anyway — quite as if what he thought of her had nothing to do with it. It was actually moreover as if he did n't think of her at all, as if he could think of nothing but the passion, mature, abysmal, pitiful, she represented, and the possibilities she betrayed. She was older for him to-night, visibly less exempt from the touch of time; but she was as much as ever the finest and subtlest creature, the happiest apparition, it had been given him, in all his years, to meet; and yet he could see her there as vulgarly troubled, in very truth, as a maidservant crying for her young man. The only thing was that she judged herself as the maidservant would n't; the weakness of which wisdom too, the dishonour of which judgement, seemed but to sink her lower. Her collapse, however, no doubt, was briefer and she had in a manner recovered herself before he intervened. "Of course I'm afraid for my life. But that's nothing. It is n't that."

He was silent a little longer, as if thinking what it might be. "There's something I have in mind that I can still do."

But she threw off at last, with a sharp sad headshake, drying her eyes, what he could still do. "I don't care for that. Of course, as I've said, you're acting, in your wonderful way, for yourself; and what's for yourself is no more my business — though I may reach out unholy hands so clumsily to touch it — than if it were something in Timbuctoo. It's only that

286

you don't snub me, as you've had fifty chances to do —
it's only your beautiful patience that makes one forget one's manners. In spite of your patience, all the
same," she went on, "you'd do anything rather than
be with us here, even if that were possible. You'd do
everything for us but be mixed up with us — which is
a statement you can easily answer to the advantage
of your own manners. You can say 'What's the use
of talking of things that at the best are impossible?'
What *is* of course the use? It's only my little mad-
ness. You'd talk if you were tormented. And I don't
mean now about *him*. Oh for him —!" Positively,
strangely, bitterly, as it seemed to Strether, she gave
"him," for the moment, away. "You don't care
what I think of you; but I happen to care what you
think of me. And what you *might*," she added.
"What you perhaps even did."

He gained time. "What I did —?"

"Did think before. Before this. *Did n't* you
think —?"

But he had already stopped her. "I did n't think
anything. I never think a step further than I'm
obliged to."

"That's perfectly false, I believe," she returned
— "except that you may, no doubt, often pull up
when things become *too* ugly; or even, I'll say, to
save you a protest, too beautiful. At any rate, even
so far as it's true, we've thrust on you appearances
that you've had to take in and that have therefore
made your obligation. Ugly or beautiful — it does n't
matter what we call them — you were getting on
without them, and that's where we're detestable.

We bore you — that's where we are. And we may well — for what we've cost you. All you can do *now* is not to think at all. And I who should have liked to seem to you — well, sublime!"

He could only after a moment re-echo Miss Barrace. "You're wonderful!"

"I'm old and abject and hideous" — she went on as without hearing him. "Abject above all. Or old above all. It's when one's old that it's worst. I don't care what becomes of it — let what *will;* there it is. It's a doom — I know it; you can't see it more than I do myself. Things have to happen as they will." With which she came back again to what, face to face with him, had so quite broken down. "Of course you would n't, even if possible, and no matter what may happen to you, be near us. But think of me, think of me —!" She exhaled it into air.

He took refuge in repeating something he had already said and that she had made nothing of. "There's something I believe I can still do." And he put his hand out for good-bye.

She again made nothing of it; she went on with her insistence. "That won't help you. There's nothing to help you."

"Well, it may help *you*," he said.

She shook her head. "There's not a grain of certainty in my future — for the only certainty is that I shall be the loser in the end."

She had n't taken his hand, but she moved with him to the door. "That's cheerful," he laughed, "for your benefactor!"

"What's cheerful for *me*," she replied, "is that we

might, you and I, have been friends. That's it —
that's it. You see how, as I say, I want everything.
I've wanted you too."

"Ah but you've *had* me!" he declared, at the
door, with an emphasis that made an end.

III

His purpose had been to see Chad the next day, and he had prefigured seeing him by an early call; having in general never stood on ceremony in respect to visits at the Boulevard Malesherbes. It had been more often natural for him to go there than for Chad to come to the small hotel, the attractions of which were scant; yet it nevertheless, just now, at the eleventh hour, did suggest itself to Strether to begin by giving the young man a chance. It struck him that, in the inevitable course, Chad would be "round," as Waymarsh used to say — Waymarsh who already, somehow, seemed long ago. He had n't come the day before, because it had been arranged between them that Madame de Vionnet should see their friend first; but now that this passage had taken place he would present himself, and their friend would n't have long to wait. Strether assumed, he became aware, on this reasoning, that the interesting parties to the arrangement would have met betimes, and that the more interesting of the two — as she was after all — would have communicated to the other the issue of her appeal. Chad would know without delay that his mother's messenger had been with her, and, though it was perhaps not quite easy to see how she could qualify what had occurred, he would at least have been sufficiently advised to feel he could go on. The day, however, brought, early or late, no word from

290

him, and Strether felt, as a result of this, that a change had practically come over their intercourse. It was perhaps a premature judgement; or it only meant perhaps — how could he tell? — that the wonderful pair he protected had taken up again together the excursion he had accidentally checked. They might have gone back to the country, and gone back but with a long breath drawn; that indeed would best mark Chad's sense that reprobation had n't rewarded Madame de Vionnet's request for an interview. At the end of the twenty-four hours, at the end of the forty-eight, there was still no overture; so that Strether filled up the time, as he had so often filled it before, by going to see Miss Gostrey.

He proposed amusements to her; he felt expert now in proposing amusements; and he had thus, for several days, an odd sense of leading her about Paris, of driving her in the Bois, of showing her the penny steamboats — those from which the breeze of the Seine was to be best enjoyed — that might have belonged to a kindly uncle doing the honours of the capital to an intelligent niece from the country. He found means even to take her to shops she did n't know, or that she pretended she did n't; while she, on her side, was, like the country maiden, all passive modest and grateful — going in fact so far as to emulate rusticity in occasional fatigues and bewilderments. Strether described these vague proceedings to himself, described them even to her, as a happy interlude; the sign of which was that the companions said for the time no further word about the matter they had talked of to satiety. He proclaimed sati-

ety at the outset, and she quickly took the hint; as
docile both in this and in everything else as the
intelligent obedient niece. He told her as yet nothing
of his late adventure — for as an adventure it now
ranked with him; he pushed the whole business
temporarily aside and found his interest in the fact
of her beautiful assent. She left questions unasked —
she who for so long had been all questions; she gave
herself up to him with an understanding of which
mere mute gentleness might have seemed the sufficient expression. She knew his sense of his situation
had taken still another step — of that he was quite
aware; but she conveyed that, whatever had thus
happened for him, it was thrown into the shade by
what was happening for herself. This — though it
might n't to a detached spirit have seemed much —
was the major interest, and she met it with a new
directness of response, measuring it from hour to
hour with her grave hush of acceptance. Touched
as he had so often been by her before, he was, for his
part too, touched afresh; all the more that though
he could be duly aware of the principle of his own
mood he could n't be equally so of the principle of
hers. He knew, that is, in a manner — knew roughly
and resignedly — what he himself was hatching;
whereas he had to take the chance of what he called
to himself Maria's calculations. It was all he needed
that she liked him enough for what they were doing,
and even should they do a good deal more would still
like him enough for that; the essential freshness of
a relation so simple was a cool bath to the soreness
produced by other relations. These others appeared

to him now horribly complex; they bristled with fine points, points all unimaginable beforehand, points that pricked and drew blood; a fact that gave to an hour with his present friend on a *bateau-mouche*, or in the afternoon shade of the Champs Elysées, something of the innocent pleasure of handling rounded ivory. His relation with Chad personally — from the moment he had got his point of view — had been of the simplest; yet this also struck him as bristling, after a third and a fourth blank day had passed. It was as if at last however his care for such indications had dropped; there came a fifth blank day and he ceased to enquire or to heed.

They now took on to his fancy, Miss Gostrey and he, the image of the Babes in the Wood; they could trust the merciful elements to let them continue at peace. He had been great already, as he knew, at postponements; but he had only to get afresh into the rhythm of one to feel its fine attraction. It amused him to say to himself that he might for all the world have been going to die — die resignedly; the scene was filled for him with so deep a death-bed hush, so melancholy a charm. That meant the postponement of everything else — which made so for the quiet lapse of life; and the postponement in especial of the reckoning to come — unless indeed the reckoning to come were to be one and the same thing with extinction. It faced him, the reckoning, over the shoulder of much interposing experience — which also faced him; and one would float to it doubtless duly through these caverns of Kubla Khan. It was really behind everything; it had n't merged in what he had done; his final appreciation of what he had done — his appreciation on the spot — would provide it with its main sharpness. The spot so focussed was of course Woollett, and he was to see, at the best, what Woollett would be with everything there changed for him. Would n't *that* revelation practically amount to the wind-up of his career? Well, the summer's end would show; his suspense had meanwhile exactly the sweetness of vain delay; and he had with it, we should mention, other pastimes than Maria's company — plenty of separate musings in which his luxury failed him but at one point. He was well in port, the outer sea behind him, and it was only a matter of getting ashore. There was a question that came and went for him, however, as he rested against the side of his ship, and it was a little to get rid of the obsession that he prolonged his hours with Miss Gostrey. It was a question about himself, but it could only be settled by seeing Chad again; it was indeed his principal reason for wanting to see Chad. After that it would n't signify — it was a ghost that certain words would easily lay to rest. Only the young man must be there to take the words. Once they were taken he would n't have a question left; none, that is, in connexion with this particular affair. It would n't then matter even to himself that he might now have been guilty of speaking *because* of what he had forfeited. That was the refinement of his supreme scruple — he wished so to leave what he had forfeited out of account. He wished not to do anything because he had missed something else, because he was sore or sorry or impoverished, because he was maltreated or desperate; he wished to do everything because he was lucid and quiet, just the same for himself on all essential points as he had ever been. Thus it was that while he virtually hung about for Chad he kept mutely putting it: "You've been chucked, old boy; but what has that to do with it?" It would have sickened him to feel vindictive.

These tints of feeling indeed were doubtless but the iridescence of his idleness, and they were presently lost in a new light from Maria. She had a fresh fact for him before the week was out, and she practically met him with it on his appearing one night. He hadn't on this day seen her, but had planned presenting himself in due course to ask her to dine with him somewhere out of doors, on one of the terraces, in one of the gardens, of which the Paris of summer was profuse. It had then come on to rain, so that, disconcerted, he changed his mind; dining alone at home, a little stuffily and stupidly, and waiting on her afterwards to make up his loss. He was sure within a minute that something had happened; it was so in the air of the rich little room that he had scarcely to name his thought. Softly lighted, the whole colour of the place, with its vague values, was in cool fusion — an effect that made the visitor stand for a little agaze. It was as if in doing so now he had felt a recent presence — his recognition of the passage of which his hostess in turn divined. She had scarcely to say it — "Yes, she has been here, and this time I received her." It wasn't till a minute later that she added: "There being, as I understand you, no reason *now*—!"

THE AMBASSADORS

"None for your refusing?"

"No—if you've done what you've had to do."

"I've certainly so far done it," Strether said, "as that you need n't fear the effect, or the appearance of coming between us. There's nothing between us now but what we ourselves have put there, and not an inch of room for anything else whatever. Therefore you're only beautifully *with* us as always — though doubtless now, if she has talked to you, rather more with us than less. Of course if she came," he added, "it was to talk to you."

"It was to talk to me," Maria returned; on which he was further sure that she was practically in possession of what he himself had n't yet told her. He was even sure she was in possession of things he himself could n't have told; for the consciousness of them was now all in her face and accompanied there with a shade of sadness that marked in her the close of all uncertainties. It came out for him more than ever yet that she had had from the first a knowledge she believed him not to have had, a knowledge the sharp acquisition of which might be destined to make a difference for him. The difference for him might not inconceivably be an arrest of his independence and a change in his attitude — in other words a revulsion in favour of the principles of Woollett. She had really prefigured the possibility of a shock that would send him swinging back to Mrs. Newsome. He had n't, it was true, week after week, shown signs of receiving it, but the possibility had been none the less in the air. What Maria accordingly had had now to take in was that the shock had descended and

296

that he had n't, all the same, swung back. He had
grown clear, in a flash, on a point long since settled
for herself; but no reapproximation to Mrs. Newsome had occurred in consequence. Madame de
Vionnet had by her visit held up the torch to these
truths, and what now lingered in poor Maria's face
was the somewhat smoky light of the scene between
them. If the light however was n't, as we have hinted,
the glow of joy, the reasons for this also were perhaps
discernible to Strether even through the blur cast over
them by his natural modesty. She had held herself
for months with a firm hand; she had n't interfered
on any chance — and chances were specious enough
— that she might interfere to her profit. She had
turned her back on the dream that Mrs. Newsome's
rupture, their friend's forfeiture — the engagement,
the relation itself, broken beyond all mending —
might furnish forth her advantage; and, to stay her
hand from promoting these things, she had, on
private, difficult, but rigid, lines, played strictly fair.
She could n't therefore but feel that, though, as the
end of all, the facts in question had been stoutly
confirmed, her ground for personal, for what might
have been called interested, elation remained rather
vague. Strether might easily have made out that she
had been asking herself, in the hours she had just
sat through, if there were still for her, or were only
not, a fair shade of uncertainty. Let us hasten to add,
however, that what he at first made out on this occasion he also at first kept to himself. He only asked
what in particular Madame de Vionnet had come
for; and as to this his companion was ready.

"She wants tidings of Mr. Newsome, whom she appears not to have seen for some days."

"Then she has n't been away with him again?"

"She seemed to think," Maria answered, "that he might have gone away with *you*."

"And did you tell her I know nothing of him?"

She had her indulgent headshake. "I've known nothing of what you know. I could only tell her I'd ask you."

"Then I've not seen him for a week — and of course I've wondered." His wonderment showed at this moment as sharper, but he presently went on. "Still, I dare say I can put my hand on him. Did she strike you," he asked, "as anxious?"

"She's always anxious."

"After all I've done for her?" And he had one of the last flickers of his occasional mild mirth. "To think that was just what I came out to prevent!"

She took it up but to reply. "You don't regard him then as safe?"

"I was just going to ask you how in that respect you regard Madame de Vionnet."

She looked at him a little. "What woman was *ever* safe? She told me," she added — and it was as if at the touch of the connexion — "of your extraordinary meeting in the country. After that *à quoi se fier?*"

"It was, as an accident, in all the possible or impossible chapter," Strether conceded, "amazing enough. But still, but still —!"

"But still she did n't mind?"

"She does n't mind anything."

BOOK TWELFTH

"Well, then, as you don't either, we may all sink
to rest!"

He appeared to agree with her, but he had his
reservation. "I do mind Chad's disappearance."

"Oh you'll get him back. But now you know,"
she said, "why I went to Mentone." He had sufficiently let her see that he had by this time gathered
things together, but there was nature in her wish to
make them clearer still. "I did n't want you to put
it to me."

"To put it to you —?"

"The question of what you were at last — a week
ago — to see for yourself. I did n't want to have to
lie for her. I felt that to be too much for me. A man
of course is always expected to do it — to do it, I
mean, for a woman; but not a woman for another
woman; unless perhaps on the tit-for-tat principle, as
an indirect way of protecting herself. I don't need
protection, so that I was free to 'funk' you — simply
to dodge your test. The responsibility was too much
for me. I gained time, and when I came back the
need of a test had blown over."

Strether thought of it serenely. "Yes; when you
came back little Bilham had shown me what's expected
of a gentleman. Little Bilham had lied like one."

"And like what you believed him?"

"Well," said Strether, "it was but a technical lie
— he classed the attachment as virtuous. That was
a view for which there was much to be said — and
the virtue came out for me hugely. There was of
course a great deal of it. I got it full in the face, and
I have n't, you see, done with it yet."

"What I see, what I saw," Maria returned, "is that you dressed up even the virtue. You were wonderful — you were beautiful, as I've had the honour of telling you before; but, if you wish really to know," she sadly confessed, "I never quite knew *where* you were. There were moments," she explained, "when you struck me as grandly cynical; there were others when you struck me as grandly vague."

Her friend considered. "I had phases. I had flights."

"Yes, but things must have a basis."

"A basis seemed to me just what her beauty supplied."

"Her beauty of person?"

"Well, her beauty of everything. The impression she makes. She has such variety and yet such harmony."

She considered him with one of her deep returns of indulgence — returns out of all proportion to the irritations they flooded over. "You're complete."

"You're always too personal," he good-humouredly said; "but that's precisely how I wondered and wandered."

"If you mean," she went on, "that she was from the first for you the most charming woman in the world, nothing's more simple. Only that was an odd foundation."

"For what I reared on it?"

"For what you did n't!"

"Well, it was all not a fixed quantity. And it had for me — it has still — such elements of strangeness. Her greater age than his, her different world, traditions, association; her other opportunities, liabilities, standards."

His friend listened with respect to his enumeration of these disparities; then she disposed of them at a stroke. "Those things are nothing when a woman's hit. It's very awful. She was hit."

Strether, on his side, did justice to that plea. "Oh of course I saw she was hit. That she was hit was what we were busy with; that she was hit was our great affair. But somehow I could n't think of her as down in the dust. And as put there by *our* little Chad!"

"Yet was n't 'your' little Chad just your miracle?"

Strether admitted it. "Of course I moved among miracles. It was all phantasmagoric. But the great fact was that so much of it was none of my business — as I saw my business. It is n't even now."

His companion turned away on this, and it might well have been yet again with the sharpness of a fear of how little his philosophy could bring her personally. "I wish *she* could hear you!"

"Mrs. Newsome?"

"No — not Mrs. Newsome; since I understand you that it does n't matter now what Mrs. Newsome hears. Has n't she heard everything?"

"Practically — yes." He had thought a moment, but he went on. "You wish Madame de Vionnet could hear me?"

"Madame de Vionnet." She had come back to him. "She thinks just the contrary of what you say. That you distinctly judge her."

He turned over the scene as the two women thus

placed together for him seemed to give it. "She might have known —!"

"Might have known you don't?" Miss Gostrey asked as he let it drop. "She was sure of it at first," she pursued as he said nothing; "she took it for granted, at least, as any woman in her position would. But after that she changed her mind; she believed you believed —"

"Well?" — he was curious.

"Why in her sublimity. And that belief had remained with her, I make out, till the accident of the other day opened your eyes. For that it did," said Maria, "open them —"

"She can't help" — he had taken it up — "being aware? No," he mused; "I suppose she thinks of that even yet."

"Then they *were* closed? There you are! However, if you see her as the most charming woman in the world it comes to the same thing. And if you'd like me to tell her that you do still so see her —!" Miss Gostrey, in short, offered herself for service to the end.

It was an offer he could temporarily entertain; but he decided. "She knows perfectly how I see her."

"Not favourably enough, she mentioned to me, to wish ever to see her again. She told me you had taken a final leave of her. She says you've done with her."

"So I have."

Maria had a pause; then she spoke as if for conscience. "She wouldn't have done with *you*. She feels she has lost you — yet that she might have been better for you."

"Oh she has been quite good enough!" Strether laughed.

"She thinks you and she might at any rate have been friends."

"We might certainly. That's just" — he continued to laugh — "why I'm going."

It was as if Maria could feel with this then at last that she had done her best for each. But she had still an idea. "Shall I tell her that?"

"No. Tell her nothing."

"Very well then." To which in the next breath Miss Gostrey added: "Poor dear thing!"

Her friend wondered; then with raised eyebrows: "Me?"

"Oh no. Marie de Vionnet."

He accepted the correction, but he wondered still. "Are you so sorry for her as that?"

It made her think a moment — made her even speak with a smile. But she did n't really retract. "I'm sorry for us all!"

IV

HE was to delay no longer to re-establish communication with Chad, and we have just seen that he had spoken to Miss Gostrey of this intention on hearing from her of the young man's absence. It was not moreover only the assurance so given that prompted him; it was the need of causing his conduct to square with another profession still — the motive he had described to her as his sharpest for now getting away. If he was to get away because of some of the relations involved in staying, the cold attitude toward them might look pedantic in the light of lingering on. He must do both things; he must see Chad, but he must go. The more he thought of the former of these duties the more he felt himself make a subject of insistence of the latter. They were alike intensely present to him as he sat in front of a quiet little café into which he had dropped on quitting Maria's entresol. The rain that had spoiled his evening with her was over; for it was still to him as if his evening *had* been spoiled — though it might n't have been wholly the rain. It was late when he left the café, yet not too late; he could n't in any case go straight to bed, and he would walk round by the Boulevard Malesherbes — rather far round — on his way home. Present enough always was the small circumstance that had originally pressed for him the spring of so big a difference — the accident of little Bilham's appearance on the

304

balcony of the mystic troisième at the moment of his
first visit, and the effect of it on his sense of what
was then before him. He recalled his watch, his wait,
and the recognition that had proceeded from the
young stranger, that had played frankly into the air
and had presently brought him up — things smoothing
the way for his first straight step. He had since had
occasion, a few times, to pass the house without going
in; but he had never passed it without again feeling
how it had then spoken to him. He stopped short to-
night on coming to sight of it: it was as if his last day
were oddly copying his first. The windows of Chad's
apartment were open to the balcony — a pair of them
lighted; and a figure that had come out and taken up
little Bilham's attitude, a figure whose cigarette-spark
he could see leaned on the rail and looked down at
him. It denoted however no reappearance of his
younger friend; it quickly defined itself in the tem-
pered darkness as Chad's more solid shape; so that
Chad's was the attention that, after he had stepped
forward into the street and signalled, he easily engaged; Chad's was the voice that, sounding into the
night with promptness and seemingly with joy,
greeted him and called him up.

That the young man had been visible there just in
this position expressed somehow for Strether that,
as Maria Gostrey had reported, he had been absent
and silent; and our friend drew breath on each land-
ing — the lift, at that hour, having ceased to work —
before the implications of the fact. He had been for
a week intensely away, away to a distance and alone;
but he was more back than ever, and the attitude in

which Strether had surprised him was something more than a return — it was clearly a conscious surrender. He had arrived but an hour before, from London, from Lucerne, from Homburg, from no matter where — though the visitor's fancy, on the staircase, liked to fill it out; and after a bath, a talk with Baptiste and a supper of light cold clever French things, which one could see the remains of there in the circle of the lamp, pretty and ultra-Parisian, he had come into the air again for a smoke, was occupied at the moment of Strether's approach in what might have been called taking up his life afresh. His life, his life! — Strether paused anew, on the last flight, at this final rather breathless sense of what Chad's life was doing with Chad's mother's emissary. It was dragging him, at strange hours, up the staircases of the rich; it was keeping him out of bed at the end of long hot days; it was transforming beyond recognition the simple, subtle, conveniently uniform thing that had anciently passed with him for a life of his own. Why should it concern him that Chad was to be fortified in the pleasant practice of smoking on balconies, of supping on salads, of feeling his special conditions agreeably reaffirm themselves, of finding reassurance in comparisons and contrasts? There was no answer to such a question but that he was still practically committed — he had perhaps never yet so much known it. It made him feel old, and he would buy his railway-ticket — feeling, no doubt, older — the next day; but he had meanwhile come up four flights, counting the entresol, at midnight and without a lift, for Chad's life. The young man, hearing him by this time, and with Baptiste sent to rest, was already at the door; so that Strether had before him in full visibility the cause in which he was labouring and even, with the troisième fairly gained, panting a little.

Chad offered him, as always, a welcome in which the cordial and the formal — so far as the formal was the respectful — handsomely met; and after he had expressed a hope that he would let him put him up for the night Strether was in full possession of the key, as it might have been called, to what had lately happened. If he had just thought of himself as old Chad was at sight of him thinking of him as older: he wanted to put him up for the night just because he was ancient and weary. It could never be said the tenant of these quarters was n't nice to him; a tenant who, if he might indeed now keep him, was probably prepared to work it all still more thoroughly. Our friend had in fact the impression that with the minimum of encouragement Chad would propose to keep him indefinitely; an impression in the lap of which one of his own possibilities seemed to sit. Madame de Vionnet had wished him to stay — so why did n't that happily fit? He could enshrine himself for the rest of his days in his young host's *chambre d'ami* and draw out these days at his young host's expense: there could scarce be greater logical expression of the countenance he had been moved to give. There was literally a minute — it was strange enough — during which he grasped the idea that as he *was* acting, as he could only act, he was inconsistent. The sign that the inward forces he had

obeyed really hung together would be that — in de-
fault always of another career — he should promote
the good cause by mounting guard on it. These
things, during his first minutes, came and went; but
they were after all practically disposed of as soon as
he had mentioned his errand. He had come to say
good-bye — yet that was only a part; so that from
the moment Chad accepted his farewell the question
of a more ideal affirmation gave way to something
else. He proceeded with the rest of his business.
"You'll be a brute, you know — you'll be guilty of
the last infamy — if you ever forsake her."

That, uttered there at the solemn hour, uttered in
the place that was full of her influence, was the rest
of his business; and when once he had heard himself
say it he felt that his message had never before been
spoken. It placed his present call immediately on
solid ground, and the effect of it was to enable him
quite to play with what we have called the key. Chad
showed no shade of embarrassment, but had none
the less been troubled for him after their meeting in
the country; had had fears and doubts on the subject
of his comfort. He was disturbed, as it were, only
for him, and had positively gone away to ease him
off, to let him down — if it wasn't indeed rather
to screw him up — the more gently. Seeing him now
fairly jaded he had come with characteristic good
humour, all the way to meet him, and what Strether
thereupon supremely made out was that he would
abound for him to the end in conscientious assurances. This was what was between them while the
visitor remained; so far from having to go over old

ground he found his entertainer keen to agree to everything. It could n't be put too strongly for him that he 'd be a brute. "Oh rather! — if I should do anything of *that* sort. I hope you believe I really feel it."

"I want it," said Strether, "to be my last word of all to you. I can't say more, you know; and I don't see how I can do more, in every way, than I 've done."

Chad took this, almost artlessly, as a direct allusion. "You 've seen her ?"

"Oh yes — to say good-bye. And if I had doubted the truth of what I tell you —"

"She 'd have cleared up your doubt ?" Chad understood — "rather" — again! It even kept him briefly silent. But he made that up. "She must have been wonderful."

"She *was*," Strether candidly admitted — all of which practically told as a reference to the conditions created by the accident of the previous week.

They appeared for a little to be looking back at it; and that came out still more in what Chad next said. "I don't know what you 've really thought, all along; I never did know — for anything, with you, seemed to be possible. But of course — of course —" Without confusion, quite with nothing but indulgence, he broke down, he pulled up. "After all, you understand. I spoke to you originally only as I *had* to speak. There 's only one way — is n't there ? — about such things. However," he smiled with a final philosophy, "I see it 's all right."

Strether met his eyes with a sense of multiplying thoughts. What was it that made him at present, late

at night and after journeys, so renewedly, so substantially young? Strether saw in a moment what it
was — it was that he was younger again than Madame de Vionnet. He himself said immediately none
of the things that he was thinking; he said something
quite different. "You *have* really been to a distance?"

"I've been to England." Chad spoke cheerfully
and promptly, but gave no further account of it than
to say: "One must sometimes get off."

Strether wanted no more facts — he only wanted
to justify, as it were, his question. "Of course you
do as you're free to do. But I hope, this time, that
you did n't go for *me*."

"For very shame at bothering you really too much?
My dear man," Chad laughed, "what *would n't* I do
for you?"

Strether's easy answer for this was that it was a
disposition he had exactly come to profit by. "Even
at the risk of being in your way I've waited on, you
know, for a definite reason."

Chad took it in. "Oh yes — for us to make if possible a still better impression." And he stood there
happily exhaling his full general consciousness. "I'm
delighted to gather that you feel we've made it."

There was a pleasant irony in the words, which
his guest, preoccupied and keeping to the point, did n't
take up. "If I had my sense of wanting the rest of
the time — the time of their being still on this side,"
he continued to explain — "I know now why I
wanted it."

He was as grave, as distinct, as a demonstrator
before a blackboard, and Chad continued to face him

like an intelligent pupil. "You wanted to have been put through the whole thing."

Strether again, for a moment, said nothing; he turned his eyes away, and they lost themselves, through the open window, in the dusky outer air. "I shall learn from the Bank here where they're now having their letters, and my last word, which I shall write in the morning and which they're expecting as my ultimatum, will so immediately reach them." The light of his plural pronoun was sufficiently reflected in his companion's face as he again met it; and he completed his demonstration. He pursued indeed as if for himself. "Of course I've first to justify what I shall do."

"You're justifying it beautifully!" Chad declared.

"It's not a question of advising you not to go," Strether said, "but of absolutely preventing you, if possible, from so much as thinking of it. Let me accordingly appeal to you by all you hold sacred."

Chad showed a surprise. "What makes you think me capable — ?"

"You'd not only be, as I say, a brute; you'd be," his companion went on in the same way, "a criminal of the deepest dye."

Chad gave a sharper look, as if to gauge a possible suspicion. "I don't know what should make you think I'm tired of her."

Strether didn't quite know either, and such impressions, for the imaginative mind, were always too fine, too floating, to produce on the spot their warrant. There was none the less for him, in the very manner of his host's allusion to satiety as a thinkable

311

motive, a slight breath of the ominous. "I feel how much more she can do for you. She has n't done it all yet. Stay with her at least till she has."

"And leave her *then*?"

Chad had kept smiling, but its effect in Strether was a shade of dryness. "Don't leave her *before*. When you've got all that can be got — I don't say," he added a trifle grimly. "That will be the proper time. But as, for you, from such a woman, there will always be something to be got, my remark's not a wrong to her." Chad let him go on, showing every decent deference, showing perhaps also a candid curiosity for this sharper accent. "I remember you, you know, as you were."

"An awful ass, was n't I?"

The response was as prompt as if he had pressed a spring; it had a ready abundance at which he even winced; so that he took a moment to meet it. "You certainly then would n't have seemed worth all you've let me in for. You've defined yourself better. Your value has quintupled."

"Well then, would n't that be enough — ?"

Chad had risked it jocosely, but Strether remained blank. "Enough?"

"If one *should* wish to live on one's accumulations?" After which, however, as his friend appeared cold to the joke, the young man as easily dropped it. "Of course I really never forget, night or day, what I owe her. I owe her everything. I give you my word of honour," he frankly rang out, "that I 'm not a bit tired of her." Strether at this only gave him a stare: the way youth could express itself was again and again a wonder. He meant no harm, though he might after all be capable of much; yet he spoke of being "tired" of her almost as he might have spoken of being tired of roast mutton for dinner. "She has never for a moment yet bored me — never been wanting, as the cleverest women sometimes are, in tact. She has never talked about her tact — as even they too sometimes talk; but she has always had it. She has never had it more" — he handsomely made the point — "than just lately." And he scrupulously went further. "She has never been anything I could call a burden."

Strether for a moment said nothing; then he spoke gravely, with his shade of dryness deepened. "Oh if you did n't do her justice —!"

"I *should* be a beast, eh?"

Strether devoted no time to saying what he would be; *that*, visibly, would take them far. If there was nothing for it but to repeat, however, repetition was no mistake. "You owe her everything — very much more than she can ever owe you. You've in other words duties to her, of the most positive sort; and I don't see what other duties — as the others are presented to you — can be held to go before them."

Chad looked at him with a smile. "And you know of course about the others, eh? — since it's you yourself who have done the presenting."

"Much of it — yes — and to the best of my ability. But not all — from the moment your sister took my place."

"She did n't," Chad returned. "Sally took a place, certainly; but it was never, I saw from the first moment, to be yours. No one — with us — will ever take yours. It would n't be possible."

"Ah of course," sighed Strether, "I knew it. I believe you 're right. No one in the world, I imagine, was ever so portentously solemn. There I am," he added with another sigh, as if weary enough, on occasion, of this truth. "I was made so."

Chad appeared for a little to consider the way he was made; he might for this purpose have measured him up and down. His conclusion favoured the fact. "*You* have never needed any one to make you better. There has never been any one good enough. They could n't," the young man declared.

His friend hesitated. "I beg your pardon. They *have*."

Chad showed, not without amusement, his doubt. "Who then?"

Strether — though a little dimly — smiled at him. "Women — too."

"'Two'?" — Chad stared and laughed. "Oh I don't believe, for such work, in any more than one! So you 're proving too much. And what *is* beastly, at all events," he added, "is losing you."

Strether had set himself in motion for departure, but at this he paused. "Are you afraid?"

"Afraid — ?"

"Of doing wrong. I mean away from my eye." Before Chad could speak, however, he had taken himself up. "I *am*, certainly," he laughed, "prodigious."

"Yes, you spoil us for all the stupid —!" This might have been, on Chad's part, in its extreme emphasis, almost too freely extravagant; but it was full,

BOOK TWELFTH

plainly enough, of the intention of comfort, it carried with it a protest against doubt and a promise, positively, of performance. Picking up a hat in the vestibule he came out with his friend, came downstairs, took his arm, affectionately, as to help and guide him, treating him if not exactly as aged and infirm, yet as a noble eccentric who appealed to tenderness, and keeping on with him, while they walked, to the next corner and the next. "You need n't tell me, you need n't tell me!" — this again as they proceeded, he wished to make Strether feel. What he need n't tell him was now at last, in the geniality of separation, anything at all it concerned him to know. He knew, up to the hilt — that really came over Chad; he understood, felt, recorded his vow; and they lingered on it as they had lingered in their walk to Strether's hotel the night of their first meeting. The latter took, at this hour, all he could get; he had given all he had had to give; he was as depleted as if he had spent his last sou. But there was just one thing for which, before they broke off, Chad seemed disposed slightly to bargain. His companion need n't, as he said, tell him, but he might himself mention that he had been getting some news of the art of advertisement. He came out quite suddenly with this announcement, while Strether wondered if his revived interest were what had taken him, with strange inconsequence, over to London. He appeared at all events to have been looking into the question and had encountered a revelation. Advertising scientifically worked presented itself thus as the great new force. "It really does the thing, you know."

315

They were face to face under the street-lamp as they had been the first night, and Strether, no doubt, looked blank. "Affects, you mean, the sale of the object advertised?"

"Yes — but affects it extraordinarily; really beyond what one had supposed. I mean of course when it's done as one makes out that, in our roaring age, it *can* be done. I've been finding out a little; though it doubtless doesn't amount to much more than what you originally, so awfully vividly — and all, very nearly, that first night — put before me. It's an art like another, and infinite like all the arts." He went on as if for the joke of it — almost as if his friend's face amused him. "In the hands, naturally, of a master. The right man must take hold. With the right man to work it *c'est un monde.*"

Strether had watched him quite as if, there on the pavement, without a pretext, he had begun to dance a fancy step. "Is what you're thinking of that you yourself, in the case you have in mind, would be the right man?"

Chad had thrown back his light coat and thrust each of his thumbs into an armhole of his waistcoat; in which position his fingers played up and down. "Why, what is he but what you yourself, as I say, took me for when you first came out?"

Strether felt a little faint, but he coerced his attention. "Oh yes, and there's no doubt that, with your natural parts, you'd have much in common with him. Advertising is clearly at this time of day the secret of trade. It's quite possible it will be open to you — giving the whole of your mind to it — to make the whole place hum with you. Your mother's appeal is to the whole of your mind, and that's exactly the strength of her case."

Chad's fingers continued to twiddle, but he had something of a drop. "Ah we've been through my mother's case!"

"So I thought. Why then do you speak of the matter?"

"Only because it was part of our original discussion. To wind up where we began, my interest's purely platonic. There at any rate the fact is — the fact of the possible. I mean the money in it."

"Oh damn the money in it!" said Strether. And then as the young man's fixed smile seemed to shine out more strange: "Shall you give your friend up for the money in it?"

Chad preserved his handsome grimace as well as the rest of his attitude. "You're not altogether — in your so great 'solemnity' — kind. Have n't I been drinking you in — showing you all I feel you're worth to me? What have I done, what am I doing, but cleave to her to the death? The only thing is," he good-humouredly explained, "that one can't but have it before one, in the cleaving — the point where the death comes in. Don't be afraid for *that*. It's pleasant to a fellow's feelings," he developed, "to 'size-up' the bribe he applies his foot to."

"Oh then if all you want's a kickable surface the bribe's enormous."

"Good. Then there it goes!" Chad administered his kick with fantastic force and sent an imaginary object flying. It was accordingly as if they were once

317

more rid of the question and could come back to what really concerned him. "Of course I shall see you to-morrow."

But Strether scarce heeded the plan proposed for this; he had still the impression — not the slighter for the simulated kick — of an irrelevant hornpipe or jig. "You're restless."

"Ah," returned Chad as they parted, "you're exciting."

V

HE had, however, within two days, another separation to face. He had sent Maria Gostrey a word early, by hand, to ask if he might come to breakfast; in consequence of which, at noon, she awaited him in the cool shade of her little Dutch-looking dining-room. This retreat was at the back of the house, with a view of a scrap of old garden that had been saved from modern ravage; and though he had on more than one other occasion had his legs under its small and peculiarly polished table of hospitality, the place had never before struck him as so sacred to pleasant knowledge, to intimate charm, to antique order, to a neatness that was almost august. To sit there was, as he had told his hostess before, to see life reflected for the time in ideally kept pewter; which was somehow becoming, improving to life, so that one's eyes were held and comforted. Strether's were comforted at all events now — and the more that it was the last time — with the charming effect, on the board bare of a cloth and proud of its perfect surface, of the small old crockery and old silver, matched by the more substantial pieces happily disposed about the room. The specimens of vivid Delf, in particular, had the dignity of family portraits; and it was in the midst of them that our friend resignedly expressed himself. He spoke even with a certain philosophic humour. "There's nothing more to wait for; I seem to have done a good day's work. I've let them have it all

319

round. I've seen Chad, who has been to London and come back. He tells me I'm 'exciting,' and I seem indeed pretty well to have upset every one. I've at any rate excited *him*. He's distinctly restless."

"You've excited *me*," Miss Gostrey smiled. "*I'm* distinctly restless."

"Oh you were that when I found you. It seems to me I've rather got you out of it. What's this," he asked as he looked about him, "but a haunt of ancient peace?"

"I wish with all my heart," she presently replied, "I could make you treat it as a haven of rest." On which they fronted each other, across the table, as if things unuttered were in the air.

Strether seemed, in his way, when he next spoke, to take some of them up. "It would n't give me — that would be the trouble — what it will, no doubt, still give you. I'm not," he explained, leaning back in his chair, but with his eyes on a small ripe round melon — "in real harmony with what surrounds me. You *are*. I take it too hard. You *don't*. It makes — that's what it comes to in the end — a fool of me." Then at a tangent, "What has he been doing in London?" he demanded.

"Ah one may go to London," Maria laughed. "You know *I* did."

Yes — he took the reminder. "And you brought *me* back." He brooded there opposite to her, but without gloom. "Whom has Chad brought? He's full of ideas. And I wrote to Sarah," he added, "the first thing this morning. So I'm square. I'm ready for them."

She neglected certain parts of this speech in the interest of others. "Marie said to me the other day that she felt him to have the makings of an immense man of business."

"There it is. He's the son of his father!"

"But *such* a father!"

"Ah just the right one from that point of view! But it isn't his father in him," Strether added, "that troubles me."

"What is it then?" He came back to his breakfast; he partook presently of the charming melon, which she liberally cut for him; and it was only after this that he met her question. Then moreover it was but to remark that he'd answer her presently. She waited, she watched, she served him and amused him, and it was perhaps with this last idea that she soon reminded him of his having never even yet named to her the article produced at Woollett. "Do you remember our talking of it in London — that night at the play?" Before he could say yes, however, she had put it to him for other matters. Did he remember, did he remember — this and that of their first days? He remembered everything, bringing up with humour even things of which she professed no recollection, things she vehemently denied; and falling back above all on the great interest of their early time, the curiosity felt by both of them as to where he would "come out." They had so assumed it was to be in some wonderful place — they had thought of it as so very *much* out. Well, that was doubtless what it had been — since he had come out just there. He was out, in truth, as far as it was possible to be, and must

now rather bethink himself of getting in again. He
found on the spot the image of his recent history; he
was like one of the figures of the old clock at Berne.
They came out, on one side, at their hour, jigged along
their little course in the public eye, and went in on the
other side. He too had jigged his little course — him
too a modest retreat awaited. He offered now, should
she really like to know, to name the great product of
Woollett. It would be a great commentary on everything. At this she stopped him off; she not only had
no wish to know, but she would n't know for the world.
She had done with the products of Woollett — for all
the good she had got from them. She desired no further news of them, and she mentioned that Madame
de Vionnet herself had, to her knowledge, lived exempt
from the information he was ready to supply. She
had never consented to receive it, though she would
have taken it, under stress, from Mrs. Pocock. But
it was a matter about which Mrs. Pocock appeared
to have had little to say — never sounding the word
— and it did n't signify now. There was nothing
clearly for Maria Gostrey that signified now — save
one sharp point, that is, to which she came in time.
"I don't know whether it's before you as a possibility that, left to himself, Mr. Chad may after all go
back. I judge that it *is* more or less so before you,
from what you just now said of him."

Her guest had his eyes on her, kindly but atten-
tively, as if foreseeing what was to follow this. "I
don't think it will be for the money." And then as
she seemed uncertain: "I mean I don't believe it
will be for that he'll give her up."

"Then he *will* give her up ?"

Strether waited a moment, rather slow and deliberate now, drawing out a little this last soft stage, pleading with her in various suggestive and unspoken ways for patience and understanding. "What were you just about to ask me ?"

"Is there anything he can do that would make you patch it up ?"

"With Mrs. Newsome ?"

Her assent, as if she had had a delicacy about sounding the name, was only in her face; but she added with it: "Or is there anything he can do that would make *her* try it ?"

"To patch it up with me ?" His answer came at last in a conclusive headshake. "There's nothing any one can do. It's over. Over for both of us."

Maria wondered, seemed a little to doubt. "Are you so sure for her ?"

"Oh yes — sure now. Too much has happened. I'm different for her."

She took it in then, drawing a deeper breath. "I see. So that as she's different for *you* —"

"Ah but," he interrupted, "she's not." And as Miss Gostrey wondered again: "She's the same. She's more than ever the same. But I do what I didn't before — I *see* her."

He spoke gravely and as if responsibly — since he had to pronounce; and the effect of it was slightly solemn, so that she simply exclaimed "Oh!" Satisfied and grateful, however, she showed in her own next words an acceptance of his statement. "What then do you go home to ?"

323

He had pushed his plate a little away, occupied with another side of the matter; taking refuge verily in that side and feeling so moved that he soon found himself on his feet. He was affected in advance by what he believed might come from her, and he would have liked to forestall it and deal with it tenderly; yet in the presence of it he wished still more to be — though as smoothly as possible — deterrent and conclusive. He put her question by for the moment; he told her more about Chad. "It would have been impossible to meet me more than he did last night on the question of the infamy of not sticking to her."

"Is that what you called it for him — 'infamy'?"

"Oh rather! I described to him in detail the base creature he'd be, and he quite agrees with me about it."

"So that it's really as if you had nailed him?"

"Quite really as if —! I told him I should curse him."

"Oh," she smiled, "you *have* done it." And then having thought again: "You *can't* after that propose —!" Yet she scanned his face.

"Propose again to Mrs. Newsome?"

She hesitated afresh, but she brought it out. "I've never believed, you know, that you did propose. I always believed it was really she — and, so far as that goes, I can understand it. What I mean is," she explained, "that with such a spirit — the spirit of curses! — your breach is past mending. She has only to know what you've done to him never again to raise a finger."

"I've done," said Strether, "what I could — one

can't do more. He protests his devotion and his horror. But I'm not sure I've saved him. He protests too much. He asks how one can dream of his being tired. But he has all life before him."

Maria saw what he meant. "He's formed to please."

"And it's our friend who has formed him." Strether felt in it the strange irony.

"So it's scarcely his fault!"

"It's at any rate his danger. I mean," said Strether, "it's hers. But she knows it."

"Yes, she knows it. And is your idea," Miss Gostrey asked, "that there was some other woman in London?"

"Yes. No. That is I *have* no ideas. I'm afraid of them. I've done with them." And he put out his hand to her. "Good-bye."

It brought her back to her unanswered question. "To what do you go home?"

"I don't know. There will always be something."

"To a great difference," she said as she kept his hand.

"A great difference — no doubt. Yet I shall see what I can make of it."

"Shall you make anything so good — ?" But, as if remembering what Mrs. Newsome had done, it was as far as she went.

He had sufficiently understood. "So good as this place at this moment? So good as what *you* make of everything you touch?" He took a moment to say, for, really and truly, what stood about him there in her offer — which was as the offer of exquisite service, of lightened care, for the rest of his days — might well have tempted. It built him softly round, it roofed him warmly over, it rested, all so firm, on selection. And what ruled selection was beauty and knowledge. It was awkward, it was almost stupid, not to seem to prize such things; yet, none the less, so far as they made his opportunity they made it only for a moment. She'd moreover understand — she always understood.

That indeed might be, but meanwhile she was going on. "There's nothing, you know, I would n't do for you."

"Oh yes — I know."

"There's nothing," she repeated, "in all the world."

"I know. I know. But all the same I must go." He had got it at last. "To be right."

"To be right?"

She had echoed it in vague deprecation, but he felt it already clear for her. "That, you see, is my only logic. Not, out of the whole affair, to have got anything for myself."

She thought. "But with your wonderful impressions you'll have got a great deal."

"A great deal" — he agreed. "But nothing like you. It's you who would make me wrong!"

Honest and fine, she could n't greatly pretend she did n't see it. Still she could pretend just a little. "But why should you be so dreadfully right?"

"That's the way that — if I must go — you yourself would be the first to want me. And I can't do anything else."

BOOK TWELFTH

So then she had to take it, though still with her defeated protest. "It is n't so much your *being* 'right' — it's your horrible sharp eye for what makes you so."

"Oh but you're just as bad yourself. You can't resist me when I point that out."

She sighed it at last all comically, all tragically, away. "I can't indeed resist you."

"Then there we are!" said Strether.

THE END